RAKES OF THE CARIBBEAN

Sun, sand and sizzling seduction

Notorious rogues Ren Dryden and Kitt Sherard
used to cut a swath through the *ton*,
but they were too wild to be satisfied with
London seasons and prim debutantes.

Now they've ventured to the sultry Caribbean
to seek their fortunes...
and women strong enough to tame them!

Ren meets his match in spirited Emma Ward.
Relish their seductive battle of wits in
PLAYING THE RAKE'S GAME
Already available

Kitt has never met a woman as unconventional as
Bryn Rutherford. Enjoy their scorching chemistry in
BREAKING THE RAKE'S RULES
Available now

And look for the
Harlequin® Historical Undone! ebook
CRAVING THE RAKE'S TOUCH
Already available

You won't want to miss this sizzling new series
from Bronwyn Scott!

Author Note

I hope you're enjoying the Rakes of the Caribbean mini-series featuring my sexy new heroes: Ren Dryden and Kitt Sherard. Kitt's story is set against the riskier side of life in a British colony in the nineteenth century. Not nearly as regulated as life in England, the Caribbean offers plenty of room for adventure and rule breaking—two things Kitt is very good at. You may have met him first in Ren's story, *Playing the Rake's Game*.

I always like to learn a little something when I read, so let me share the historical setting for Kitt's story. It is an economical one. Up until 1836, English pounds were not allowed for import to the Caribbean, so most debts and purchases were paid for in barter and trade (usually rum or sugar) or with Spanish or Dutch currencies. In June of 1836, a charter was granted to establish a British bank in Barbados. I've placed the fictional Rutherford as the envoy charged with carrying out that commission and organizing a board of directors. It is true that the bank would have been a joint stock bank, which means it's an investment bank. History shows that the bank in Barbados soon led to the establishment of a network of British banks through the Eastern Caribbean.

Stay tuned at my blog or website for more Bronwyn Scott updates, bronwynswriting.blogspot.com and bronwynnscott.com.

Bronwyn Scott

Breaking the Rake's Rules

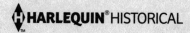

Recycling programs
for this product may
not exist in your area.

ISBN-13: 978-0-373-29820-4

Breaking the Rake's Rules

Printed in U.S.A.

Bronwyn Scott is a communications instructor at Pierce College in the United States, and is the proud mother of three wonderful children (one boy and two girls). When she's not teaching or writing she enjoys playing the piano, traveling—especially to Florence, Italy—and studying history and foreign languages. Readers can stay in touch on Bronwyn's website, bronwynnscott.com, or at her blog, bronwynswriting.blogspot.com—she loves to hear from readers.

Books by Bronwyn Scott

Harlequin® Historical and Harlequin® Historical Undone! ebooks

Rakes of the Caribbean

Playing the Rake's Game
Breaking the Rake's Rules
Craving the Rake's Touch (Undone!)

Rakes Who Make Husbands Jealous

Secrets of a Gentleman Escort
London's Most Wanted Rake
An Officer But No Gentleman (Undone!)
A Most Indecent Gentleman (Undone!)

Ladies of Impropriety

A Lady Risks All
A Lady Dares
A Lady Seduces (Undone!)

Castonbury Park

Unbefitting a Lady

Visit the Author Profile page at Harlequin.com for more titles.

For Flo, my awesome editor, who really massaged this book into excellence and took time to make it a meaningful story with a strong life lesson: you can't outrun your past, so you might as well embrace it. Thanks to Flo, Kitt Sherard does it in style.

And thanks to my agent, Scott Eagan at Greyhaus Literary Agency, who also had to put up with all my rewrites. There were lots of fits and starts and you were kind enough, patient enough to argue with me about all of them. It is much appreciated.

Chapter One

The Caribbean—June 1836

'**P**rotect the rum!' Kitt Sherard raced forward on the beach to throw himself between the oncoming attackers and the newly unloaded cargo of precious barrels. 'It's a trap!' A pistol flashed in one hand, his knife in the other as the words left his mouth, the cry carrying down the line to be taken up by his men. 'Protect the rum! Protect the rum!' He felt his men surge behind him, his first mate, Will Passemore, at his right, digging his bare feet into the sand, ready to take on the thick of the fighting.

Anger fuelled Kitt, pumping through his body over the betrayal. This was supposed to have been a standard trade done in the light of broad day; rum for farming supplies. The afternoon sun beating down on them was proof enough of that, but somewhere, something had gone wrong. There was no time to sort through it at present.

Cries echoed throughout the deserted cove as the first of the attackers emerged from the pack. Kitt took aim at the man's shoulder and fired, hoping the draw of first blood would cause the bandits to retreat. He meant business when rum was on the line, especially when that rum belonged to a friend, but he never liked to take a life.

The man clutched his arm and fell back, only to be overrun by his fellow outlaws. So much for deterrence. 'Get ready, this means war,' Kitt muttered under his breath. 'These bastards won't go easily.'

'We'll manage them, Captain.' Beside him, Passemore's jaw was set with grim determination.

The horde was on them, then. With one roar, Kitt's men met the mêlée. Kitt threw aside his pistol. This was knife work now. He stabbed wherever he could, quick, sharp jabs to shoulders, thighs, an occasional belly when there was no choice. Sweat ran in his face and he fought the urge to wipe it away with a hand. The bandits were tenacious, Kitt would give them that. At last they began to fall back—the sight of their fallen comrades was persuasion enough that whatever they were being paid wasn't worth it. 'Come on, boys, we've got them on the run!' Kitt yelled over the fighting, leading the charge to drive the bandits from the cove.

They fled with relative speed, dragging their wounded with them. Will was ahead of him, firing a pistol into the fleeing rabble. A man went down and Will leapt on him, blade drawn. 'No!' Kitt swerved to Will's side. 'We need him alive. Get him back to the ship and get him patched up. I want to know who is behind this.'

'Aye, aye!' Will said with a relish that made Kitt grin. The younger man reminded him of himself six or so years ago when he'd begun this adventure. Will hefted the man over a shoulder with a grunt. 'C'mon, you stupid bastard.'

With Will headed back to the bumboats with the wounded man and the bandits scrambling the island hills to protection, Kitt organised the beach. 'Let's get the barrels back on board, men! Look lively—we don't want them thinking about organising a counter-attack.' Kitt doubted they would. His men had given them quite a drubbing, but he knew from experience one did not take chances in this business.

Even though he'd not expected trouble this afternoon, he'd come armed, just in case. Kitt helped roll a barrel towards the bumboats, his thoughts chasing each other around in his mind. There'd been reports these last four months of bandit crews operating in the area, stealing rum and sugar from small merchant trading ships that sailed between the islands.

For the most part, Kitt hadn't taken those reports seriously. Small merchant ships, many of them more like boats and not in the best of shape, were often unarmed and undermanned when it came to fighting. They made easy targets, unlike his ship, *Queen of the Main*. Small-time bandits would prefer small-time targets. Only today, they hadn't.

Kitt ran a hand through his hair, surveying the beach. All the barrels were loaded and the men were ready to go. Kitt gave the signal to shove off and leapt into the bow of the nearest boat. It had been the worst of luck the bandits had chosen today, when he'd been hauling his friend Ren Dryden's rum. Ren would be disappointed.

Kitt had protected the rum, which was no small thing in this part of the world where rum and sugar were still the currency of the land. But on the downside, Ren had been counting on this trade to purchase much-needed farming supplies. Now, Ren was without a sale and without the goods he and his wife needed for the upcoming harvest. He didn't relish telling Ren he'd failed.

Ahead in the water, Kitt could see the first boat bump up against the side of the *Queen*. He could make out Will hauling their prisoner up to the deck in a rope sling. Kitt hoped the prisoner would provide some answers.

Aboard ship, Will had bad news. 'I don't think we can save him, Captain. He took the ball in the back. It's lodged in his spine. You'd better come quick. It's beyond O'Reilly's skill.' Not surprising news given that O'Reilly's 'skill' was relegated to stitching knife wounds.

The man was laid out on the deck, unable to be moved any further. The pain of his injury was evident in the pallor of his skin. Fear was evident, too, Kitt thought as he knelt beside him. The man knew death was coming. Kitt saw it in his eyes. 'Aye, man, it won't be long now,' Kitt said softly, motioning for his crew to give them room.

Kitt lay a hand on the man's forehead. 'Is there anything you want to tell me? Anyone you want me to notify?'

The man—or was he a boy?—shook his head. Up close, beneath the dirt and sweat, he didn't look as old as Passemore. Or perhaps they all looked like boys when they died, all pretence of bravery stripped away when it came right down to it. His brother had looked very much the same way in the last hour they'd spent together, the enormity of what was about to transpire etched in every ashen line of his face.

'All right then,' Kitt soothed him. 'May I ask who sent you? Who paid you?'

The man struggled to speak as the pain took him. There was urgency in his gaze. His words were halting. 'They. Are. Waiting. For. You. If. We. Failed. Don't. Go. Back.' His features relaxed, his breathing rattled. 'Am. I. Forgiven?' The question of every dying man.

Kitt pressed a kiss to the man's forehead and gave him the only absolution he could. 'Your debt is paid. Rest in peace.' The man breathed once more and was gone. Kitt rose. His crew was solemn around him. Kitt clapped a hand on O'Reilly's shoulder, his tone sombre. 'You know what to do, take it from here. Make sure I have anything of note that he carried.' In case there was a message to convey after all, or a clue as to who 'they' were, or even the man's name.

Shadows were falling by the time they put into port at Carlisle Bay and rowed ashore. Bridgetown was quiet for the evening, all the shops closed, people at home with their families. Out at Sugarland, Ren and Emma would be preparing to sit down to an evening meal. Kitt smiled, thinking of his friend and Ren's newfound happiness as a husband, a landowner, a man in charge of shaping his own destiny. It was what Ren wanted out of life. It was what Kitt had once assumed would have been his, too, by right, a future he'd been raised to expect without question up until the hour it was snatched away, no longer an option. Six years in and he was still grasping just how long for ever was.

Don't think on it, remembering can't change anything. The dying man had made him maudlin. Tonight, such ruminations were best set aside in light of the dead man's warning. He couldn't afford the distraction no matter what sentiments the man had conjured.

Normally, this was a time of day Kitt enjoyed, for a while anyway. Dusk was a break between the hustle of his days and the activity of his nights. Staying busy was critical in keeping his mind focused on the present. Too much solitude, too much quiet, and he knew from experience his mind would drift to less pleasant considerations best left in the past. This evening, though, the usual peace of dusk was absent. Menace stalked the stillness.

Maybe he was paranoid. Did he believe the dying man's warning? Or was it one last lie? If so, it was certainly a powerful one. Kitt could hardly afford to ignore it. He dipped his hand into the top of his boot and drew his knife. If there was an attack, there'd be no time to draw it later. He had rooms in a boarding house just off Bay Street past the governor's mansion for nights when it was too late to go home or when business detained him in town, as it did this evening. He was due at the Crenshaws' for dinner. The distance wasn't far, although tonight it seemed like miles.

At the end of Bay Street, the shadows moved. In one stealthy motion, they were upon him, three against one. One of them leapt on his back, trying to push him down, but Kitt was ready. He smashed the body into the wall of a nearby building, stunning the first attacker. His back to the wall, Kitt whirled, knife in hand, to face the other two. They were big, swarthy men. Kitt assessed the situation instantly. They would want to make the first move, would want to crowd him against the wall so that he had no room to move. They were operating under the assumption that he would fight. Kitt grinned. He would seize the advantage and take them by surprise. Knife at the ready, head lowered like a bull, he rushed them, pushing one aside with enough of a shove to keep the man off balance, and then he kept going.

But the men were fast and willing to give chase. They were closing on him. Kitt spied a house with lights on. That would do. He tore through the little gate separating the house from the street and streaked through the garden. He needed to get up and in. Ah, a trellis! A balcony! Perfect.

Kitt planted his foot on the bottom rung of the trellis and climbed upward, feeling the trellis bend under the pressure of his weight at every step. He grabbed the railing of the balcony and hauled himself up, his foot kicking the trellis to the ground as a precaution just in case the men were fool enough to try. Kitt threw himself over the railing and drew a breath of relief. He lay on his back, looking up at the sky and exhaled. It had been one hell of a day. Maybe he *was* getting too old for this.

He'd just got to his feet, feeling assured the would-be assassins had given up and ready to think about what to do next, when the balcony door opened. 'Who's there?' A woman in a white-satin dressing gown stepped outside, her mouth falling open at the sight of him.

Only quick thinking and quicker reflexes prevented a scream from erupting. Kitt grabbed the woman and pulled her to him, his mouth covering hers, swallowing her scream. He'd only meant to silence her, but God, those soft, full breasts of hers felt good against him. She was naked beneath the dressing robe, a fact every curve and plane of her pressed against him made evident.

Maybe it was the adrenaline of the day, but all he wanted to do was fall into her. His intrepid lady didn't seem to mind. She'd not shut her mouth against his invasion, her body had not tried to pull away. It was all the invitation he needed. His lips started to move, his tongue caressing the inside of her mouth, running over her teeth. Ah, his lady had a sweet tooth! She tasted of peppermints and smelled of her bath, all lemon and lavender where he breathed in her skin. She was all womanly heat against him, her tongue answering him with an exploration of its own.

Kitt nipped at her lower lip, eliciting a surprised gasp. His hand moved to cup her breast, kneading it through the slippery satin, the belt of her robe coming loose. He slipped a hand inside, making contact with warm, lemon-and-lavender-scented skin, his arousal starting to peak. He had no doubt she could feel it against her thighs where their bodies met.

An ill-timed knock on her door interrupted the pleasant interlude, followed by worried masculine tones. 'Is everything all right in there?' Kitt knew a moment's panic. There were only so many explanations for a voice like that. A father? A brother? A fiancé? Or worst of all, a husband?

His lady jumped away, her grey eyes wide as she mouthed the words, *My father*! But she was cool under pressure. Panic was already receding as she stared at him, assessing her choices and their advantages. Would she give him away? Kitt gave her a wicked smile to indicate there were definite benefits to keeping his secret. She smiled back. Apparently the decision was made.

She called into the room, loud enough to be heard through the door. 'Everything's fine, I heard a crash. It's nothing, just the trellis again.' And then, perhaps realising someone might come in anyway to be sure she was safe, she added hastily, 'I'm, um, getting dressed. I'll be down in a moment.'

Satisfied she would be left alone, she turned towards Kitt, hands on hips. 'Now, for the question of the night, who are you and what are you doing in my bedroom?'

Kitt grinned, letting his eyes appreciably roam the length of her. His rescuer was strikingly attractive. Long chestnut hair hung down her back in a heavy, shiny curtain, the sharp planes of her cheek bones and cool grey eyes creating the impression of intelligence. This was no unseasoned Miss. Maybe things were starting to look up. His cock certainly thought so. He leaned back against the railing, arms crossed over his chest, making no attempt to hide his arousal. 'My name is Kitt and what I'm doing in your bedroom is entirely up to you.'

Chapter Two

If there was a more blatant invitation to sin, Bryn Rutherford had yet to hear it. Or see it, for that matter. The blond, tanned, mass of male muscle leaning on the rail of her balcony was temptation personified. Even sweaty and wearing the dirt of the day—and from the looks of it, his day, whatever it had been, had been pretty dirty—she could tell he was delicious. He'd tasted delicious, too, like an adventure—all wind and salt as if he'd spent a day at sea.

She probably should have slapped him for his unorthodox silencing, but that would assume she hadn't liked it, or that she hadn't willingly participated in it. She was honest enough to admit that she had. And why not? It wasn't every day a handsome man climbed into a girl's bedroom. The question now was what was she going to do about it? She ought to throw him back down the trellis, but her curiosity simply wouldn't allow it, nor would the fact that he'd apparently knocked the trellis over.

Bryn returned his stare with a frank appraisal of her own, running her gaze down the length of him in return. Two could play this game. 'There isn't time for what you propose, sir. I have a dinner to attend. My father is expecting me downstairs momentarily.' As if *not* having a dinner engagement would have changed her decision. One look at him had told her he would not appreciate a reticent Miss who shirked from stolen kisses. He wanted the woman she'd been in his arms, all courage and fire.

'Another time perhaps?' Bryn dared, enjoying this moment of boldness, of not worrying about the rules. Men who climbed trellises were beyond the rules to start with. She needn't worry about him telling anyone what they'd done. Such a confession would force him to the altar and that was the last thing he wanted. This man was not husband material, he was fantasy material, but she needed him to depart. Her maid would be up any minute to help her finish dressing. He would be rather hard to explain. 'As lovely as the interlude has been, I do need to ask you to leave.'

He made a show of looking around, past her into the bedroom, down at the garden below and up at the sky for good measure. 'Exactly how do you propose I do that?'

'It would have been easier if you hadn't kicked over the trellis.' Easier, but far less exciting. It was rather arousing to imagine those arms of his flexing as he pulled himself over the balcony without the help of any support. Whatever he did all day, it was no doubt 'exerting'. He fairly oozed good health from the pores of that tanned skin. Probably what he did all night was exerting, too. He wasn't the kind to sleep alone.

Bryn looked over the railing at the ground. 'Easier, but not impossible without it. If you lowered yourself over the balcony and extended to your full length, you could safely make the drop without any harm, I think.'

'Or I could hide under your bed until you've left,' he suggested with another sexy smile that sent a decadent trill down her spine. This was the most fun she'd had in ages: no chaperon, very nearly no clothes and this wicked man all to herself. She'd forgotten how much fun flirting was.

She trailed her hand down the open vee at the neck of her dressing gown, watching his eyes follow the motion. 'What a most erotic suggestion, letting you watch me undress. I must decline out of fear you will rob us blind after I leave. I can't let a stranger have unsupervised access to the house.' She flicked her eyes towards the door in warning, a reminder that discovery was imminent if he continued to delay. 'I really must ask that you go or this time I will scream.'

He laughed and made her a little bow before throwing a leg over the railing. She held her breath. She didn't want him to be hurt, but she had to get rid of him and she was fairly sure the drop wouldn't be injurious. He gave her a wink as he levered himself into position. 'Don't worry, I'm sure your estimations are correct.' Then he disappeared. A moment later, she heard a quiet thud. She risked a look over the edge and saw him rise up, brush off the dirt and trot out the garden gate into the night. In the falling darkness, her conscience might have imagined the limp.

Bryn wished he'd trot out of her thoughts just as easily. He might have if the dinner had been more entertaining. Although to be fair, it would had to have been extremely diverting in order to compete with the episode on her balcony. As it was, the most exciting thing about dinner was the empty chair across from her. It most certainly wasn't the man on her left, a Mr Orville, a successful importer, who simply wasn't up to it with his paunchy belly and habit of excessively using the term 'my dear' to start most of his sentences. The man on her right was not much better, only younger. But she understood the importance of making a decent first impression, of stroking the feathers of a man's ego. The nuances of being a lady had been drilled into her quite thoroughly by her mother, a testament to her upbringing, since she'd turned fourteen. She knew how to be a lady and how to use it to her advantage. That didn't mean she liked it.

Quite frankly, being a lady was boring, a discovery she'd made her first Season out. She preferred to think she was far more adventurous than dancing twice with the same man at a ball. She also preferred to think she was more like the woman she'd been on the balcony. However, she was smart enough to know that woman, full of fire and passion, had no place at a dining table full of her father's potential business partners. As much as it chafed, tonight she had to play the lady.

She and her father had only been ashore for three days and everyone was eager to make their acquaintance given her father's mission. The men gathered at the Crenshaws' this evening were the influential cream of Bridgetown society, the men with connections and knowledge that would be critical in carrying out the crown's charter.

These were the men she needed to impress, not sweaty, blond rogues caught in the likely act of housebreaking. The man today was nothing more than a com-

mon criminal and she'd carried on like a common hussy
with him. No matter how exciting he might have been,
such behaviour was not what her father needed from
her. He would be scandalised if he knew what had transpired. She supposed she should be disappointed in herself. She'd set aside the teachings of girlhood at the
merest temptation. But when that temptation kissed like
her balcony god, it was hard to be penitent.

Bryn sipped from her wine glass and smiled at the
man on her right, a Mr Selby, very aware that he was
trying to sneak a glimpse of her bosom while he talked
about the island's sights. Heaven forbid he actually talk
about banking with a woman. She had the impression
her unexpected visitor wouldn't make such a distinction.
He'd talk about whatever he liked, with whomever he
liked. Kitt-with-no-last-name wouldn't 'sneak' a peek at
her bosom, he'd make no secret of appreciating it with
a rather frank and forthright blue-gazed assessment.

'What do you think, Miss Rutherford?' Mr Selby
asked, catching her unawares.

'I'm sorry, about what?' Bryn apologised, trying to
look penitent, an emotion she was apparently having
difficulty conjuring with any sincerity tonight.

He smiled patiently, too much of a gentleman to protest her inattention, but not too much of a gentleman
to look down her dress. 'About a picnic. I thought you
might enjoy a tour of the parish.'

Coward. The man from the balcony would have made
her accountable for her distraction. The thought of how
he might do that sent a pleasant shiver down her spine.
Then again, if it had been him, her attention wouldn't
have lapsed in the first place.

'I would, although perhaps it could wait until Father

and I are settled. There's quite a lot to do at the moment with unpacking.' She smiled and turned back to Orville, signalling the discussion was closed.

It became the pattern of the evening. Bryn listened intently, and responded appropriately, playing the dinner game adequately if not adroitly. By the time the cheese course arrived, signalling the end of dinner, she'd come to the disappointing conclusion evenings here weren't unlike the evenings in London. She'd hoped they would be different. She'd hoped the men would be different, too.

A little smile tugged at her lips. In that regard, at least one of them was. She wondered if she'd see him again or *how* she *could* see him again. Perhaps he ran a business in town? Perhaps it was possible to arrange a chance meeting? She almost laughed aloud at that. Her logic was failing her. He'd given her no last name, very likely on purpose. Men like him didn't want to be found. Her balcony Romeo was no businessman. Just a few minutes ago she was thinking him a criminal. Besides, businessmen looked like Mr Orville on her left, they simply didn't look like *Kitt*: part-beach god, part-pirate.

Be careful where your thoughts are leading you, her conscience warned. *This is a new start for your father. Your father needs you. You can't run around risking a scandal. This is too important for him. Besides, you promised.*

But it's a new start for me, too, her heart argued in return. She could have stayed in London with relatives where life was safe and predictable. She'd had enough of that. If she was discreet, perhaps there would be a way to have both. After all, was it wrong to want a little adventure? She'd been good for so very long. Years, in fact. Surely she was due some reward.

Eleanor Crenshaw, their hostess, rose, indicating the ladies should follow her into the drawing room. Bryn gathered her skirts and cast a last glance up the table where her father was nodding and answering questions. She hoped it was going well. She still didn't know quite how her father had managed the royal appointment. She suspected well-meaning relatives had had a hand in it. Her father's older brother was the Earl of Creighton and well-connected politically.

It wasn't that she doubted her father's abilities. Even as a younger son, he'd had his own ambitions, albeit they'd always been more of a local bent. Still, she wasn't sure it was fair to equate his experience as a country financier on the same level as the banking interests of an empire. She adored her father. She didn't want to see him set up to fail, but this had not been a consideration when the mighty Rutherfords had lobbied for the lucrative post to Bridgetown. They'd seen only the advantages.

Her father's success would see the Rutherfords strategically placed to take advantage of the crown's banking monopoly in the Caribbean. It served the grand Rutherford design to send her father overseas to expand the family interests, but Bryn hoped for more than that from this appointment. She hoped the change would give him a chance to rebuild his life after the death of his wife. For over a year her father had moped about, showing interest in nothing since her mother's death. It was time for him to move on. He was too vibrant, too intelligent of a man to simply give up on life when there was still much he could do for his family and for others.

The ladies' conversation in the drawing room politely danced around that very issue with feminine delicacy. What could her father do for their husbands? How much authority did her father have to act on his own? Was her father going to run some of his own investments? Bryn hoped not, if for no other reason than she wanted him to start slow, follow the crown's directive to the letter and complete his mission with success. It was simple enough if he stuck to the plan. But she also knew his brother had encouraged him to make some private investments as well.

Bryn was about to turn the conversation a different direction and ask about the empty chair at the dinner table when a footman entered. The man whispered something to her hostess, bringing a smile to the woman's face. 'By all means, Bradley, show him in.' She beamed at the women seated around her. It was the smug smile of a woman who has just pulled off a social coup. Bridgetown or London, apparently the look was universal. 'Our dear captain has arrived.'

Everyone burst into smiles and there were even a few titters behind painted fans. Good Lord, this Captain Whoever-he-was had the women acting positively swoony, even the married ones who ought to know better. To Bryn's left, the daughter of one of the women—a Miss Caroline Bryant—blushed and looked down at her hands in an attempt at modesty. Bryn thought it only a moderate effort at subtly calling attention to herself and whatever she wished the gesture to imply about her and the captain. In London, a girl Miss Bryant's age would have been out for a few Seasons and far better schooled in the art of dissembling.

'Ladies,' the footman intoned, coming back into the room, 'Captain Christopher Sherard.'

Bryn's gaze went to the door out of curiosity over the hubbub, her mind wrapping around the name. Captain Sherard was one of the investors on her father's list of potential hopefuls and one of the men they had not met yet. He'd been highly recommended by the Earl of Dartmoor through a friend back in London. Her father was pinning a lot of his hopes on this particular investor who had yet to materialise.

At first glance, the man who stepped into the room was striking. At second glance, he was horrifying familiar. *Kitt. Christopher.* No, it couldn't be. Her heart began to hammer as her mind connected the names with this golden god and then connected the implications. The man from the balcony was her father's prime investor!

Unexpected didn't begin to cover it. Bryn looked a third time, desperate to be sure, or was it to be 'not sure'? She wasn't certain if her heart pounded from fear of impending disaster or from the excitement of seeing him again. The way it was racing at present it might be both. Maybe she should simply wipe her sweaty palms on her skirts, ascribe it to the fact that he looked extraordinary and leave it at that.

Surely it couldn't be the same man? Long golden hair was slicked back into a thick tail tied with black ribbon. His sweat-streaked shirt had been exchanged for immaculate linen. A subtle diamond winked in his cravat as a statement of wealth and good taste. His evening clothes were well fitted enough to have done any Bond

Street tailor proud, their tight fit showing off broad shoulders, lean hips and long legs.

The physique certainly suggested he was the same man. It was the clothes that differed. They were expensive and tasteful, two traits she didn't associate with her balcony visitor. She knew a moment's disappointment. Perhaps it wasn't him after all, just a strong similarity simply because she'd been thinking of him. It would be an easy enough trick for her mind to play on her. Her pulse settled back into its usual rhythm. It was for the best. Business and pleasure never mixed, at least not well, and what sort of investor climbed balconies and kissed strange women? Not one her father could trust and not one she should trust either.

But wait… She studied his face, the strong line of his jaw, the razor straightness of his nose, features she'd seen up close today. It was the eyes that gave him away. Her heart bucked in her chest. It *was* him! The very same man who'd climbed up to her balcony, kicked over her trellis and kissed her senseless without even knowing her name.

All the fine tailoring in the world couldn't disguise the wildness in his blue eyes as they roamed the room, taking in the occupants one by one until they rested on her. Recognition fired in their cobalt depths ever so briefly, his mouth twitching with a secret smile.

Her breath caught as she suffered his silent scrutiny. Would he expose their little secret? She'd not worried about the man on the balcony exposing anything, it didn't suit that man to be caught in a compromising position. She understood him. But this one in fine evening clothes who acted like a gentleman and was supposed to be a banker? *This* was going to be tricky. He had destroyed all her assumptions and that left her feeling far too vulnerable at the moment.

A scandal was the last thing she needed. She knew very well her behaviour reflected on her father. Rutherfords were taught from birth the actions of the individual reflected on the family. Men would be reluctant to do business with a man who couldn't control his daughter. Besides, she'd made a promise and Bryn Rutherford *never* went back on her word.

His gaze left her and he moved towards Eleanor Crenshaw, making their hostess the focus of all his blue-eyed attention. Gone was the sweaty, dirty pirate prince. This new version came complete with requisite manners. He would dazzle in any ballroom, let alone Mrs Crenshaw's provincial parlour. He took their hostess's hand. 'Please forgive me for being late. I hope the numbers at the table weren't terribly upset.'

Bryn fought the urge to gape, her thoughts catching up to the implication of his statement. He was the empty chair. This grew more curious by the minute. Questions spun off into more questions. If he was supposed to have been here, why had he been scaling balconies? It was hardly standard banker behaviour.

Mrs Crenshaw was murmuring some inanity about forgiving him anything as long as he was here now to entertain them. 'Perhaps you and Miss Caroline would play another duet for us. You are both so excellently talented at the piano.' Her balcony intruder played the piano? The oh-so-modest Miss Caroline blushed again as Kitt acquiesced and escorted her to the piano, which stood suspiciously ready for such an occasion, further proof that his presence tonight was no accident. He'd been expected and in fact was expected regularly. This was no random occurrence. Well, Miss Caroline and her blushes were welcome to him, Bryn told herself. She hardly knew the man well enough to be jealous. A few stolen kisses hardly constituted a relationship. She really ought to feel sorry for Miss Caroline, who was clearly labouring under the assumption Kitt Sherard was somehow a respectable gentleman.

Bryn should count herself lucky. She'd seen his true colours this afternoon. She knew what he'd been doing and why he was late.

However, by the time the tea cart arrived and the men joined them, she liked Miss Caroline a little less than she had the hour before.

'When you said another time, I didn't think it would be so soon.' The smooth voice at her ear made her jump. She salvaged her tea cup just barely without spilling.

'I didn't imagine this party to be your sort of venue— no trellises to climb,' Bryn replied smoothly, keeping her gaze fixed forward on the other guests, but her body was aware of his closeness, the clean vanilla scent of his cologne and the sandalwood of his bath soap. He'd bathed after he'd left her, a thought that brought a flood of prurient images to mind. Hardly the sort of thing one should think about over evening tea.

'Pity, I would have pegged you for having a rather good imagination earlier this evening.' Laughter bubbled under the low rumble of his voice as if he had somehow followed her train of thought straight to his bath and knew exactly what she was thinking. 'There's plenty to climb here, just trellises of a different sort.' She ought to be put out by his innuendo, but instead all she could do was fight back a smile. If she did smile, people would be bound to notice and wonder.

His breath feathered her ear in a seductive tickle. 'Your failing imagination aside, I fear you have me at a disadvantage.'

She smiled down into her tea cup, unable to suppress it any longer. 'Oh, I doubt that very much, Mr Sherard. I don't think you ever find yourself at a disadvantage where women are concerned.'

He grinned in agreement, his teeth white against the tan of his face. 'In this case I most definitely am. Might you do me the honour of your name? You know mine, but I don't know yours.'

He would know soon enough. Island communities were small. 'It's Bryn, Bryn Rutherford.' She felt him stiffen slightly, the pattern of his breathing hitching infinitesimally in recognition, signs that he knew her already, or perhaps knew *of* her. She turned to catch sight of his reaction, wanting to confirm she'd guessed right. She nearly missed it.

He hid the reaction well. Had he not been standing so close, she wouldn't have noticed it, but she'd not been wrong in its attribution. He recognised the name. How odd that a simple fact like a name could provoke surprise between strangers. Or perhaps it wasn't so surprising. Bridgetown was a small society and news must travel fast. Every merchant, every businessman in town would know by now her father was coming, and why. It was intriguing to count Kitt Sherard among their number since she had so quickly dismissed him on those grounds earlier that evening. Did she proceed with the fiction that she hadn't noticed his surprise or did she confront him?

She opted for a bit of both. 'Does the earl know what you do in your spare time?' She was having difficulty reconciling this rogue of a man with a gentleman who'd have the ear of an earl. She was starting to think Dartmoor must have owed him an extraordinary favour to make this recommendation. Although, dressed as he was tonight, Captain Sherard might be mistaken for a lord, too.

He was studying her, hot blue eyes raking the length of her evening gown. He crooked his arm. 'Miss Rutherford, perhaps you would accompany me out to the veranda for some fresh air?' There was going to be a price. Bryn saw the subtle negotiation immediately. He wasn't going to talk in here where they could be overheard, but he would be pleased to trade information for the privacy of the veranda and whatever might evolve out there.

Say yes, the adventurer in her coaxed without hesitation. If his impromptu kisses were that good on a balcony, what might they be like on a veranda with moonlight and a little premeditation behind them? The lady in her knew better and tonight the lady held sway. *But only for tonight*, her naughty side prompted. She wouldn't always have to be the lady. She'd promised herself that, too, among other things.

Bryn decided to challenge him. 'Why? So I can risk a dagger in the back from the lovely Caroline Bryant for stealing your attentions or so that you can manoeuvre your way into my father's good graces through me? It'll take more than a kiss and a trellis to wring a recommendation from me, Captain.'

The women had been trying to lobby her all night. As much as a starlit veranda stroll with Kitt Sherard appealed to the adventurer in her, she wasn't naive enough to think romance was the captain's sole motivation. Rutherford girls were taught early to detect an opportunist at fifty paces. With dowries like theirs, it was a necessity for surviving London ballrooms crawling with genteel fortune hunters.

Bryn let her eyes lock with his over her tea cup as she raised it to her lips. 'I never mix business with pleasure. It would be best if we said goodnight, Captain, before one of us makes any faulty assumptions about the other.' Goodness knew what he must think of her after the balcony. If it was anything akin to what she thought of him, there'd been plenty of assumptions made already. Hardly the first impression either of them would have chosen to make.

His eyes glittered with humour, giving her the impression that while she had got the last word, he still had the upper hand. He gave her a small bow like the one he'd given her on the balcony, elegant and exaggerated in a subtly mocking manner. 'I have a meeting with your father in the afternoon. Afterwards, we could walk in the garden. You can decide then if it's business or pleasure.'

A meeting with her father? She knew what he thought. It would be a meeting where she was relegated to some far part of the house while men did business. Who was she to correct his assumptions? Bryn smiled, hoping the wideness of her grin didn't give her away. 'Until tomorrow, then, Captain Sherard.' The arrogant man might think he had the upper hand and the last word, but she had a few surprises of her own.

Chapter Three

Damn and double damn! Of all the balconies in Bridgetown, he'd climbed up Bryn Rutherford's, the daughter of the man who'd come to induct the crown's currency into the Caribbean and the man on whom Kitt's future business interests depended. Kitt couldn't believe his luck. What he couldn't decide was if that luck was good or bad. He was still debating the issue the next afternoon when he set out for his meeting with her father.

A certain male part of him had concluded it was very good luck indeed. Bryn Rutherford was a spitfire of a goddess. She had the lips to prove it, and the tongue, and the body, and everything else, including an insightful amount of intelligence. She'd immediately seen the ramifications of going out on the veranda with him.

Her refusal made her something of a cynic, too. For all the spirit she'd shown on the balcony, she was wary of consequences or maybe it was the other way around: consequences had made her wary. Perhaps it simply made her a lady, a woman of discernment and responsible caution. Not everyone had a past chequered with regrets just because he did. Then again, this was the Caribbean, a far-flung, remote outpost of the British empire. In his experience, which was extensive, *ladies* didn't sail halfway around the world without good reason. Did Bryn Rutherford have something to hide, after all?

It was an intriguing thought, one that had Kitt thinking past the interview with her father and to the walk in the garden that would follow. How did a girl with a well-bred, and very likely a sheltered, upbringing end up with the ability to kiss like seduction itself?

No, not a girl, a *woman*. There was no girlishness about Bryn Rutherford. She was past the first blush of debutante innocence. The green silk she'd worn last night communicated that message with clarity, even if he hadn't already seen her in that sinfully clingy satin dressing robe, felt her uncorseted curves, or tasted her unabridged tongue in his mouth giving as good as it got. Thoughts like that had him thinking he was a very lucky man. Thoughts like that also had kept him up half the night.

The other half of the night belonged to another set of less pleasant thoughts—who wanted him dead this time? The candidates for that dubious honour were usually different, but the motives were always the same. Was this latest attacker simply one of his less savoury business associates who felt cheated or was it more complicated than that? Had someone from his past found him at last and bothered to cross the Atlantic for revenge? He'd been so careful in that regard. Discovery risked not only him, but his family. He'd cast aside all he owned including his name to keep them safe. Of course, discovery was always possible, although not probable. But he was alive today because he planned for the former. It wasn't enough to just play the odds. Not when the people he loved and who loved him were on the line.

His mind had been a veritable hive of activity last night. He supposed he should feel fortunate he'd got any sleep, all things considered. There'd been critical business thoughts claiming his attention, too: would Bryn Rutherford hold the balcony interlude against him? If she did, how would that skew the business opportunities a bank in Barbados would provide? Those questions were still plaguing him when he knocked on the Rutherfords' front door.

He was taken down a long hall by a stately butler who must have come with them from England. The butler, Sneed, fit the surroundings perfectly with his air of formality. In the short time they'd been in residence, the Rutherfords had already left their aristocratic mark on the house. They'd come loaded with luxuries; carpets and paintings adorned the floors and walls in testimony to the Rutherfords' prestige to say nothing of the butler.

Kitt always made it a habit to study his surroundings. How a man lived offered all nature of insight. This house, the décor and its accessories were all designed to communicate one message: power and authority. Kitt approved of the intent. It was precisely the message a man charged with the crown's banking interests in the new world should convey. But, did the message match the man? That remained to be seen.

The door to the study was open, revealing the same luxury and wealth that dominated the hall. The butler announced him to the room in general and Kitt was surprised to see that Rutherford was not alone. James Selby, an aspiring local importer, was already present. The weasel. He must have come early. Well, Selby's limitations would speak for themselves sooner or later. Hopefully sooner.

The surprise didn't end there. Selby wasn't the only other person present. By a set of open French doors that let in the light and the breeze, her head demurely bent over an embroidery hoop, sat Bryn Rutherford. She looked up for the briefest of moments, long enough to let a coy smile slip over her lips when she met his gaze, her eyes communicating silent victory.

The minx! She'd known all along she was sitting in on the meeting. *Until tomorrow, then.* He could still see the wide smile on her face, the cat's-got-the-cream look in those grey eyes. He hadn't quite understood at the time. He understood now. She'd been laughing at him, getting a little of her own back.

'You look well settled for a man who has just arrived,' Kitt said affably, shaking hands with The Honourable Bailey Rutherford. Today, he would finally have a chance to take the man's measure more closely than he'd been able to do last night during their quick introduction at the Crenshaws'. The man was in his early fifties, with faded chestnut hair starting to thin, although once it must have been the rich colour of his daughter's. His face betrayed weariness in its lines and there was a trace of sadness in his eyes. He exuded none of his daughter's confidence.

Bailey Rutherford waved a dismissive hand in the air, the gesture showing off a heavy gold ring on one finger, another subtle sign of wealth and power. 'I can't take credit for any of this. I wouldn't know where to begin when it comes to setting up a house. My wife always handled these things. Now my daughter does.' He smiled in Bryn's direction. 'Did you meet her last night? Of course you must have.' There was pride in those last words and sorrow in the first. The sentence told Kitt volumes about Bailey Rutherford.

He was playing catch-up in that regard. Kitt would have liked to have talked to Rutherford prior to this meeting, would have preferred getting to know the man so he could assess Rutherford's character more thoroughly. Missing dinner had been unfortunate, but there'd been nothing for it. After leaving Bryn on her balcony, he'd taken a circuitous route home to avoid another encounter with the would-be assassins and then he'd absolutely had to bathe. By the time he was presentable, it had been too late for dinner.

'You already know Mr Selby?' Rutherford enquired, indicating that Kitt should take the empty chair. 'We were just talking about the geography of the islands.' They proceeded to continue that discussion, Kitt adding a bit of advice here and there, but Selby was in full glory, espousing his latest hobby; cataloguing the island's butterflies for a book. It would be a rather difficult book to write, Kitt thought. Barbados wasn't known for its butterflies. Beyond Rutherford's shoulder, Bryn rolled her eyes. Good. She found Selby as ridiculous as he did.

Thanks to Selby's windbag tendencies, there was plenty of time to let his gaze and his thoughts drift towards Bryn, who was trying hard to look demure in her quiet day dress of baby-blue muslin and white lace, her hair done up in a braided coronet, her graceful neck arched over her hoop. She wasn't fooling him for a minute.

Her very presence at such a meeting was provoking. Certainly, she'd planned to be here from the start, but in what capacity? She was no mere innocent attendee sitting here for her health, no matter that she'd dressed for the part. Most men wouldn't look beyond the dress and the sewing. They'd see her embroidery hoop for what it was—a woman's occupation.

Kitt saw it as much more—a ploy, a distraction even. He knew better. He had kissed her and a woman kissed her truth, *always*. Kitt had kissed enough women to know. He knew, too, that Bryn Rutherford's truth was passion. One day it would slip its leash—passion usually did. Kitt shifted subtly in his seat, his body finding the prospect of a lady unleashed surprisingly arousing.

Rutherford finally turned the conversation towards banking and Kitt had to marshal his attentions away from the point beyond his host's shoulder. 'I've been meeting with people all day. Now that the royal charter for a bank has been granted, everything is happening quickly. By this time next year, we'll have a bank established in Barbados and branches opening up on the other islands.' He smiled. His eyes, grey like his daughter's but not as lively, were faraway. 'That seems to be the way of life. We wait and wait for years, thinking we have all the time in the world and when the end comes, it comes so fast. So much time and then not nearly enough.'

Kitt leaned forward, wanting to focus on the bank before time for the interview ran out and all they'd discussed were butterflies. 'It's an exciting prospect, though. A bank will change the face of business and trade here,' he offered, hoping the opening would give Rutherford a chance to elaborate on the possibilities. At present, sugar and rum were as equally valid as the Dutch and Spanish currencies used as tender because the crown had not permitted the export of British money to its Caribbean colonies. As a result, actual money was in scarce supply. Plenty of people settled their debts in barter. Currency would make payment more portable. Casks of rum were heavy.

When all Rutherford did was nod, Kitt went on. 'The presence of an English bank would allow British pounds in Barbados. It would create alternatives for how we pay for goods and how we can settle bills, but it will also affect who will control access to those funds.' Kitt was not naive enough to think the crown had established the charter out of the goodness of its royal heart. The crown and those associated with it stood to make a great deal of money as a result of this decision. Kitt wanted to be associated. The charter would give the crown a monopoly not just on banking, but over the profits of the island.

'Exactly so,' Rutherford agreed, his eyes focused on a faceted paperweight.

It was Kitt's understanding Mr Rutherford's job was to make sure the charter was settled and the right players were in place. Rutherford would decide who those players would be. Although right now, Rutherford hardly seemed capable of making such weighty decisions. Then again, it might also be the effects of travel and late nights. Rutherford was not the youngest of men. Yet another interesting factor in having chosen him. Still, the bottom line was this: the interview was not going well.

It occurred to Kitt that Rutherford's disinterest might

have something to do with him personally. Maybe the man had already decided not to include him in the first tier of investors. Perhaps his daughter had told him certain things about balconies and kisses after all.

Kitt decided to be blunt. He had worked too hard for this invitation. He knew very well he'd only got his name on the list of potential investors because of his connections to Ren Dryden, Earl of Dartmoor. It had been Ren who'd put his name forward. 'What kind of bank will it be?' Kitt asked. He had his ideas, but clarification was important. There were savings banks and joint stock banks—quite a wide variety, really, since the banking reforms a few years ago—and when it came to money, not all banks were equal.

Rutherford showed a spark of life. 'Joint stock, of course. There are backers in London already assembled, waiting for counterpart investors to be assembled here. It will be like the provincial bank I was on the board for in England.'

Kitt nodded his understanding. This was good. The man had some experience. He would need it. These sorts of arrangements weren't without risk. Joint stock meant two things. First, it meant that the investors would share in the profits and in the losses. What the bank chose to invest in would be important, so would the level of risk. The less risk the better, but the less risk the fewer the profits, too. Second, it meant that shares could be traded on the exchange. They'd operate essentially like a business. This was not just a mere savings bank, it was a venture capital bank.

'Would we be loaning money to plantations?' Kitt asked, thinking of how that would change the current loan system. Right now, private merchants were primarily responsible for advancing the planters loans against the upcoming harvest so planters could buy supplies. It was what he'd done for Ren, or had tried to do for Ren before the bandits had upended the rum sale yesterday. A bank would reduce the opportunity for single merchants to finance planters. For those not on the board it would eliminate an avenue of income. No wonder there was competition for these spots.

Out of the corner of his eye, he caught Bryn reaching for something under her skeins of threads. No, not reaching. *Writing.* She was writing on a notebook. She'd been taking notes the entire time. Like Selby, he'd got so caught up in the discussion, in assessing Rutherford's assets, he'd not taken time to notice. Her part in all this was growing more interesting by the moment.

'It would depend,' Rutherford explained, 'on their collateral. Property cannot be taken as security.'

Kitt was thoughtful for a moment. Rutherford knew his banking vocabulary. That was reassuring. 'What do we mean by property, exactly?' Property, was a pretty wide term.

'It means the obvious, of course; homes and farms cannot be used as security.' Rutherford paused for a long moment and Bryn looked up, neatly inserting herself into the conversation.

'But it also means the less obvious, too, doesn't it, Father? That merchandise like rum or sugar can't be used as security either?' Kitt recognised immediately it wasn't a question as much as a prompt.

'It's not really a question of collateral then, is it?' Kitt surmised, flashing Bryn an inquisitive glance. 'We're to invest and hope there's profit. If there isn't, we're unlucky. There's no recouping of funds.' There would be no collateral. The charter had just couched it in different terms.

'Yes. Certainly, we can invest in the plantations, we just can't expect anything in return beyond a piece of the profits,' Rutherford said, regaining his confidence. 'Still, there's money to be made here.'

Kitt raised his eyebrows, encouraging the man to say more about what that money might be. Rum certainly, sugar and even tobacco in places were good cash crops. Then there was the merchandising end of things if a man acted quickly enough and knew when to get out. There was a boom going on currently, riding the wave of emancipation. Freed slaves meant more wage-earning consumers and that meant more demand for goods. Kitt knew that boom would not last, but for now it was spawning a retail layer that had originally been focused only on wholesale to large plantations.

'There's land, for starters,' Rutherford offered, looking pleased with himself.

'There's some,' Kitt said evenly, but he found the choice odd. It wouldn't have been his first option. But a non-native Englishman would. A newcomer wouldn't understand. 'Most of the land in Barbados is already under cultivation.' He'd been here for six years and knew first-hand there wasn't much left to claim unless it was bought from a previous owner. It was something the freedmen were struggling with. They wanted to be their own farmers, but there wasn't any land. This was an area where only time could teach a newcomer the realities of property ownership on an island where land was definitely a finite commodity.

Sneed entered to announce the next appointment was waiting. Rutherford nodded and turned to Kitt. 'I will be assembling the board of directors over the next few weeks. I hope we'll have a chance to talk further. I hear you're a successful businessman in these parts. You come recommended. Your expertise of the area would be useful in determining the right investments for us.'

'Quite possibly.' Kitt rose and shook the man's hand. The veiled invitation was progress enough for today. It confirmed he had not been ruled out. He also appreciated he wasn't being asked to commit today. The bank was going to happen. It was already a *fait accompli*. That was assured. What wasn't assured was the bank's success. If the bank was going to do well, it would need someone knowledgeable and strong at its helm. A weaker man might easily be led astray and subsequently Rutherford, too.

Selby rose as well. 'I was hoping I might have a private word with you before I go?' he said to Rutherford, shooting a pointed look in Kitt's direction. In general, Selby didn't like him. He was too reckless for the young man's more conservative tastes. A plainer plea for privacy could not have been made. Kitt might have been offended over the dismissal if it hadn't suited his purposes.

Kitt glanced over at Bryn. 'Perhaps you could show me the gardens? You mentioned them last night and I'm eager to see them.' He turned towards Rutherford. 'If it's all right with you, of course?'

Rutherford beamed and nodded. 'Absolutely. Bryn dear, show our guest the gardens. I didn't know you were a botanist, Captain?'

Kitt gave a short nod of his head. 'I'm a man of diverse interests, Mr Rutherford.' He offered Bryn his arm, feeling a smug sense of satisfaction at the disapproving frown on Selby's face. It served him right for coming early and then asking for a private audience on top of that. 'Shall we, Miss Rutherford? I want to see the trellis you've told me so much about. It's a climbing trellis, if I remember correctly?'

Chapter Four

'You're a wicked man to bring up the incident in such company,' Bryn scolded him as soon as they stepped outside. She wasn't truly upset with him, at least not about the potential for exposure anyway. She'd reasoned away those concerns last night. He had nothing to gain but an unwanted wife from telling.

Kitt merely grinned. 'Harmless fun only, I assure you. It means nothing to anyone but us.' Drat him, he was enjoying teasing her and that grin of his said he wasn't done yet. 'But you, miss, are another story entirely. *You* knew you would be at the meeting. I feel quite taken advantage of.' He feigned hurt, then added with a wink, 'I can't let you have all the surprises.'

Bryn gave him a coy smile to indicate she understood his game. He no more liked losing the upper hand than she did. There was safety in having control. Control meant protection against the unexpected. 'Ah, it's to be retribution then?' She couldn't resist teasing him in return. His humour was infectious, even if she needed to remember it was deceiving. It would be too easy to forget that his good-natured response veiled something more, as did her own clever answers. They were both after the same thing—to take the other's measure. What was fact and what was fiction when it came to the faces they showed society?

Bryn slanted him a sideways look as they walked. If she asked, would he give her the answer she wanted? What had he been doing in this same garden yesterday under significantly different circumstances? Twenty-four hours ago, he'd been an uninvited intruder. Today, he was received as a highly sought guest, a man whose favour her father would do well to curry. 'It hardly seems fair for you to hold me accountable for such a small thing when you were the one who invaded my balcony. If we're keeping a tally of surprises, you seem well ahead of me in that regard.'

Kitt stopped and turned towards her, his free hand covering hers where it rested on his sleeve. The simple gesture, something countless gentlemen had done on countless walks before, made her keenly sensitive to the intimacy of bare skin on bare skin. It was his eyes that made it different, how they followed his gesture, forcing her gaze to do the same until they rested on the point where his hand met hers. 'Surprises or secrets, Bryn?'

His voice was a low rumble, his eyes lifting briefly to hers as he said her name. 'I find the difference between the two to be slim indeed.' This was how sin started, with a sharp stab of awareness igniting between them over the intimate caress of a name. Oh, he did not play fair! She'd meant to be interrogating *him* and here he was flirting with her, although flirting was not nearly a strong enough word for what he was doing.

'Secrets?' Bryn feigned ignorance of his intent.

'Don't play coy with me, I much prefer your bold

mouth.' Kitt's gaze lingered on her lips. He was a master indeed at conjuring seduction out of thin air if he could turn the slightest of gestures into something more.

'What were you doing in that meeting?' It was said with the quality of a caress, but no less lethal for its intimacy. All seductions had their price.

'What were you doing on my balcony?' Bryn challenged in a breathy whisper. Now that they'd come to the crux of the conversation, the one subject they'd been dancing around, it was hard to concentrate. Most of her mind was focused on the fact they were only inches apart, inches from another kiss, from tasting the boldness of their mouths as he so bluntly put it. Her body knew it, hungered for it after only one taste.

Anticipation hummed through her, but Bryn steeled her resolve. Had he no sense of caution? Had *she*? Sneed *could* be coming out with lemonade this very minute. Maybe. The lady in her wouldn't risk it, but the adventurer would. Sneed would be terribly busy this afternoon. The odds of getting away with a stolen kiss beneath the palms were probably in her favour...

Stop it! She had to quit thinking like this, although Kitt Sherard clearly thought like this on a very regular basis if the episode yesterday was anything to go on. Bryn took mental hold of herself: *Make him accountable. Answers before kisses. Your father's business depends on it.* 'What I was doing by the window is simple. The light is best by the window—' Bryn began.

'For writing? You were taking notes,' he interrupted, his accusation implied in his tone. Kitt stopped his tracing, his hand closing over her wrist in a harsh grip. His blue eyes were harder now, their seductiveness gone.

'You can fool Selby, but not me. I know what I saw. You were there for a purpose.'

'It hardly matters,' Bryn answered sharply. She did not have to stand here and validate her presence at that meeting to this man she barely knew just because he could turn her insides to mush and ruin any hopes of logical thought. All things considered, she was holding her ground well.

Kitt shrugged, his grip relaxing on her wrist. He gave her a slow smile. It was not a pleasant smile, it was a warning. Somewhere, she'd made a mistake and he was about to capitalise on it. 'Perhaps you're right and it hardly matters. What happened on the balcony stays on the balcony, after all.'

Bryn saw the trap too late. She'd walked right into it for all her careful play up until now. He was casting her as the hypocrite. How else could she argue the balcony mattered, but her presence at the meeting did not? There was nothing for it but to answer. She met his gaze, giving no sign of having contradicted herself. 'My father needs reliable men in this venture.'

'Men like James Selby?' Kitt put in with an arch of his blond brow. 'Selby wouldn't know an opportunity if it jumped up and bit him in the arse.'

'And you would?' Bryn countered sharply, only to receive one of his disarming grins.

'Nothing bites me in the arse, princess, opportunity or otherwise.'

His candour made her blush. Her mind had run right down that rather provocative path created by his words, just as it had last night at the the thought of his bath, as he'd likely intended. 'I'm not worried about the balcony,' Bryn said staunchly, keeping an eye on the bright coral hibiscus across the yard to maintain her composure. It was far less distracting than the man beside her. 'I want to know because you will be doing business with my father. That worries me more than a few stolen kisses. If he is to trust you, he needs to *know* you.' And what about her? Could she trust him?

The question was merely one of many which had plagued her last night long after she'd returned from the Crenshaws'. What sort of man climbed balconies in sweat-streaked shirts and then turned up in expensive evening clothes a few hours later at an exclusive soirée, only to sit down at the piano and entertain the ladies as if he had manners.

'Ah, perhaps this is more about *you* than it is about your father,' Kitt said shrewdly. 'You needn't worry, I won't blackmail you with the balcony.'

'Of course not,' Bryn retorted. 'You'd be doing nothing more than compromising yourself into a marriage if my father found out and that can hardly be what a man like you wants.'

His eyes narrowed, the air about them crackling with tension. 'A man like me?' He became positively lethal in those moments. She'd trodden on dangerous ground with her hot words. 'What do you know about men like me?'

She held her ground. 'Enough to know you're not the marrying kind.' This had become a perilous verbal *pas de deux*. What had started as a probe into the nature of his business character had rapidly become personal.

'I assume you mean one without a moral code, who takes what he wants without thought for the consequences, someone who serves only himself?' He was riveting like this, a sleek, predatory animal, stalking her with his eyes. No gentleman had ever behaved thusly with her. They were all too busy pandering to her, to her fortune.

His hand reached up to cup her jaw, the pad of his thumb stroking the fullness of her lower lip with a hint of roughness to match his words. 'Your logic fails you, if you believe there's nothing to fear from a "man like me".'

'You don't frighten me.' Far from it. He excited her. Bryn swallowed hard, more aroused than insulted at being called into account for her words.

'Maybe I should.' His voice was a low rumble, part-seduction, part-intimidation. She couldn't decide which. 'I would think my sort would be *extraordinarily* interested in a woman like you: beautiful, wealthy, well positioned socially, kisses like the naughtiest of angels.' He bent close, close enough to put his mouth to her ear, for his lips to brush the shell of it. 'Princess, I am the epitome of everything you've been warned about.'

All she had to do was make the smallest of movements to fall into him and whatever he was offering. She leaned towards him, into him, but too late.

Kitt stepped back, releasing her. 'Now that's settled, if you'll excuse me? I have another appointment.'

A more cautious woman would retreat the field and admit defeat, but not Bryn. She was determined to not let him get away without an answer. A man who wouldn't give one was definitely hiding something. 'You're really not going to tell me?' She gave him a last chance to confess. 'About the balcony?'

He swept her a bow, eyes full of mischief. 'You have my permission to let your imagination run free.'

She would not let him get away with boyish charm

after the rather adult heat of the previous moments. Bryn fixed him with a hard stare. 'I can imagine quite a lot of reasons, none of them good.' Perhaps if he thought she would imagine the worst, he'd rush to amend that image. Having a poor impression of him could hardly be what he wanted when a position on the bank board was on the line. She was not naive. She knew what sort of men came to the Caribbean: adventurers, men who were down on their luck, men who wanted to make new lives. Certainly there were a few like James Selby who was here for decent opportunities as a merchant, but he was not the norm.

Kitt gave her a sly smile. 'Then I leave you with this: you're a smart woman. You already know men who scale balconies are up to no good. You don't need me to tell you that.'

The garden was quiet after he left and somehow less vibrant, as if he'd taken some of the bright, tropical colour with him. Bryn took a seat on a stone bench near the hibiscus, not wanting to go in, not wanting to encounter any of her father's business partners. She wanted time to think first.

Kitt was right. She *had* known. She'd just hoped for better. Or perhaps, more accurately, she'd hoped it wouldn't matter and it hadn't until he'd walked into the Crenshaws'. Now, she had a dilemma. Should she stay silent and let her father discover Kitt Sherard for himself or should she warn her father off before real harm could be done? Could she even do that without exposing what had happened on the balcony?

Bryn plucked at a bright orange blossom. Current evidence suggested the latter was not possible at this point without risking the consequences. Current evidence also suggested Kitt was hiding something. Her hand stalled on the blossom. No, he wasn't hiding anything, he was all but admitting to it, whatever 'it' was—further proof she needed more evidence. She was working off supposition and kisses only. She needed more than that. Too much hung in the balance. A man who compromised her, compromised her father. Likewise, if she voiced her concerns, she could ruin Kitt's investment chances.

It all boiled down to one essential question: could Kitt Sherard be trusted? There was only one way to find out. She would have to get to know him—a prospect that was both dangerous and delicious since he'd made it abundantly clear he was not above mixing business with pleasure.

Chapter Five

'I don't have pleasant news.' Kitt kept his voice low as he and Ren Dryden, the Earl of Dartmoor, his mentor in this latest banking venture, but more importantly, his friend, enjoyed an after-dinner brandy in Ren's study at Sugarland. Night had fallen and Ren's French doors were open to the evening breeze. The dinner with Ren and Emma had been delicious, their company delightful, both well worth the five-mile ride out to the plantation from Bridgetown. Kitt hated returning their hospitality with bad news.

'Tell me, there's no use holding back. I'm not the pregnant one.' Ren pitched his voice low, too, aware of how sound carried in the dark Caribbean night. With Emma expecting, Kitt knew Ren was eager nothing upset her, yet another reason Kitt was reluctant to be the bearer of such news. Ren shared everything with his wife. Kitt didn't think he'd be able to keep this from her.

'It was a trap.' Kitt still couldn't believe it, couldn't *understand* it, no matter how many times he replayed the ambush in his mind. 'They waited until we'd unloaded the barrels and then they charged, right there, on the beach in daylight.' Not that it made much difference if it was night or day on a deserted beach. There was no one to see either way. Things like this happened to others who were less meticulous, less prepared, less cynical. But he had a certain reputation, which made him all the more suspicious about the motives behind the attack. What had he missed? It was a simple run, the kind he made all the time. What had he missed? The words had become a restless, uncontainable mantra in his mind that obliterated other thought.

Kitt rose and began to pace the length of Ren's French doors, some small part of him registering Ren's eyes on him. But most of his mind was focused internally, replaying the ambush, running through potential scenarios, potential suspects responsible for the attack. *What had he missed? This had been the first deal with a new client he'd contracted with a couple weeks ago. Someone, it appeared, who might not have been who he claimed to be.*

Kitt stopped pacing and leaned his arm against the frame of the doors. He felt dirty, as if he'd unknowingly picked up a disease and then unwittingly spread it to a friend. *Who? Who? Who?* pounded relentlessly in his head, his mind was determined to solve this mystery. Kitt closed his eyes, thoughts coming hard and fast. It wouldn't be the first time someone had given a false name to their agent. *Follow that line of thought, Sherard,* his mind urged. He was aware of Ren talking as if from a distance. He couldn't concentrate on Ren's words just now, but four managed to break through.

'They took the rum?' Ren asked quietly, neutrally.

Kitt's eyes flew open in disbelief. The day second-rate bandits took a cargo from him was the day he'd quit the business. 'Of course not! We fought like berserkers to protect your rum. You should have seen young Passemore with his knife, stabbing away like he fought the fiends of hell for his very soul.'

'Stop!' Ren's interruption was terse, his eyes hard as he grasped the implications. 'You *fought* to protect the rum? Are you *insane*?'

'They were bandits, Ren, they had weapons,' Kitt answered one-part exasperated, one-part incredulous. Did Ren not know him at all? Did Ren think he'd give up his friend's cargo without a fight when he knew how much Ren and Emma were counting on it? *On him?* Kitt pushed a hand through his hair. He owed Ren a debt of friendship he could never truly repay.

'We had to do *something*, Ren.'

'You should have let them have it, that's what you should have done. It's only rum, after all,' Ren scolded.

Only rum? Kitt almost laughed, but Ren would not have appreciated the humour. Ren had only been here a year. Island nuances, or the lack of them, were still relatively new to him. Rum was Caribbean gold. Taking a man's rum in Barbados was like robbing the Bank of England in London. People did indeed die for it, although Kitt didn't plan on being one of them.

Kitt looked out into the night, his mind working hard. Behind him, he heard the shift of his friend rising from his chair and crossing the room to him, determination in Ren's footfalls. 'Dear God, Kitt, you could have been killed and for what? *For rum?*' Indignation rolled off Ren. Kitt didn't have to see him to feel it.

'What would you have me do? Do you think so little of me that I would give up your cargo when I know how much you and Emma were counting on it? Counting on *me*? I couldn't just let them take it.'

The bandits had known that. Kitt's mind lit on those last words. Or at least whoever had hired them had known, had guessed that he would fight. It had been what they'd wanted. He recalled now how, after he'd shot the man leading the charge, the bandits had not been deterred. He remembered muttering to Passemore, 'This means war.' Those bandits had been spoiling for a fight, looking for one even. He remembered being surprised by their fierceness, their determination to go up against Kitt Sherard and his men—something most were unwilling to do. The rum had been a cover to get to him, or had it?

Beside him, Ren was still bristling. 'I'd never forgive myself if you died over one of my cargoes, neither would Emma. Promise me you won't take such a chance again. I don't want you dead.'

But someone did. That was the part that niggled at him. He'd had five deliveries this week. If whoever had hired the bandits had wanted him, they could have taken him any time that week and had better opportunities to do it. *All right, where does that lead you? If that's true, what does it mean?* His brain prompted him to make the next connection. It meant the rum was *not* a cover or a coincidence. Kitt tried out his hypothesis on Ren. 'They weren't trying to kill me over just any rum. They were after me and *your* rum.' And when that had failed, they'd been happy to settle for just him in a back alley of Bridgetown.

Ren blew out a breath and withdrew to the decanter. 'I'm going to need more brandy for this. What aren't you telling me?' Kitt could hear the chink of the heavy crystal stopper being removed, the familiar splash of brandy in a glass, but he didn't turn, didn't move his gaze from the opaque darkness of the night, not wanting any sensory distractions to interrupt his thoughts. He was close now, so close, if he could just hold on to the ideas whirling through his head and form them into a cohesive whole.

'There were two men waiting for me back in port,' Kitt said.

Ren moaned and gave the decanter a slosh to judge the remainder. 'I don't think I have enough. Is that why you were late to the Crenshaws'? And here you had me believing it was because you were out carousing.'

Well, that and a certain woman on a certain balcony—not that Ren needed to know that part. The carousing part wasn't entirely untrue. The fewer people who knew about Bryn's balcony the better, especially Ren, who had done so much to get him on the list of potential bank investors. Ren had enough bad news tonight without hearing he'd been kissing Mr Rutherford's daughter, no matter how accidental.

'Would it be fair to conclude those men are still out there?' Ren returned to him and handed him the glass. Kitt nodded and waited for the other conclusion to hit. It did. 'And you travelled out here *alone*? They could have had you any time on the road. Dammit, Kitt, have you any sense?'

The thought had occurred to Kitt, too. Traffic on the road between Sugarland and Bridgetown was light, especially during the heat of the late afternoon. There were places where an attack would draw no attention even if anyone chanced along. 'I was prepared for them.' Kitt shrugged, thinking of the knife in his boot and the pistols he'd slung over his saddle. Part of him had been hoping they'd try again, hoping he could wring some answers from the bastards when they did.

They were standing close together now, Ren's gaze on his face searching for answers he didn't have yet. 'Who would do such a thing? Do you have any idea who wants you dead?' There was real concern in Ren's tone and it touched him. Until last year, he'd been alone, cut off from all he knew, all social ties gone except the ones he'd created in this new life of his, but they would never be close, would never be allowed to replace the ones he'd given up. It was too dangerous. Closeness created curiosity and that was a commodity he could not afford. Then Ren had shown up and it was like coming back to life. Here was one of the two people left who knew *him* and it was gift beyond measure. 'Who, Kitt?' Ren asked again.

Kitt shook his head. 'That's not the question to be asking.' That list was rather long, definitely distinguished and would result in a needle-in-the-haystack sort of search. 'The real question is who would want revenge against *both* of us?' *That* list was considerably shorter. Ren was well liked and an earl besides. There were few who would dare to be his enemy. But there was one...

Suddenly Kitt knew with the starkest of clarity who it was and *why* it was. It was the scenario that made the most sense, and frankly, it was the scenario he preferred to the other possibilities. The other scenarios were far worse to contemplate, like the one where his past came to the island and destroyed everything he'd built, everything he'd become. If that happened, he wasn't sure he could protect himself.

He felt better now, back in control. There was relief in the knowing, in having a concrete enemy, although he doubted Ren would share that relief. It was all fairly simple now that all the pieces had come together. He faced Ren. 'I know who it is. It's Hugh Devore.'

'No, it couldn't be,' Ren answered in almost vehement denial, but his face was pale. 'Devore is gone, he promised to leave the island, to leave us alone.'

'A man will promise any number of things when his life is on the line,' Kitt said. 'He's had a year to rethink that promise and it probably didn't mean much to him anyway.' Last year, he and Ren had forcibly exiled three planters from the island after Arthur Gridley had assaulted Emma and attempted to burn down Sugarland. Gridley was dead now, shot by one of his own, but the others were at large, a deal he and Ren had struck with them to avoid exposing Emma to the rigours of testifying at a public trial.

'Do you know where?' Ren asked quietly.

Kitt shook his head. He had been the one to sail them to another island and leave them to their exile. The island had been rather remote, barely populated. They'd been free, of course, to leave that island, as long as they didn't return to Barbados.

'Cunningham went back to England,' Kitt said. It wasn't Cunningham he was worried about. Cunningham had been the one to shoot Gridley, the ringleader. He was done with the group. It was the other two, Elias Blakely, the accountant, and Gridley's right hand, Hugh Devore, whom Kitt was worried about. 'I have no idea where the others might have gone.' Devore would be dangerous. Exile had cost him everything: his fortune, his home and even his wife. Devore's wife had refused to go with him. She'd taken Cunningham's cue and gone back to her family in England.

Ren's face was etched with worry, as well it should be. Devore was vindictive and cruel and Ren had a family now; a wife and a new baby on the way, beautiful things to be sure, but liabilities, too. Devore would not hesitate to use those treasures against him and Ren knew it.

Kitt clapped a hand on Ren's shoulder in comfort. 'I'll find them.' He could handle trouble of this nature. He would protect Ren with every breath in his body. It had been Ren who had hidden him that long last night in the dark hours before the tide, Ren who had stood against the watch when they'd come. Kitt would never forget.

'You don't need to protect me,' Ren said with quiet steel. 'This is not England, Kitt, and I'm not your addle-pated brother. You do not need to sacrifice yourself for me.'

Kitt dropped his hand, his gaze holding Ren's. Ren was one of the few who could make that comment, in part because it took a certain boldness to remind Kitt of his family, and in part because there were only two people outside of that family who knew the truth. Ren was one, Benedict Debreed was the other. Kitt blinked once and looked away, the only concession to emotion he would make. 'Perhaps not sacrifice, but you'll need me to watch your back and Emma's.'

Ren grinned. '*That* offer I will take.'

The emotion eased between them and Kitt smiled back. The crisis, the bad news, had passed for now. 'In the meanwhile, I'll set up another deal for your rum and you can tell Emma everything will be fine.'

Ren's eyes drifted to the clock on the desk at the mention of his wife. Kitt laughed. Even after a year of marriage, Ren was thinking about bed, about Emma. 'You don't have to stay up with me,' Kitt assured him with a wolfish grin. 'I can finish my brandy all by myself.'

Ren hesitated. 'I can wait a few more minutes—you haven't told me about the new banker in Bridgetown yet.'

'No, you can't wait. It's written all over your face how much you want to be with her.' Kitt chuckled. 'Go, the rest of my news can keep until morning. We'll have another good talk before I leave tomorrow.' He shooed Ren off with a gesture of his hand.

'Well, if you're sure?' Ren set down his glass, already halfway to the door.

'I'm sure. Goodnight,' Kitt called after him with a laugh.

Kitt took a swallow, listening to the tick of the clock. The room was quiet without Ren and he let all the dangerous thoughts come, the ones he'd struggled to suppress these last few days, the surge of envy at all Ren had and that he could never have. It wasn't that he coveted Emma or the baby or the plantation. It was that he could never have such a family himself. Nor could he ever claim the family he'd once had.

In the last year both Ren and Benedict had married happily and against no small odds. That wasn't the strange part. Men like them, men with titles and obligations, got married all the time. They were expected to. They were expected—required even—to stand at stud for the benefit of their great families and procure the next generation in exchange for dowries that would sustain the financial burden of expanding the family line. The strange part was, despite those expectations, Ren and Benedict had managed to marry for love, to marry beyond their obligations.

In doing so, they'd turned marriage into something otherworldly, something Kitt had not thought possible when he'd made his sacrifice. But now, seeing that it *was* possible, well, that changed everything. Only it was six years too late to change anything for him. He was Kitt Sherard, adventurer extraordinaire, lover nonpareil, a man who lived on the edge of decency in his occupation as a rum runner among other things. He didn't pretend all his cargoes were legal, just some of them, *enough* of them, to massage Bridgetown society into tolerating him among their midst. He had only what he'd created for himself: a home, a ship, even his name. He was a self-fashioned man who came from nowhere, belonged to no one, was claimed by no one. This identity as a man from 'nowhere' suited him, even if it made him socially questionable. It wasn't the sort of background mamas wanted their daughters to marry into. Nor would he allow them to. That meant he should leave Bryn Rutherford alone. There was no need, no point, in tempting them both into foolishness.

She had been right today. More right than she knew. He wasn't the marrying kind. She'd only been talking about his flirtatious behaviour. The life he lived was dangerous and unpredictable, enemies lurking in the shadows, as illustrated by the latest turn of events. But he didn't have a choice, not a real choice anyway. It had to be this way. He was destined to be alone. Alone kept him safe, kept others safe.

His life kept him busy, made him rich enough to buy any pleasure he wanted, any distraction he needed to keep his mind off the past, because it wasn't just the past he remembered, it wasn't just the sacrifice he remembered, but also the guilt—he'd run to save himself when perhaps he should have stayed and saved others first.

Kitt poured a third glass, trying hard to push away the memories. He could not imagine bringing a wife and a family into the mire of his past or the peril of his present. Indeed, they would only be liabilities and they would always be at risk. He'd not be able to concentrate on his work if he was always worried about them. What was the point of having a wife, a family, if he *didn't* care enough to worry about them? He knew himself well enough to know he'd *want* to worry. It had been concern over another that had brought him to this state of life in the first place. His thoughts went to the man Passemore had shot. Was there a wife and children waiting for the dead man even now? Were people wondering and worrying when he didn't come home?

He saw his own family in the sad picture such an image painted; his once-brilliant, sparkling family. Had they learned to laugh again without him? He hoped so. He didn't want to imagine them grey and wilted—the way they'd looked the last time he'd seen them. The scandal had broken them. Did they still wait expectantly for some small piece of news about him from Benedict the same way he coveted the mail packet?

Benedict's letters were the only connection he allowed himself, the only risk he allowed himself where his family was concerned. He cherished each scrap of news. His brother, his *twin*, was courting Viscount Enderly's daughter. An engagement was in the offing.

Kitt had rejoiced over that in the last letter. It proved his choice had been worth it. The scandal had been survived, by them at least. But there was pain, too. He wouldn't be there for the wedding, wouldn't be there to stand beside his brother as a witness, wouldn't be there to act as uncle to the children that would follow. Only in the dark, fortified with brandy, did Kitt ever permit himself to admit how much he missed his brother. But to see him, to contact him, would be to condemn him and Kitt loved him far too much to risk it even if it had killed him to sever that tie. To those who suspected he still lived, he was a pariah. To those in London who believed him dead, his death was considered a good riddance and a just one.

Kitt couldn't imagine a woman who would be willing to risk stepping into his life once she truly understood it. His bed, on a temporary basis, was one thing. A woman needn't know too much about him to enjoy his bed. He had a woman in every port and in some places, he had two. But permanently? Therein lay the risk.

A hazy, brandy-induced thought came to him. What would Bryn Rutherford do if she knew how he'd amassed his fortune? Would she run screaming to her father or would she throw caution to the wind like she had yesterday? One had to wonder if Bryn Rutherford was in the habit of living recklessly when no one was looking or if it was merely a momentary lapse in judgement? Kitt hoped for the latter.

It had been rather heady business today in the garden, sparring with her, the lightness of their banter cleverly interspersed with a more serious hunt for information. She'd been a rather tenacious opponent, shrewd enough to know he was not all he seemed. He'd actually found arguing with her a bit arousing, watching those grey eyes flash, knowing her mind was working as they stood close enough to do something other than argue. He'd thought about it—about silencing her with a kiss—she'd thought about it, too. He'd seen it in her eyes. She'd been aware of his intentions when his eyes had dropped to those full, kissable lips of hers.

Here in the dim room, the darkness encroaching, the memory had the power to pleasantly rouse him. But Kitt decided against it. Kissing her would have been the easy answer and a belittling one for such a fine opponent. If he couldn't have her trust, he'd at least have her respect. It was a starting point at least. Ren had used his title, his English influence via Benedict back in London, to get his name on the list of potential investors. Kitt would not let the opportunity go languishing for the sake of a few kisses.

Kitt shifted in his chair to a more comfortable position, letting his mind drift. Bryn Rutherford was something of a conundrum. She'd been fire in his arms, eager to meet him on equal ground. Yet the woman he'd encountered at the dinner party had been concerned with propriety, which posed a most certain dichotomy to passion. Under usual circumstances, such juxtaposition would be worth exploring, intriguing even. But circumstances were not 'usual', not even for him. He had a cargo of rum to trade, new investments to consider and an assassin on his heels.

As tempting as an *affaire* was, it was too distracting for him and too dangerous for her. His safety and hers demanded he keep her at arm's length. If ever there was a time to pursue a new flirtation, this was definitely not it. He needed all his wits about him.

Chapter Six

One certainly needed their wits about them to keep up
with the Selbys, or even just to be *up* with them. Bryn
had awakened to the surprise—and not the good sort
of surprise either—of finding James and his mother
at the breakfast table. Breakfast had become a time of
day reserved just for she and her father, a time to talk
plans. Having the Selbys present felt like an intrusion
into intimate territory.

But there they were, with plates filled full of eggs
and sausage and more than enough talk to go around.
James and his mother leapt from topic to topic with
lightning speed in an attempt, no doubt, to show off
their conversational acuity. But it was bloody difficult
to follow, with an unladylike emphasis on the 'bloody'.
It was a dizzying array of subjects, really, ranging from
butterflies to weather to books and back again to butterflies. The book had been about butterflies so perhaps
they'd never truly left the topic.

'Butterflies are a rarity in Barbados, which makes
studying them a challenge. It has something to do with
our position in the Atlantic that I don't pretend to un-

derstand.' James waved a fork in the air to punctuate his point. 'But it does make their presence here special. The Mimic is one of my favourites. It looks like a Monarch, but it's the story behind it that makes it so extraordinary. Scholars believe it came from Africa and was brought over on the slave ships or perhaps it was blown here on the currents of a storm.'

Not unlike many of the people who'd sought the sanctuary of the island, Bryn thought. Certainly there was the literal application of the idea. The recent abolition of slavery meant that many of the freedmen had come here as slaves. There was a figurative application, too. People like she and her father, people looking for a fresh chance, blown here metaphorically on the winds of their personal storms. Men, perhaps, like Kitt Sherard.

'I've just recently been able to add an Orion to my collection,' James told the table at large. 'An Orion is grey and blends in terrifically with things like old leaves, which makes catching one difficult.'

For an instant, the image of a butterfly garden filled Bryn's mind. It was the first interesting thing James Selby had said. She was rather surprised he had such a garden. She wouldn't have guessed it of him. A butterfly garden would be so bright and colourful, a perfect tropical accessory. She could imagine all the little butterflies gaily fluttering around.

Selby's next words shattered the image. 'I finally caught one up near Mont Michael a few weeks ago. I took it home and pinned it in the centre of my display case, I'm that proud of it.'

Pinned. Trapped. Dead. Bryn discreetly lowered her fork of eggs and opted for a sip of tea instead. Her vision had been a moment's fancy. She silently chastised herself. James Selby didn't have a butterfly garden, it had been silly to think so. Lepidopterists pinned things. It was what they did. It was what men like Selby did. He wasn't a cruel man, merely young and shallow. He'd probably not even thought to consider what his actions would mean to the butterfly even though they'd impact the butterfly considerably more than they'd ever impact Selby.

She'd met men like Selby before. They were thick on the ground in London's ballrooms. Selby would waltz through life never considering the impact he would have on others. He was an earl's grandson. He didn't have to. No one would expect it of him, not even his wife, who would only be a butterfly of a different sort to Selby; something to pin to his arm, to display in his home, another decoration along the same lines as his fine taste in carpets.

She must have had a distasteful look on her face. When she looked down the length of the table, her father gave her an inquisitive arch of his eyebrow. She immediately pasted on a smile and received one from him in return. In fact, his was positively beaming. Uh-oh. She didn't like that smile. She scaled back hers to something more aloof and polite.

She had to be careful here. She didn't want to foster false hopes and she knew exactly what was afoot: a match and one, that on paper, would be regarded as perfect in every way. Selby was young, in his mid-twenties, not unattractive in a well-kept sort of way, someone who with the right guidance could be moulded into a successful gentleman. She'd seen his file before they'd left England. She'd seen *all* of the investors' files. She'd spent the voyage studying each of the recommended investors and there'd been countless letters and communications between them and her father even before that. When she'd met Selby it wasn't as if she was meeting a stranger. In many ways she'd known him months before the actual meeting.

He was the grandson of an earl with a small inheritance of his own from his father. He was in the Caribbean managing the family's sugar interests, cutting his teeth before taking over properties in England that would come to him upon his thirtieth birthday. His prospects were not much different than those of a second son and entirely respectable. His situation and expectations were very much akin to hers.

Oh, yes, she knew precisely where this was going and why. She wasn't the only one who'd made promises to her mother. Her father had made them, too. But she'd also made a vow to herself, one that would inevitably collide with her father's plans. She only hoped when it did that her father would concede. He'd always been the permissive parent, growing up. He'd been the one who allowed her to ride astride, to swim in the swimming hole, to spend the afternoons hunting with Robin Downing, the squire's son, although he probably shouldn't have.

Selby kept talking. It was easy to smile when she thought of those afternoons with Robin. They'd both been reckless sorts—it was what had made them such good friends. As they'd grown up, though, that recklessness had transformed from dares over climbing trees to something wilder, more dangerous. More than one kiss had been stolen on those adolescent hunting trips. Perhaps there had even been a time when she'd fancied marrying Robin, but a squire's son wasn't an adequate match for the Earl of Creighton's niece and her mother knew it. Young Robin turned twenty-one and found himself off on a Grand Tour. Then her mother had taken ill and her little family was off on a tour of their own, albeit less grand, from spa to spa searching for a cure that didn't exist.

Now she and her father were here. This was to be a new beginning for them both. Bryn was honest enough to admit she didn't know what she wanted from that new start, but she did know what she *didn't* want and that was a copy of London only with different scenery. She could not be James Selby's latest butterfly, no matter what promises had been made.

'I think Selby's plantation opportunity sounds like the perfect investment.' Her father's words drew her back into the conversation with an alarming jolt, the words 'Selby' and 'opportunity' reminding her rather poignantly of Kitt Sherard's comment in the garden. *Selby wouldn't know an opportunity if it jumped up and bit him in the arse.* Now here were those same two words again in a different, even contradictory context. They couldn't both be right. What had she missed while she was busy letting her thoughts wander behind a pseudo-smile?

Selby took her silence for ignorance and leapt into the breach with an explanation couched in slightly patronising terms as if she couldn't be expected to fully understand. 'Plantation stocks are a popular method for making money. One doesn't have to do more than write the cheque. We invest, someone else manages and we pick up the profits at the end of the season. There are countless smaller islands that might support a single large plantation if one can stand the isolation.' Selby gave her an indulgent smile. 'The best part is, we might never have to set foot on the island. All the work is done by someone else.'

'If it works out—' her father picked up the conversation, his face more animated than it had been in a year '—we could have the board look into a larger investment once it's assembled. This will be a trial run.'

We. She didn't think for a moment her father meant her in that pronoun. By 'we' he meant Selby. He'd certainly taken to Selby quickly enough. She supposed it was natural. He'd exchanged letters with many of the investors months before leaving England, Selby included. Only Sherard had not written directly. All of his correspondence had come through the Earl of Dartmoor's brother-in-law, Benedict DeBreed. Like her, her father felt that he knew many of the men before actually meeting with them in person. The two of them had spent countless hours on board ship discussing each one until the faceless investors had taken on a certain familiarity.

She might have been jealous of all the attention her father lavished on James Selby if it wasn't for the fact that she knew her father needed her. They were partners in this venture—silent partners: the men were not the kind to tolerate the presence of a woman in finance. But she had a job to do that only she could do. She was to vet the ladies and determine what sort of wives and lives these potential investors had.

Investors had to be more than the sum of their chequebooks. Money might get one in the door, but one needed ethics and a particular quality about oneself to stay, especially when they would be putting other men's money on the line. That's where the mystery of Kitt Sherard came in. He had money and connections. Did he have the ethics, too? Those were the questions she'd be attempting to answer today on her shopping trip with Martha Selby, Alba Harrison and Eleanor Crenshaw.

Sneed entered the breakfast room to announce the arrival of her shopping guests and her pulse speeded up. Time to go to work and, if she was lucky, time to play a little, too. Her outing today wasn't just about vetting the women. At the very least, she hoped to draw the women out about him and where he fit in all of this. If she had her way—and she almost always got her way—she'd 'accidentally' meet up with the captain. Bryn rose and smoothed the folds of her white-sprigged skirts. This was one of her favourite gowns with its tiny apple-green flowers and wide matching green sash that set off her waist. She had a certain effect on men when she wore it. She was confident Kitt Sherard would be no different. She was very good at getting what she wanted and today she wanted answers.

She needed to be careful what she wished for. Three hours into shopping, Bryn had all the answers she wanted and more. Alas, none of them were about the more interesting subject of Captain Sherard. However, she had all the impressions she needed of Eleanor Crenshaw, Alba Harrison and Martha Selby, which also meant she had got more than an earful of the merits associated with her son. She'd not quite believed someone could be bored to death, but she was a believer now.

Selby's mother had spent a good portion of the day chattering about James's attributes, a sure sign that whoever married him would have to answer to Martha. It was also clear that Martha was more than happy to turn the financial aspects of life over to her son. She'd mentioned more than once what a relief it was to have James manage everything for her. 'A proper woman should never have to worry over things like money,' she said with a flutter of her fan. Bryn could almost hear the unspoken words that followed the statement: *and I am a most proper woman, thanks to James.*

To that, Alba Harrison had given a soft smile and agreed. 'Edward handles everything except my household budget.' There was pride behind that smile, as if ignorance was anything to be proud of. Bryn's temper started to rise. It might have been fuelled by her disbelief that wives of investors could be so blasé about their own financial ignorance or it might simply have been that she was in a peevish mood, brought on by Martha Selby's incessant prattle.

Couldn't they see such ignorance wasn't in their best interest? The lessons of her childhood surged to the fore. Her mother had schooled her early in life on the subject and importance of a woman's financial independence. That was one lesson that had taken. When men lost fortunes they could rebuild them or put a gun to their heads in a discreet room at a gambling hell, but it was the women who paid, the women who lost their homes, their security. A woman risked far more by relying on a man's good sense. For that reason alone, a woman should be an informed and active participant in a family's financial dealings.

Bryn knew her attitude wasn't popular, but her temper had the better of her. Before she could rethink the wisdom of her comment, the temptation to goad their thoughts was tumbling out of her mouth. 'Don't you ever want to know where your money comes from and where it goes? How much it makes? Isn't it a little bit dangerous to be so blind?' In her opinion, it was *more* than a little bit dangerous. Both her parents had instilled in her the belief that a strong financial acumen showed no preference in gender. Her father had been proud of how quickly she'd grasped the concepts of investment banking.

The ladies stared at her with identical looks of confusion. 'No, it's a relief really, my dear. It's one less thing to worry about,' Mrs Harrison said softly, her tone somewhere between polite correction and gentle instruction. Mrs Selby seemed to be making a mental note, probably something to the extent of her being an unsuitable bride for James. That stung.

Bryn squared her shoulders, stood a little taller and told herself it was for the best. She had no intentions of being a suitable bride for James. But it still hurt. She was a Rutherford. As such, she was used to being found eminently suitable. That James Selby's mother, a woman who had only a few of the barest claims to true society, would find her lacking was a bit of a blow to the ego.

They stepped into a shop on Swan Street that handled imported European furniture. The interior was dim after the brightness outdoors and it took a moment for Bryn's eyes to adjust. Even with her wide-brimmed hat on for protection today, the sun had played havoc with her vision, something she had yet to get used to after the perpetual grey skies of London.

She was still blinking when the man at the counter finished his discussion with the proprietor and turned towards them. 'Ladies, good day.' He gave them a little bow she'd recognise anywhere for its slightly sardonic nature, even in the interior of a dim little furniture shop. Then he turned the full force of his attentions in her direction, so urbane, so polite, it was hard to reconcile him with the ruthless seducer-interrogator he'd been in her garden, challenging her with his words, his body. 'Miss Rutherford, how are you besides sun-blinded?'

Kitt Sherard! Her first thought was that the fates had decided to smile on her after all. She was beginning to think they'd deserted her entirely after enduring three hours of tedious discussion *and* Martha Selby's indirect disapproval. Her second thought was that she must look like an owl. Bryn tried to stop blinking, it was hardly going to impress him. 'I'm fine, thank you. These kind ladies have been showing me the shops. And yourself?' Mrs Selby stiffened beside her. The latest of her *faux pas* coming too soon after the first. Apparently such a question from a young lady was too bold. Yet another strike against her. Perhaps she'd make a game of it and see how thoroughly she could antagonise Martha Selby. But, no, she'd promised her father better.

'I am picking up a chair Mr Friberg has repaired for me,' Kitt answered her, his smile defrosting the ladies. 'If I could offer some advice, Miss Rutherford, you need a pair of *lunettes de soleil*. They'll make your sojourn in the sun more comfortable.' He reached into an inside pocket and unfolded a pair of spectacles with green-glass lenses. 'Here, take mine until you can find a pair that suits you better.'

'I couldn't deprive you,' Bryn refused politely, aware that Mrs Selby was watching the two of them with interest. A few strikes against her were a positive deterrent. Too many, though, and she'd be a social pariah, which was not what her father needed.

'Yes, you could. I insist. I have other pairs at home, drawers full of them, in fact.' He said 'drawers' as if

he meant an entirely different sort of drawers. She felt
her cheeks heat. Dear lord, what was wrong with her
that she saw innuendo in everything he said? 'I make
them myself, it's a very useful hobby in this part of the
world. It would be an honour if you accepted them as
a welcome gift to the island.' Kitt would brook no refusal and surely the ladies could see that she'd resisted
as much as she could without being downright rude.

But then, when she might have escaped the situation with minimal scathing, Kitt pushed his advantage
too far. He didn't just hand them over, he put them on
himself.

Kitt stepped forward and reached beneath the brim
of her hat to fit the arms of the glasses over her ears and
to adjust the lenses on the bridge of her nose with his
thumbs; an act that hardly involved impassioned touch
any more than tying someone's shoe or the casual ad-
justing of a piece of clothing, yet the act seemed alarm-
ingly intimate for such a public spot. She knew without
looking in the woman's direction that Mrs Selby found it
positively lurid. She was going to kill him for this. Secret
balcony kisses were one thing, as were hot looks in the
garden where no one could see. Discretion, discretion,
discretion. Even the wild child in her knew that much.

Maybe it was because there were onlookers and Mrs
Selby had puckered her mouth up into a sour frown
or maybe it was simply the intimacy of the act that
made her entirely self-conscious. She noticed everything acutely in those brief moments of contact: Kitt's
face close to hers, blue eyes laughing as if he knew Mrs
Selby's mouth currently resembled a prune, Kitt's fingers sweeping down the curve of her jaw as he stepped
back. 'There, that will do for now.' The smile on his

face suggested he was up to mischief with this latest endeavour and she was not in on the entire joke.

To be sure, she was in on part of it. He'd enjoyed getting a self-righteous rise out of Mrs Selby and he divined correctly that she wouldn't mind a little fun at Mrs Selby's expense. But there was more to it than that, Bryn would bet on it. She'd bet, too, that Kitt wouldn't be around when the other proverbial shoe fell. But it would fall, she could feel it. Mrs Selby was fairly bristling beside her as Kitt took his leave and conversation was forced as the ladies finished their errands. The shoe would fall soon and she would bear the brunt of it all on her own even though she hadn't asked for his attentions.

It fell over tea in the lobby of the hotel. 'I am sorry for the distasteful instance with Captain Sherard,' Mrs Selby said, trying to sound casual and sympathetic as she passed Bryn a teacup when in reality she was neither. 'He's quite the ladies' man in these parts.' She smiled, trying to appear friendly. 'It's not your fault, my dear. You're new, you couldn't possibly know what sort of man he is.'

'What sort of man is that, Mrs Selby?' Bryn asked bluntly.

That had her nonplussed, Bryn was gratified to note. Mrs Selby hesitated, weighing her options before answering with a hedge. 'Of course, the men like him a great deal as does a certain sort of lady, but a young woman like yourself needs to take care. He has a way of turning heads without really meaning to. I wouldn't want you to read too much into his gesture this morning.'

Or his kisses on my balcony. You know he's had his hand on more than my face, Mrs Selby. Bryn smiled politely. 'Surely he's not as bad as all that. He appeared quite the gentleman a couple of nights ago at the Crenshaws'.' She smiled at Eleanor Crenshaw, hoping to engage an ally. Eleanor had invited him, after all. 'Where does he fit in? Is he a gentleman or a rebel?' Bryn asked point blank.

All three of them were stymied, exchanging awkward looks. It was Eleanor Crenshaw who answered, 'We tolerate him, of course, because he's rich and there's so little society in the islands, but he has no people. No one really knows where he's from.' She said the last in a little whisper as if it were the gravest of sins.

Bryn decided to bedevil the subject a bit further. 'Miss Caroline Bryant didn't seem to mind.' She might disagree with Mrs Selby's assessment of Kitt Sherard, but Bryn wasn't about to let this conversational opening go unused. It was the perfect chance to learn more about one of her father's investors.

Alba Harrison pitched her voice low. 'Caroline is the quartermaster's daughter.' She arched dark brows as if emphasising Miss Bryant's connection to the quartermaster explained everything. 'Captain Sherard strings her along because it's good for his business,' Alba Harrison added when it was clear the emphasis was lost on Bryn. Alba Harrison leaned forward, her words coming fast, her brown eyes intense. 'He'll do the same to you as well if you're not careful. He wants in on the joint stock bank and he'll use your influence with your father to ensure his place. It's the truth, I don't mean to be cruel.'

Yes, you do. Bryn met Alba Harrison's gaze evenly. This was nothing different than the catty politics between women in London ballrooms: the endless battle between those who held a man's attention and those who wanted it. How much of this was jealousy and how much was truth? 'I see. Thank you.' She did see, far more than Alba Harrison realised. Alba's rather vociferous condemnation of Kitt Sherard was not in character with the woman who earlier this morning had softly advised leaving all sense of finance and business to the men.

That was when Bryn realised two things: One, Alba Harrison had lied. She *was* into the family finances as deep as her husband, no matter what she professed publicly. She understood perfectly well what was riding on this opportunity with the bank. There was no doubt in Bryn's mind, Alba had come shopping with one goal in mind—secure a place on the board of investors. Second, Kitt had used her. He'd known his actions would provoke this sort of conversation. The question was, had he done it to expose Alba Harrison's true nature or to expose his? Now Bryn understood why he'd smiled. She just didn't understand the reason behind it. But she was going to.

If Alba had thought to gain favour with her warning about Kitt, she'd be surprised to note it had just the opposite effect. Bryn made up her mind on the spot. When tea was done, she would find Sherard and confront him. He would soon learn she did not care for the role of unwitting accomplice. He'd set her up and he would have to pay.

Chapter Seven

The rum at his hand was cold and the stones on his back were hot. Life was perfect. For the moment. Perfection never lasted and he knew better than most that life could change without notice or warning. He'd learned to take the moments where he could find them. Today there were no bandits, no knife fights on beaches, no assassins in the shadows.

Kitt shifted beneath the thin white sheet draped over his buttocks, the only part of him that was covered as he lay in his open-air pavilion on a raised bed that looked out over the white carpet of sand and turquoise expanse of ocean. *This* was Paradise on earth, maybe even Paradise period. And it was all his: a private home, a pristine beach, bought and paid for with rum money and danger. *C'est la vie*—such is life, the French would say. Everything, Paradise included, had a price.

'How does that feel, Mr Kitt?' The Bajan beauty working him over placed the last of the small heated stones on his back, her accented English a gentle lilt at his ear, quite a different earful than the sharp tongue of Miss Rutherford who'd likely want to skewer him the next time she saw him.

'Like heaven, love.' Kitt gave a groan of appreciation as the masseuse kneaded away the tension that had taken up residence between his shoulder blades. A gentle breeze passed through the open-air pavilion, mixing deliciously with the heat of the stones against his bare skin. After the last two days, he deserved this. When he'd finished in town, he'd come here straight away with strict instructions to Passemore that he not be disturbed. This was his own private hideaway, a place where he could relax, plan or think as the mood suited.

Right now, a little of all three suited that mood. With Devore on the loose, he couldn't allow himself to relax entirely no matter how tempting it was. Even in the safety of his home, his body tensed at the thought of Devore. The man was evil incarnate, a man who calculated his cruelty to exact every possible ounce of suffering from his victims. He would never be completely able to rid his mind of images of what Devore and Gridley had done to Emma. He probably should have put a bullet in Devore when he'd had the chance.

He took comfort in knowing there was little Devore could do to him. Outside of Ren and Emma, he had no other interpersonal attachments and Ren would protect Emma. It was one of the benefits of having reinvented himself. No one relied on him. He had no one to worry over. Still, if Devore was on the move, he'd be watching, looking for some weakness, some sort of leverage to use against him. Devore would not hesitate to strike at any chink in his armour, perceived or otherwise, further proof this was not the time to pursue anything that remotely resembled familiarity with Bryn Rutherford. Kitt would not tolerate an innocent bystander caught in the crossfire of revenge.

His behaviour in town had been all about convincing Bryn to keep her distance without ruining his business chances with her father. His behaviour had been outrageous, but not out of character and it should have served as a final reminder of the sort of man he was; completely unsuitable for a princess like her. He'd warned her earlier with words, now he'd warned her with actions.

Right about now, the shrewd Miss Rutherford should be heading home, ready to mull over all the news the ladies of Bridgetown had imparted about him. He felt a smile of satisfaction creep across his mouth. She would be coming to her senses while he was basking in Paradise, enjoying the quiet and…*the sound of footsteps?* What the bloody hell?

Kitt reared up, dislodging the hot stones, his hand sweeping under the pillow for his knife as he leapt off the bed, his body immediately alert to danger. There was relaxation and then there was stupidity, after all. He preferred not to face an attacker in his altogether, but it was too late to do anything about the latter now.

'Passemore!' Kitt lowered his knife, the adrenaline induced tension ebbing from his body as he recognised his first mate. 'Dammit, I told you I wasn't to be disturbed. Cleo will have to start all over now. This had better be good.'

A snatch of green and a flicker of white skirts garnered Kitt's attention on the path over Passemore's shoulder. Good God! Passemore had not come alone. Kitt waved the knife in her direction with a growl at Passemore. 'What is *she* doing here?' But he knew. She'd got one over on Passemore. He almost felt sorry for William. Almost.

'I couldn't stop her,' Passemore stammered, unusu-

ally unsure of himself. 'She insisted she ride along with
me when I brought the supplies out.' Kitt had left his
first mate in town to load up the wagon, never guessing
Bryn would want to track him down so quickly, if at all.
The magpies were supposed to have sent her running
the other direction with their gossip, not draw her here.

'You need to get laid, William,' Kitt muttered under
his breath. He wasn't surprised his first mate hadn't
been match enough for Bryn Rutherford, but he was
surprised she was here. So much for keeping her at
arm's length.

'Mr Sherard, I need a word with you,' Bryn began
before she even came to a full stop. 'If you think you
can set me up like that…' She paused mid-sentence, her
eyes dropping down his length as the scene hit her full
force. 'You're naked.'

'And you're staring.' Kitt grinned, enjoying taking the edge off what was likely a well-planned tirade
she'd rehearsed all the way out. He'd stood naked before plenty of women and he had nothing to be ashamed
of. As for Miss Rutherford, he was probably her first.
His grin widened. 'See anything you like, princess?'

Of course she was staring, how could she not? He
was as gorgeous as he was arrogant and Kitt Sherard
was arrogant in the extreme. Not without reason. That
tan, sleek body of his rivalled the gods of Olympus.
Arms bulged with muscle, his torso an atlas of ridges and
planes as it tapered to narrow, defined hips and a rather
robust phallus announcing its presence. It was hard to
look away. A girl didn't have such a fine specimen of
manhood displayed for her every day. But she would
not let him thwart her efforts at conversation with this
rather bawdy display of man flesh. First, however, she

had to find her voice. Bryn cleared her throat with what she hoped was the sound of authority and not nerves.

'Is this how you greet guests? Armed and naked?' With nearly superhuman effort, she managed to flick a cool glance at the knife in his hand. She was trying so very hard not to look, to pretend that she conversed with naked men all the time. Heaven knew what she'd interrupted. The cocoa-skinned woman had discreetly withdrawn, but not before Bryn had been aware of her presence. There were only so many conclusions one could draw about a woman and a naked man without being completely obtuse.

'Perhaps you and I disagree on what constitutes a guest, Miss Rutherford. Where I come from, guests are *invited.*' He held his arms out to his sides, giving her eyes free rein. '*This* is how I greet people who take me by surprise in the middle of a massage. Technically, that makes you a trespasser.' He gave a wicked grin that sent a tremor of excitement through her. 'There's a forfeit for trespassing.'

Yes, please, I'll pay it, the rather heated part of her imagination all but yelled in her mind. Part of her knew she shouldn't have come here. Decently bred ladies didn't seek out gentlemen and they certainly didn't go barging into a gentleman's private quarters. She was getting her just deserts for intruding. The other part of her thought those deserts not only just, but delicious. But she had to play this coolly, had to be aloof, had to appear unfazed by this blatant display of nudity. 'It hardly seems fair that you can climb my balcony, but I can't walk on your beach.'

'You want to "walk on my beach"?' He had a way of making even a simple statement sound erotic. 'There's a forfeit for that, too, princess. This is turning into a pretty expensive visit. Make sure you can afford it.'

It was her turn to laugh. If he meant to frighten her off, he was doing a poor job of it. 'You don't scare me, Sherard.' Just the opposite. He was exactly the sort of gentleman who would indulge her wild fantasies, who would be her lover without exacting marriage, but their situation was anything but ideal. She could not mix his brand of pleasure with her father's business. She needed absolute objectivity in order to help her father select the right men.

He arched a blond brow. 'If we're to go, ah, "walking", as you like to call it, we should dispense with the formalities. It sounds like a bad romance novel: *Miss Rutherford and the Captain*. I prefer Kitt.'

Kitt, reached for the sheet and wound it about his middle with a pointed glance at her feet. 'You might want to take off your shoes. And your stockings.' He paused, considering her hem. 'You might want to tuck up your skirts, too, if you want to stay dry.'

It was Bryn's turn to raise a brow. 'Anything else you'd like me to take off?'

'Not at the moment, no.' Kitt laughed. 'But I reserve the right to amend my suggestions.'

It was definitely the most decadent walk of her life, strolling barefoot on the beach alongside a man wrapped only in a sheet. But it was worth it to feel warm sand between her toes and the occasional wave the temperature of her bath gently lap against her ankles.

'This beach is really yours?' Bryn asked. The calm waves had taken some of the fire out of the intent of her visit. She felt less like fighting with him than simply wanting to talk with him, to learn about this enigmatic man who owned this peaceful Paradise while being anything but peaceful himself. Perhaps that's why he consented to let her walk along the shore instead of ushering her to the door. Refusing to see her would only have served to stoke her anger. This was distraction at its finest. Kitt had proven he was a shrewd tactician. She must remain alert. But what harm could there be in a walk when she *knew* what he was playing at?

Kitt stretched his arms wide, pride evident in his voice. 'All this is mine, the house and the beach as far as the eye can see. Since the house isn't on farmable land, the owner had no use for it. It was just a decoration and that was fine with me. I wanted a decoration. Somewhere I could be alone.' The last was intended as a pointed commentary on her intrusion.

'Your home is lovely.' She meant it, choosing to overlook his slur. The house resembled a Mediterranean villa with its white stucco and arches. A quick glimpse of the interior as she'd passed through with Passemore had revealed the place was well furnished. The gardens in the back leading down to the shore were immaculately groomed and full of colour. There was even a fountain that trickled enticingly into a tiled basin on a patio.

'Thank you, but that's not what you came to discuss.' They'd come to a cove with a wide, flat-topped rock formation set fifty or so yards from shore. Kitt tugged at her hand with a nod towards the rock. 'Are you game? We can sit on the top.'

There were so many reasons to decline the invitation. Well-bred ladies didn't climb rocks with men in sheets, they didn't walk beach shores with them either. It certainly wasn't part of the promise she'd made her mother. But the line of propriety had been crossed long before this latest breach. She'd crossed it the moment she'd sought out his company alone in his home. Maybe even before that, when she'd allowed him indecent liberties on her balcony instead of screaming for help.

And yet, her wild side argued as she scaled the rock with Kitt, hadn't she come to Barbados especially for this? How could she refuse the offer? Look where her choices had led so far: To a beautiful beach, to scrambling up a rock and sitting beside a half-naked man, letting the breeze off the water cool her skin while she took in the stunning view of the ocean and the coastline, half a globe away from the world she knew, the world that would condemn taking advantage of a moment like this. What did that world know anyway?

In a declarative act of defiance, Bryn took off her hat when they reached the top. She arched her neck, letting the sun and the breeze bathe her face. 'I never dreamed there was a place like this on earth.' Her legs dangled over the side of the rock alongside Kitt's. Below them, waves hit the rock, the spray tickling her legs. Her skirts would be damp no matter how far she tucked them up, but right now she didn't care.

Bryn gave herself a few minutes to enjoy the scene before returning to the subject at hand. 'This doesn't mean I'm not still upset with you about this morning. You can't bribe me.'

Kitt shrugged and played innocent. 'What did I do this morning?'

He was going to make her spell it out for him. 'You know what you did with your little *lunettes de soleil*. You made me look bad in front of Martha Selby and Alba Harrison, two women whose favour I need for my father. Martha Selby couldn't make notes fast enough regarding my unsuitability as a bride for her son.' She gave Kitt a sideways glance, watching for his reaction.

'You are. Unsuitable, that is.' Kitt tried to look penitent, something he obviously wasn't familiar with. 'I'm sorry, did you want to marry James Selby?'

'No.'

He grinned. 'Consider it a favour then. I don't know why you're upset.'

'It's the principle of the matter. You used me.'

'To your benefit.' Kitt threw a pebble into the water. 'Did you see Mrs Harrison's true colours?'

'Yes,' Bryn said slowly, trying to divine where this was headed. She didn't like the idea of owing Kitt any favours.

'Did you learn something more about me? Am I well maligned by the upstanding moral arbiters of Bridgetown society?'

'Yes, most definitely that.' Bryn narrowed her eyes. Alba Harrison's comment about Caroline Bryant notwithstanding, Kitt didn't strike her as the sort of man who did something entirely out of altruism. She cocked her head and studied him. 'What do you get out of all of this?'

Kitt laughed. 'My, my, we're quite the cynic. Perhaps I did it purely for your own benefit. Do I have to get anything out of it? '

'In my experience, yes,' Bryn answered honestly. 'I don't trust you.'

She expected him to be offended. The likes of James Selby certainly would have been. A gentleman's manners were supposed to inspire a lady's trust and confidence. Instead Kitt nodded, absorbing the revelation.

'That is as it should be, don't you think? You hardly know me well enough to trust me. For the record, I don't trust you for the same reasons.'

Now she was the one offended. 'Not trust *me*? What is there not to trust?' Bryn argued. She knew a moment's panic. 'You *are* going to invest in the bank, aren't you?' If Kitt pulled out, would he influence the others to do the same? Where would that leave her father?

Kitt seemed unconcerned. 'Maybe. I have to do my research.' He turned his blue eyes her way. 'Villas and private beaches don't come cheap. The question your father should be considering is not *if* I have money to invest, but *how* I made that money. I don't gamble, princess. I only bet on sure things.'

That did give her pause. Bryn saw the fallacy in her own reasoning. She'd been so intent wanting to learn about the potential investors that she hadn't thought about what those investors would want to learn about them.

'You see, it's not just about investing with your father and the royal charter. It's about investing *with* the other six men. Can I trust them with my money? Can I trust their investment choices?'

The tenor of their conversation had taken on a very personal cast. Bryn couldn't recall anyone ever speaking with her like this before. This was certainly not the kind of conversation one held at balls and her usual social venues where talk was interspersed between dance sets or limited to short bursts of time as people passed one another in crowded ballrooms. Even teas and at-homes kept 'decent' conversations between the sexes to fifteen-minute calls, hardly enough time to delve deeply into any subject, hardly enough time to do more than exchange pleasantries.

It seemed something of an irony to be having an honest conversation with this man, who made no pretence to being a gentleman beyond dressing like one when the part suited him. Did that mean the opposite was true as well? That she'd spent her adult life to date having dishonest conversations with gentlemen? If so, perhaps it was further proof ballrooms were a waste of time.

If people talked, really talked, they might learn something about each other. What was 'indecent' about that? There might be happier marriages. Then again, there might be a lot more pre-marital seductions, too, if people felt they knew each other. That was what she was feeling now—that she was starting to know Kitt, to see the man beyond the sharp wit and outrageous behaviour. That man was an analyst, a thinker with a stunningly shrewd command of human nature. He understood people and what drove them. *And* it was just as exciting as his kisses.

'Why don't you trust Selby?' she asked, deciding to test her hypothesis about his analytical skills.

'It's not him I don't trust, it's his judgement,' Kitt clarified. He spoke quietly, his voice nearly at her ear, although there was no one to hear. His body was close to hers on the warm rock slab, their legs occasionally brushing against each other as they dangled over the edge. 'He's ignorant of the world around him. Because of that, he makes less educated choices. He's young, he's eager to please and quite desperate to be seen as a man, as a leader, when that isn't where his skills lie at present. He hasn't the experience to be those things, only the money. Do you know the old proverb, "a fool and his money are soon separated"? That's James Selby in a nutshell.'

'Surely not all of his decisions are bad? He's invest-

ing in a plantation.' Kitt had her worrying about Selby.
If her father insisted on taking Selby on to the board,
would he bring the bank down or would he sit quietly
and let the more experienced men lead the way while
he learned for the future?

Kitt raised an eyebrow at this. 'Is he? I hadn't heard.
I was unaware there were any shares available.'

'I think it's on another island.' Selby hadn't said precisely where the plantation was.

'I hope it works out for him. Sugar prices are a bit
low right now, but sugar and rum are always decent
money in the long run,' Kitt offered vaguely.

'You sound sceptical,' Bryn pressed, picking up on
his hesitation. He wasn't the only one sitting on this
rock who knew a little something about reading people.

'I don't know enough to be otherwise.' Kitt tapped
his forehead with his index finger. 'Research, remember?' A further reminder, if she needed another one,
that Kitt Sherard was as people-savvy as they came.
He understood what people thought, *how* they thought
and that included her, as unnerving as the prospect was.
Her London beaux had never guessed at half the things
going on in her head. But Kitt seemed to guess them
all, even the ones she wished he didn't, like how much
she wanted him to kiss her again.

His eyes held hers for a long moment. 'I only bet on
sure things and you should, too.' A slow smile spread
across his face and Bryn had the distinct impression
they weren't talking about banking any more. 'Now,
about those forfeits.'

Chapter Eight

His hand cupped her jaw, tilting her mouth to his. Her body started to fire at his touch. She ought to fight this. But when his mouth moved over hers, it claimed all desire to resist. All the warnings she could muster, all the promises she had made, held no power here.

He kissed her deeply, slowly, and she wanted to drink him in as she had not drunk of him earlier. Those balcony kisses had been rough and rushed, the result of their rather spontaneous situation. He'd kissed her then to silence her surprise. These kisses were prelude to a game of a different sort. He smelled of sun and salt and prime male. Her hands anchored in his hair, tangling in its thick blond lengths as he pressed her back against the warm surface of the rock. His mouth moved down the column of her throat, kissing, nipping, his hand cupping a breast, lifting it to be caressed by his mouth through the thin muslin of her gown. She'd never thought of clothes as being erotic until now, until Kitt had his mouth on her, creating a delicious friction with the fabric and his teeth as her nipple hardened, laved into a decadent, straining peak by his tongue.

Her body arched against him, intuitively seeking his confirmation that he, too, was swept away by this. It was there in the erection that lay bold and strong against her where their bodies met, tactile evidence of what she'd seen with her eyes. The feel of him was enough to ignite other heady curiosities. What would it be like to touch him, to feel that part of him jump in her hand?

Bryn didn't think. She simply reacted out of primal instinct and reached for him. He was hot in her hand even through the negligible barrier of the sheet. She revelled in the power of him. He was long and hard beneath the linen where her hand shaped him through the cloth. Kitt gave a hungry groan, his mouth devouring hers, their bodies pressing into one another with an intensity that went far beyond any of her adolescent forays. This was pleasure at its finest and it was madness, too. Only disaster could come of this.

Bryn broke the kiss, levering on her elbows to sit up and dislodge Kitt from where he laid against her. Spray from a wave hit her ankles, reminding her there were other reasons this had to end, too. Tides came in. Even now the shore looked slightly further away.

Kitt looked past her shoulder out to sea, distracted for a moment, and then followed the direction of her gaze back to shore. 'We'd best head back in before we have to swim for it.' He seemed unbothered by the impending tide, but he didn't have skirts to worry about. She'd be a mess by the time she got home—not that she wasn't already a mess. Her hair had come down and the pristine, white dress she'd left the house in that morning was wrinkled from climbing and from kissing—lots of kissing. Wading back to shore could hardly make her look worse, but it could make her look wetter and that would be problematic.

In the end, Kitt carried her back to shore. It would have been humorous and quite a well-deserved fate for having enticed her out to the rock in the first place if the sheer, bare physicality of him hadn't served as a potent reminder of how many lines she'd crossed, how many rules and promises she'd broken by coming here today. Her mother would not be pleased.

Kitt set her down and gave her a once-over, assessing the damage, as it were. He shook his head, arriving at the same conclusion. 'You will not do. You'll have to come in while we set you to rights.' He gave her one of his wicked grins. 'Unless you don't mind everyone knowing what you've been up to? Then our task gets considerably easier.'

Another rule gone. A lady didn't enter a gentleman's house unchaperoned. But after this afternoon, what was one more rule? She'd broken so many already. It was quite the day for overturning the teachings of childhood. She should feel guilty. But she didn't. She felt intrigued instead. Truly, she couldn't say rules had done much for her in the past except create absolute tedium. Maybe it didn't count if a rule was broken and there was no one to see, sort of like the fallen tree in the woods. Broken rules only mattered if one was caught and Kitt had made it clear already he wasn't going to kiss and tell. For being alone with a rogue, she felt quite safe.

The inside of Kitt's house was as spectacular as the outside. For a man of questionable repute, the understated elegance of his home was unexpected. The hall he led her down was appropriately lined with consoles adorned with vases full of island flowers set at just the right intervals, the occasional painting hung over a console here and there. The drawing room was done in a dark blue and cream, striking a masculine tone while not being oppressive. A gorgeous piano sat in one corner, its lid up, its sleek body gleaming with polish and care.

Bryn ran an idle hand over a porcelain figurine of a dog decorating a side table. 'You have good taste.'

Kitt laughed and pulled the bell rope. 'You sound surprised. Is "good taste" a woman's domain? Are men not allowed to have any?'

Bryn sat on a damask-covered sofa done in dark blue to match the curtains. She was acutely aware of the sand on her skirts and the fineness of the upholstery. 'In my experience, men can have good taste, but many fail to exercise it.'

Kitt slouched into the chair opposite her, sheet and all, reminding her the house and its trappings of luxury were part of the illusion, just as his evening clothes had been at the Crenshaws'. Without those accessories, he was a rogue at heart. 'Or is it that a man of my dubious reputation isn't entitled to good taste?' Kitt persisted in calling her out, persisted in reminding her of the façade.

Bryn gave him a sharp look. 'I didn't say that. Don't put words into my mouth.'

'You were thinking it.' Kitt challenged her with his eyes, holding her gaze for a long moment before the butler entered. 'Ah, Stephens, there you are. We are going to need a hairbrush, a mirror and some hairpins. I need you to send someone to the pavilion as well. Miss Rutherford has left her shoes and stockings.'

Stephens nodded with a 'very good, sir' and departed without so much as batting an eye at her dishevelled state or questioning the attire of his employer. Perhaps there was no need to look astonished, perhaps Kitt entertained in a sheet regularly. Perhaps women left various items of clothes around his house regularly, too. Given what she knew of him, it wouldn't be surprising. Still, all told, his butler was extraordinarily well trained, on par with Sneed, who was a paragon.

She would not have thought a man like Kitt Sherard would have such a staff. Then again, she was starting to think she didn't know what sort of man Kitt Sherard was after all. Flirt? Seducer? Businessman? Rake? It was starting to sound like the children's nursery rhyme little girls played with their buttons: rich man, poor man, beggar man, thief... Kitt was a rich man most definitely. Exquisitely appointed houses didn't come cheap.

'It's all right to think it, Bryn.' Kitt returned to the topic of his taste, much to her mortification. He read her mind far too easily. 'It's what all the ladies think. I'm sure they've filled your head with a resounding catalogue of my sins.'

Bryn swallowed, feeling guilty. He was right, of course. She'd not left tea without being duly warned of his shortcomings. 'Does it bother you?'

He arched a sandy brow. 'My good taste? Does my good taste bother me? No, not really.' He was being obtuse on purpose. She could see the merriment lurking in his eyes. He wanted her to say it.

'I meant the ladies. Does what they think bother you?' It was a daring question no matter how delicately she asked it.

Kitt leaned back in his chair, looking wild and masculine, his hair falling about his shoulders. He was a god, someone untouchable. It was a ridiculous question to ask. Of course it didn't bother him. He was impervious to the slights of silly women. One had only to look at him to know that.

His eyes were laughing at her again. 'Oh, you mean do I mind that I am deemed "socially tolerable" at best? I have no choice really. I live my life, they live theirs. On occasion, like the bank charter, our lives intersect. On those occasions, I become momentarily acceptable. Money helps.' He paused, sobering. 'I won't be something I'm not for the likes of them.' His gaze rested on her with a look that made her mouth go dry. 'How about you, Bryn, will you?'

That, of course, was the very question she'd done battle with for the last year. Who would she be? Who would she *allow* herself to be?

By the time Stephens had returned with the hair things and she'd put on her stockings and shoes, then tidied her dress as best she could, Bryn knew what she had to do. She had to keep Kitt Sherard at a distance. He was a dangerous man with his mind-reading and kisses. He had her thinking and questioning all sorts of assumptions about him, about her, about the point of life in general. These were not assumptions she could challenge until she'd fulfilled one last promise to her mother. Kitt and his philosophies would have to wait.

She could justify this one lapse in the name of business. She'd come here to learn about him and learn she had. Now that was over. His behaviour today confirmed the incident on the balcony was not an isolated one. He was audacious in the extreme regardless of his excellent intuition. She needed to make her position clear before she left so there would be no more incidents like the one in town, so there would be no more need to confront him in visits like this.

'Alba Harrison believes you flirt with Caroline Bryant because she's the quartermaster's daughter and it's good for business.' Bryn finished with her laces and rose. 'She believes you will flirt with me for the same reason. I assure you, such behaviour will not be tolerated by me or by my father.' There would be no more stolen kisses. But she wasn't sure if she needed clarity on that point for him or for herself.

Kitt refused to be scolded. More than that, he refused to apologise. 'I think what happened on the rock went beyond flirting, don't you?'

She felt her face colour. Bryn busied herself with putting on her hat. 'I was trying to be polite.'

Kitt stood, finally. He hadn't risen with her, making no attempt at playing a gentleman. When one was dressed in a sheet, what was the point anyway? He stepped towards her, his body close and intimate and big as it invaded her space. 'I don't think lying is particularly polite and that's what you were trying to do. I am happy to admit I was quite aroused out there and I think you were, too.'

That was a mortal hit. Bryn's hands tangled in the ribbon on her hat, barely able to tie a bow. How dare he stand there, looking so smug over her discomfort, and the dratted man wasn't done yet.

'You're wrong, you know, Bryn. Yesterday in the garden you said you didn't trust me. But you do.' He took the ribbons from her and tied a more-than-adequate bow. He was far too competent with women's clothing.

She fixed him with a piercing stare and opted for the high road, hoping he didn't see her pulse leap in her neck where his hands had skimmed her skin. He got to her in so many ways no other man in her experience had. If she did anything today, it would be to best him in at least one argument. 'How, exactly, do you reason that?'

'You never would have gone out on the rock if you didn't.' He gave a smug grin.

'You seemed pretty certain I would.' A suspicion was starting to take root.

'Yes, I was.' Kitt's response was simple and succinct, his blue eyes watching her with a riveting intensity she doubted she'd ever get used to. He had a way of making her feel like the only woman worthy of his intentions when logic suggested otherwise. The truth rolled over her like the waves against the shore. *I only bet on sure things.* He'd managed to manipulate her one more time. A cold pit formed in her stomach, but his hand was warm at her back, his voice at her ear as he ushered her towards the door. 'While you study me, I study you.'

At the door, Bryn schooled her features into a mask of neutrality. On the drive, Passemore waited with the wagon to drive her back to town. She had a last chance to prove to Kitt he wasn't the only who was good at games. 'I suppose there's only one question to answer then. Are *you* a sure thing?' She looked straight ahead and walked down the steps to the waiting wagon. Sometimes the best way to get the last word was to leave.

Even then, it wasn't a guarantee. Kitt's laughter rang

in the air. 'What are you more upset about, Bryn, that I got under your skin or under your skirt?' His response burned in her ears the whole drive back. Not because it was insulting, but because it was true. He might have used her, but she'd let him.

Kitt soaked in his bath, eyes shut, his mind replaying, regretting, revelling in his parting words. He hated to leave it at that, with Bryn angry and feeling used. But she'd appreciate it in the long run, perhaps she'd even come to understand the reasons for it. He'd not expected her today. His strategy to keep her at a distance by letting the ladies do the alienating for him had wrought the opposite effect.

Instead of driving her away, it had driven her out here to invade his private abode. That had been the last thing he wanted. He was currently a target, Devore's target. Until that was resolved, anyone who was connected to him was potentially in danger, too. If that someone was the daughter of a wealthy banker, so much the worse. Devore would not hesitate to use her against him.

The timing was unfortunate. Under other circumstances, he would have found Bryn Rutherford interesting. What had happened on the rock was proof of that. Now, she could be nothing more than a liability, all kissing aside. In truth, he wasn't sure he'd planned to kiss her. He certainly hadn't planned to let things go as far as they did with hot caresses and her hand on his cock.

He wanted to justify those kisses as part of his scare strategy to convince her to stay away. But that wouldn't be entirely true. It had simply happened. She had looked so lovely, sitting on his rock in the sun. Then she'd raised her arms to take off her hat, her breasts rising high and firm with the effort as they pressed against the thin muslin of her gown and he'd swallowed hard, his groin tightening. He was human and male after all. At that point all bets had been off.

When she'd touched him, his body had sung with the thrill of it. This beautiful English rose had her hand on him. In all of his amorous pursuits, he'd not had a truly cultivated lady. She'd hesitated just enough to prove his speculation correct: bold and wild, but a lady still the same; a lady who did care about proprieties at the end of the day. London must have been hell on her. Society did not reward a woman for curiosity or intelligence and Bryn Rutherford had both. London was for hothouse roses, not wild ones, and Kitt suspected she was as wild as they came when she allowed it.

Kitt smiled to himself. Perhaps that explained what she was doing here in Barbados. How interesting. He wasn't the only one with secrets. She was welcome to keep them. The less he knew about her the better. The less she knew about him…even more so. He definitely needed to push her away for his sanity. He could not bed a lady and avoid trouble, not even in the Caribbean. Not only for his sanity, but for her safety, which he hoped it was not too late to protect.

He owned the beach, but he didn't own the waters. Today out on the rock, he'd thought he'd caught sight of a ship passing slowly. Ships passed all the time. He probably wouldn't have paid it any attention, if he hadn't caught a glimpse of sun reflecting off what was most likely glass. Whoever was on the ship was looking for something or someone. Given the other events surrounding the occurrence, Kitt couldn't afford to ignore the coincidence. Scepticism had kept him alive this long for good reason and now it would have to do for two. Whatever Bryn Rutherford was or wasn't, could or couldn't be, for him, she would not die for him.

Chapter Nine

'How is it that Sherard is still alive?' Hugh Devore's tone was deceptively calm as he surveyed the two men standing before his desk. But one had only to look in his eyes or note the tension in the beefy hands he splayed on the desk's polished surface to know better. He was angry and the two men on the other side of that desk— the inferior side—knew it. Devore had only to look in *their* eyes or watch *their* hands to know it.

The two men, big brutish men, twisted their caps. Good. He liked exercising his authority, liked watching them squirm. They had a lot to be accountable for. He'd paid them a decent sum of money to see Sherard dead and they had yet to deliver. They'd had three days, three opportunities to see their job completed.

'He ran into someone's backyard,' the taller of the two men answered. 'We couldn't follow for fear of being recognised.'

Devore steepled his hands and leaned back in his chair. These men had something more to fear than recognition if they failed in their task. 'Yes, I know. You told me that two days ago. What has happened since? Sherard has driven out to the countryside, he has shopped in town. The man has made himself an accessible target and yet the two of you have made no other move to bring him down. Is the amount of pay holding you back?'

It was a question that could only be answered in one way if they wanted to walk out of his office alive. They were lucky they hadn't lost a finger or two this morning as a reminder he meant business. He was in a relatively good mood for having received bad news and that was saying something. He had what might be considered a volatile temper.

'No, of course not, boss,' the other man answered smartly, quickly, his sense of self-preservation kicking in. Of course it wasn't the money. They'd been well paid and it was no easy thing to come up with the funds. Once, he could have paid them any amount and not felt the pinch. Now, thanks to Sherard and Dryden, he felt every pound that left his reduced coffers.

'Then what is it? The weapons?' Devore prompted although he knew very well it wasn't.

'He's just hard to catch, sir.'

Devore gave a hard laugh. 'He's one man. There are two of you and you come highly recommended. Surely you have some skill to manage him? What about yesterday? You sailed past his private beach, it would have been the perfect shot.'

'Yesterday, he was with a lady.' The two men exchanged nervous looks with one another. He had them on edge. Now he just had to push them to see the job done in short order. Desperate men worked more diligently than comfortable men and Devore wanted this done now. Actually, he'd wanted it done three days ago.

It had been disappointing in the extreme that the rum

ambush had failed so completely. Best-case scenario: he'd acquire Ren Dryden's rum, deal Dryden a financial setback and see Sherard dead in the mêlée of an ambush where no one was sure who had killed whom. Rum runners like Sherard embraced a certain level of danger with their career choice. His death would surprise no one.

But that had not happened. Sherard had foiled it all from beginning to end and now he was reduced to tracking Sherard with these two assassins. Devore stroked the dark bristles of his beard in thought. This was the first interesting piece he'd heard from these two. His mind was already contemplating the possibilities. Here was someone at last who could be levered against Sherard, the man from nowhere, the man with no attachment to anyone. Sherard had women, of course. The man was hardly a monk, according to Devore's sources. But one-night stands weren't worth dying for. Sherard's women to date weren't exactly the sort to inspire chivalry. Devore suspected Sherard kept it that way on purpose. 'A lady?'

The men nodded vigorously, no doubt thinking they'd found a point of empathy with him or maybe they hoped it would be a distraction from the real issue of their failure to kill Sherard. 'She was definitely a lady. She had fine clothes and a big hat.'

Devore gave them an icy smile. They would find no empathy here. Silly men, didn't they know by now he had nothing but enmity when it came to Sherard and Dryden or anything those two bastards touched? They'd taken his home, his wealth, even his wife when it came down to it. She hadn't been interested in staying once the home and the money were gone. To top it off, they'd exiled him to an island to make what he could of himself. Very soon they'd see exactly what that was and very soon they were going to pay. He would do it himself if these two got squeamish. 'Is the lady a problem? You can't kill in front of her?' he asked.

The two men exchanged horrified looks and he had his answer. He let displeasure rule his features. 'I didn't think you two came with scruples.' He paused, fixing each one with his stare in turn. 'This is a disappointing development at such a late stage of the game.'

One of them swallowed, his Adam's apple bobbing. 'We were thinking about witnesses. We thought you'd prefer not to have any. She was out on the rock with him when we sailed by.'

'Ah, that's the first sensible thing you've said. The issue of witnesses is easily solved. Kill them both.' If he'd read their faces aright, that should shock their apparent code of ethics. It almost qualified as entertainment to watch them react.

'But, sir,' one of them made the effort to protest, 'they were otherwise engaged. You wouldn't have us shoot a man in the middle of taking his pleasure.'

Couldn't they see how perfect it would have been? Two deaths were better than one. There would be no witnesses and less suspicion about a third party. Devore shrugged. 'Shooting them both—we could have made it appear to be a lovers' quarrel and no one would think to come looking for you. With Sherard's reputation that wouldn't be a hard fiction to sell.' Good lord, did he have to do all the thinking in this operation? Then again, he quite purposely didn't pay these men to think, only to act, only to take the fall should they be discovered.

His temper was starting to rise with his exasperation.

'Find out who she is, I want to know immediately.' He dismissed them and blew out a breath. Maybe that was the sacrifice he needed to make for success. He hated being out of society, but Sherard had threatened to kill him if he was caught in Bridgetown, so exile it was. But it meant he didn't know whom associated with whom. It weakened his ability to negotiate through leverage. If this woman was important to Sherard, by extension she was important to him. Devore wanted to know.

It wouldn't be long now before Sherard was dead, Dryden was beggared and his own riches returned, balance restored to his world. He just had to be patient a little longer.

Patience was a virtue, Bryn decided, for the simple reason it was bloody impossible to cultivate. If it was easy, everyone would do it. Her patience was definitely being exercised this afternoon at Mrs Selby's Barbadian-themed luncheon, complete with every Caribbean food imaginable from fried plantains to pig in souse. She was tired of the posturing, of everyone jockeying for position with her father. The game was nearly done, though. Her father would announce board within the next few days.

Bryn wasn't the only one who sensed it all coming to a head. Mrs Selby recognised it, too. This luncheon was one final attempt to ensure her son's place on that board. Everyone who coveted a spot was here with one notable exception. Kitt was not. Bryn was certain he'd been invited. Mrs Selby wouldn't risk jeopardising her father's favour by slighting Kitt, not when her father had made it plain he would receive Kitt even if she did not.

It had been a week since her rather precipitous visit

to his house. He'd not been to her father's house for a meeting, nor to any of the functions hosted by potential investors. She would have believed he'd withdrawn from the endeavour entirely if it hadn't been for the notes he'd sent to her father. But *she* had not seen him since their afternoon on his rock, which led her to this conclusion: he'd not withdrawn from the bank, but from her. *Which was for the best*, her conscience was fond of reminding her. Out of sight, meant out of mind. It was easier to keep promises when the temptation to break them was removed.

Her mind didn't want to leave it at that. Her mind wanted to know why? Did he not *like* her? Had she offended him? The former seemed unlikely after his reaction on the rock. He liked her plenty. The last seemed laughable. Kitt was not a man easily offended. He was honest about himself, about society and the world. He knew how the world worked. The truth would not offend him.

Still, it galled her that he'd disappeared without any word to her personally. *He was supposed to send you a note? Who appointed you his mother?* That was her practical side. Her less-practical side had developed the habit of getting distracted at this point in the argument: he had a mother? What sort of mother had this sort of son? Which led to other curiosities—did he have a family? Where were they? But when those considerations were done, her practical side was still there, mocking her. *He owes you nothing.* Men were like that. They could kiss a girl and have it mean nothing. Her London swains had seen her fortune, but not her, never her. They would have been appalled to know she'd swum naked in a swimming hole with her best friend, who happened to be male and he'd been naked, too. And that was only the beginning of her adventures. Kitt would merely laugh and say 'Is that the best you can do?' His blue eyes would spark as he teased her: 'I once climbed a trellis into a woman's room whom I didn't know.'

Why do you care so much? came the inevitable question. Bryn plucked at a blossom on one of Mrs Selby's flowering bushes. Because he represented everything she wanted. He was the gateway, the escape. Represents or *is*? Was he merely a symbol of something she craved or did she crave *him*? Of course she didn't *crave* him. That was too intense for a man she'd just met. He wasn't an addiction. Now she was being hopelessly romantic. She'd barely met him and they'd had only a few encounters, one of those a banking meeting. *But he rouses you, he makes you forget you're a Rutherford and makes you remember who you are...who you were before the rules, before the sickness took your mother and three years of your life, before you lost Robin. He makes you remember your true self.* If that was the case, it was no wonder she was desperate for him. Without meaning to, he was coaxing her back to life.

'Would you like some cake?' Selby materialised at her elbow, a real flesh-and-blood contrast to all Kitt represented: neat brown hair to Kitt's dishevelled blondness, composed manners to Kitt's insincere, mocking bows, placid security to Kitt's wildness. He offered her the plate in his hand. 'It's a chocolate rum cake, but there's coconut sugar cakes at the dessert table if you'd prefer.'

Bryn took the plate. Chocolate sounded perfect. Rum sounded better, even though she knew the spirit baked out. Martha Selby would never serve a tipsy dessert.

'Thank you.' She hoped James would politely retreat. Instead he sat down on an empty chair and motioned for her to join him and the practical lady in her head went to work.

You could have this one. A few smiles, a few light touches on the arm and he'd come up to scratch. Kitt Sherard offers no guarantees. You don't even know where he is. This one offers guarantees aplenty: marriage, security, a family, prestige, social standing that matches your own—all the things your mother wanted for you.

'Did you enjoy yourself today?' James asked. It was her first visit to his home. She understood the point of the luncheon had been for the Selbys to impress her father with their quality of living and no doubt they had. The Selbys lived just outside of town in a big home with wide verandas and shady gardens. Martha Selby had made good use of those gardens today, setting up tables and chairs under the cool palms.

'Your home is beautifully appointed,' Bryn offered neutrally, fearing where this was leading. As the only unmarried man among the coterie of her father's select investors, it had been natural to pair James with her when the group met with their wives. As a result, she'd spent a considerable amount of time with him in the interim. It hadn't necessarily improved him. *But what is there to improve? On paper, he's perfect.*

James leaned forward. 'I would like to ask you something rather personal, if I may.'

As long as it's not a proposal. It wouldn't be though, would it? It was far too soon to be making decisions of that nature. 'Of course, Mr Selby.' In truth, she didn't want to hear his 'personal' question, but a lady had no other answer. It was hardly a question at all.

'Has Captain Sherard been troubling you?' She wondered if Kitt's extended absence had emboldened him now that there was no chance of Kitt hearing him.

'He's hardly here to do any troubling.' Bryn smiled to allay his concern, but also to make the subtle point she didn't approve of asking after a man who wasn't there to defend himself. 'I hardly know him well enough to find him troubling or otherwise.' Perhaps he'd extend that message to himself as well.

James didn't smile back. He lowered his voice further. 'He will be back, though. He's out on one of his infamous runs through the islands.' There was a hint of derision in his tone. 'My mother indicated he'd been overly forward when the four of you met up with him while shopping.'

Bryn wanted to laugh. James was so very serious. She tried to answer with an appropriate amount of reserve. 'It was nothing. Your mother was just looking out for my best interest.'

'She was right to do so. Captain Sherard is in no lady's best interest,' James said with a touch of manly protection.

Probably true. James would be appalled if he knew even half of what had transpired between her and Kitt. She decided to steer the conversation in another direction. 'Where does he go on his runs?' This was something she had not heard.

'He runs cargoes between the islands. He has a fast ship, the *Queen of the Main*. Most of his cargo is rum, so you can imagine the people he deals with.' Oh, she could imagine. James would be stunned by the vivid images that conjured up: Kitt at the helm of a boat, wind his hair, his shirt open at the neck.

'It's all very unsavoury.' James's distaste was written in the scowl on his face.

Very dangerous, too. That explained the knife. The image of Kitt naked and wielding a knife was engraved on her mind for obvious reasons. It had not occurred to her until she'd got past the 'obvious' part of that image how odd it was he'd had a knife handy while getting a massage. Who kept a knife with them when they were relaxing?

Now she knew and the answer wasn't nearly as satisfying as she'd hoped. It merely spawned other questions and more curiosity. She'd been able to justify her interest in Kitt as purely business at first. But this new flare of interest was far more personal. Who was he? She knew so little about him. *And you should keep it that way. What could knowing more about him do but cause trouble?*

She was still debating this when her father walked over, smiling broadly to claim her. It was time to make their farewells to their hostess. Her father was still smiling as they left the Selbys.

'What has you so happy? Did your discussion go well?' Bryn asked, opening a parasol as the open barouche headed back towards town.

'Yes, I think the group is forming well. We should be able to send a preliminary report back to England on the next mail packet in a week or so. But I'm smiling because of you. I saw you with James. Do you like him? He's a solid young man with great potential.'

Bryn hated to spoil her father's good mood, but there was no sense in prolonging a lie or creating false hopes.

'He's nice enough, a perfect gentleman, but he's not for me. I don't think anyone is right now. It will take me some time.'

Her father nodded and leaned over to pat her knee encouragingly, misunderstanding her remark. 'There will be someone.'

'Maybe, some day.' She smiled to assure him. Until that time, there was Kitt Sherard and his audacious kisses. It occurred to her that perhaps the reason she'd behaved so badly with Kitt was that she knew nothing could come of it. In that regard, he was safe. There would be no professions of love. Just physical pleasure, just coming alive. And that was enough, more than enough. In short, there would be nothing to break: no engagements, no hearts, nothing. Just life. Just living. He offered a far simpler arrangement, which was, unfortunately, quite appealing to a woman who felt chained by complicated promises.

'You're smiling, Daughter, and that's a start.' Her father's voice held a laugh, something she hadn't heard from him in a while. 'Whatever has put that smile on your face, I'm glad for it. We are coming alive again, you and I both.'

Now if only the reason for that smile would come back, Bryn thought. Where was her pirate prince?

Chapter Ten

Kitt took the helm of the *Queen*, feeling alive at sea in a way he never quite achieved on land. The ship moved beneath him, gently bucking over the waves, like a woman finding her pleasure. He never tired of either image, the woman or the ship, although these days the image of the woman had taken the very definite shape of Bryn Rutherford as she'd been on the rock, as she'd been on the balcony: hot, curious and willing in his arms.

There were other images, too: her storming down the path full of righteous indignation only to find him nude; her untying the ribbon of her hat and lifting it from her head, her hand on him. For a woman he was trying to avoid, the list of images he carried in his mind was rather long and colourful. In short, arousing.

Of course, that might also have something to do with the fact that he'd been without one for far longer than he was used to. This trip had not allowed enough time to avail himself of his usual port-to-port favourites. There'd been business to handle, which had been hectic due to the impending cane harvests. There'd been extra business, too, like arranging another trade for Ren's rum barrels. And, as always, there'd been information to gather, which involved a lot of listening, head nodding and a judiciously placed question here and there on his part, sometimes accompanied by judiciously placed coins. The good information was never free.

Kitt turned the wheel to put the ship's nose to the wind, the sails full against the blue sky as he headed for Bridgetown and home. That was a dangerous word. Home made a man weak just as friends made a man vulnerable. It was a sign he'd been here too long. He was starting to feel comfortable. He was starting to feel hopeful. There were signs of that hope sprinkled throughout his life. He had his villa, his ship, he had Ren and soon Bridgetown would have a bank. Civilisation was coming to him and Bridgetown both. There was no escaping it and it was not the time to start feeling 'comfortable'. He should be feeling increasingly vigilant. With civilisation came more opportunity for his past to be exposed.

Perhaps he should consider leaving. The western Caribbean was still fairly untouched by the English, still fairly lawless. It would be hard to find him there. It would keep him from entertaining fantasies about Bryn Rutherford. She'd definitely be out of reach then. He was going to have to see her again. He couldn't communicate with her father by letter for ever if he wanted to be part of the investment group.

The ship entered the bay and his blood hummed. He told himself it was because he was eager to talk to Ren. Something was definitely afoot. The islands were brimming with activity. There'd been reports of new plantations trying new crops. It sounded very industrious, very interesting, even very lucrative. Plantations were the backbone of the Caribbean economy. Since the sixteen hundreds, people had been cultivating a variety of new crops, some with success, some not. These islands were seedbeds of innovation for those willing to risk it.

Kitt also knew these islands were seedbeds for other more notorious activities. When innovation was of a less-honest nature, it was called swindling. That was what had him worried. He wanted word of James Selby's plantation. When he'd been approached by an acquaintance of a regular connection on one of the smaller islands, Kitt had listened intently. The Sunwood project, he'd called it, a chance to experiment with new strains of cotton and cane. Perhaps this was the one Selby had spoken of. It would be something to start from.

Why do you care so much about what Selby invests in? his mind prodded. Selby was welcome to his own mistakes, but this time those mistakes involved Kitt's money. If he was going to invest in a bank, it had better be a good one. He wasn't going to throw money after poor investments. That was the easy answer, the one that didn't require any further thought.

The harder answer was that Bryn's father was involved, at the very least by association. Selby's foolishness would reflect poorly on the bank. If her father was involved, then she was involved, too, and that was intolerable to Kitt. He'd seen too many innocent bystanders brought down by the foolishness of others. He hadn't been able to save them. But he'd be damned if he stood by and watched it happen again if he could help it.

That was all. He put a firm lid on that analysis. It had everything to do with the past and nothing to do with Bryn personally. With that, his thoughts came full circle, back to the woman who'd started them. It was nearly impossible for him to think about the pending bank without thinking of Bryn. Had she missed him? Had she noticed he was gone? Stupid questions both, and hardly worthy of a man who'd refined the art of physical pleasure without emotional attachment.

Is that what he meant by 'Had she missed him?'? Miss as in she was sorry he was gone? Did he want her to miss him? Why? He liked her well enough. She was out of the ordinary, a challenge. But to what end? To see if he could have a woman like that without the trappings of his old life to recommend him? To see if Kitt Sherard, rum runner, could win a cultivated woman of high birth—the sort of woman who, by rights, should never look twice at such a man, a woman who was reserved for a lord? Or was she more than a game he played with himself? Neither proposition was answered easily or comfortably for a man who prided himself on remaining unattached and emotionally aloof.

Had she spent her time wondering such things, wondering about him? Or had she spent the week deciding James Selby was a better choice by far? She would have had ample opportunity to make the comparison. There would have been parties and meetings—had she sat in on any more of those? He couldn't imagine Selby finding her attendance at meetings a womanly behaviour.

In England, he wouldn't have even viewed Selby as competition. But that life was over. Here, Selby had the advantage. For all her protests to the contrary, perhaps Bryn would see that. Again came the question—why did he care? There were plenty of women who were glad to warm his bed and make no demands, yet she was the one who made his blood heat with anticipation when he thought about this evening, the reason he was back in Barbados so soon. The banking board would be announced tonight at the gala. He would be there for that, as would Ren. And Bryn. He'd see her tonight, perhaps tonight he'd test his many hypotheses about the attraction she held for him and sort this out once and for all.

It had been a difficult decision to sail with so much going on, but he had a business to continue and he wasn't worried about being left off the board. His money spoke for itself, as did his business sense. The good women of Bridgetown might look down their noses at his unorthodox methods, but their husbands were all too happy to make money with him.

Kitt called for the anchor to be lowered. As eager as he was to be home, the trip had been incomplete in some ways. There'd been no news about anyone who might be stalking him and that was decidedly unnerving for two reasons. First, he usually had a good idea of who his enemies were and why. Second, because of the first reason, it affirmed the suspicions he'd voiced to Ren. Ghosts of the past had come back to haunt them. But not for long. When he got things settled on land, he'd go do a little hunting of his own by sea. It was necessary and it might even give himself a chance to purge this growing obsession with Bryn Rutherford.

It occurred to Bryn that she might be developing an obsession for Kitt Sherard. Bryn's eyes hunted the lantern lit gardens for him, searching the crowd with her gaze from the darker perimeter. He should be here. Tonight was the bank's celebration gala and his ship had been sighted in the bay that afternoon. Not that it did her any credit to admit she was looking for him, it was just something to pass the time, a reason to disengage from the crowd for a moment.

She'd done her duty as her father's hostess and greeted all the guests. Now, she wanted a moment to step back and see the results of her planning. Although invitations had only gone out a week ago, this party had been conceived of months before. The supplies for it, including the cases of champagne, had crossed the Atlantic with them in anticipation of this precise outcome; the assembling of the bank's charter members.

Across the garden, she could see him deep in conversation with Selby and Harrison, his face animated as he spoke. Bryn couldn't help but smile. Her father had done it. Tonight was his triumph—a triumph that went beyond banking, although she was the only one present who knew it.

A server passed by, bearing icy glasses of champagne on a silver tray, the bubbly liquid sparkling like gold diamonds in the lights. She reached for one, but someone behind her was faster, whisking two glasses off the tray.

'Silver and gold, perfect colours for tonight's party, don't you think?' Kitt materialised out of the darkness beside her. He handed her a glass, bemused by her gasp of surprise.

'You do have a way of taking a girl unawares.' Bryn took a sip of the sharp, fizzy champagne, trying not to give away the excitement his presence raised in her or the fact that he'd succeeded in catching her off guard. She'd expected to see him first.

'You were looking for me. Miss me, did you?' Kitt chuckled, taking a swallow.

'Were you gone?' Bryn answered coolly, annoyed

that he'd been spying on her. He'd been here longer than she'd thought and he'd been watching her. She'd wanted to have all the control.

'Minx.' Kitt smiled and it went straight to her knees. He was even more handsome than she remembered. A week aboard ship had served to deepen his tan and bleach his hair to a sleek white-gold. He fairly vibrated with potent good health, his presence more intoxicating than the champagne. She was definitely developing an obsession.

'I must confess, I was worried,' Bryn said casually. 'You were the first asked and the last to sign.' Worried, because she'd feared somehow her secret indiscretions had affected Kitt's decision and her father's success would pay for her indiscretions, although they were hardly her fault, at least not the first one. She hadn't asked Kitt to climb her balcony and she hadn't known who he was at the time.

'I had business,' Kitt offered vaguely.

'Rum?' Bryn guessed. 'I suppose we're lucky you came back at all. The way Selby tells it, rum is a most dangerous business.'

Kitt laughed outright at that. 'It used to be—it's far tamer these days in most cases.' But he would say nothing further about what he'd spent the last week doing, and Bryn sensed there was far more to it than simply trading barrels of rum for farming supplies. Kitt Sherard was not a simple man, why would he lead a simple life?

Kitt nodded in her father's direction. 'He's done well. This is an important night for him and for England. History will mark this occasion.'

She had not thought of that. It was just the sort of

comment Kitt would make when she was convinced he was nothing more than a habitual flirt. Was he the only one who saw it? Did the others see it, too, or had they also lost the forest for the trees? Everyone had been so intent on the immediate gains of banding together for investment and personal profit. Bryn cocked her head to one side, giving Kitt a considering glance. 'Is that why you're here? Posterity?' Goodness knew he didn't need the group to make money.

Kitt raised a broad, nonchalant shoulder. 'Maybe it's my way of thumbing my nose at all of it, a little bit of irony. In the end I was good enough.'

A very telling comment and a surprisingly revealing one, too. For all his airs to the contrary, Kitt Sherard wanted to prove himself. It was there in his magnificent house and his private beach and it was here tonight in his decision to join a most respectable group of gentlemen. She did wonder why. Something else she could add to her growing list of questions about the stranger who'd climbed her balcony. She knew shockingly little about the man with whom she'd shared some rather liberal intimacies.

Across the garden her father motioned for her to join him. It was time for the official announcement. Selby was already with him, standing on at his right shoulder. 'I have to go.' It was dratted timing. She'd just got Kitt to herself. She wanted to say something, to arrange to meet afterwards, but that seemed forward. It seemed desperate, too, an admission that she had indeed missed him.

Kitt's eyes hardened, looking over to her father and Selby. 'Who do you go to? Him or Selby?'

She kept her gaze neutral, her smile mysterious. 'Who

do you think?' If he really understood her the way he intimated he did, he knew the answer. In the meanwhile, it was a novelty to know that she could summon at least the faintest stirrings of jealousy or covetousness. The idea that Kitt Sherard coveted her just a bit sent a feminine thrill down her back and maybe, just maybe, she walked away with a little more swing in her hips in case she was right.

'Is she or isn't she?' Kitt muttered, watching her go. Bryn Rutherford would give the devil a run for his money when it came to temptation.

'Is she or isn't she what?' Ren sauntered up, a glass of champagne in hand for the anticipated toast.

'You weren't supposed to hear that.' Kitt took a swallow of his champagne. At this rate, he'd need another glass.

'Then don't talk out loud.' Ren laughed. 'I presume the she in question is the lovely Miss Rutherford? May I also presume the question is: is she a temptress with experience or merely a temptress who has no idea of her skills?' Ren paused. 'I am being delicate with my terms, of course.'

'Dammit, yes, that's exactly what I'm considering. Is she or isn't she a virgin?' Kitt blew out a breath. The crowd had obscured Bryn from view and he couldn't watch those hips sway across the garden.

'Does it matter?' Ren asked, both of them watching Bryn reappear as she kissed her father on the cheek and smiled broadly at the group assembled around him.

'Only in the sense that it dictates how far I can take things and the price that might be paid for it.' It struck Kitt that it didn't really matter to him personally. Virginity had never been something he'd thought much about, but in this case it mattered.

Ren laughed and slapped him on the back. 'Oh, that I've lived to see the day Kitt Sherard is infatuated.'

'I am not infatuated,' Kitt argued in firm undertones. 'I am merely planning my next conquest.' Even as he said it, he knew it was a lie. He *was* infatuated. Ren had hit it on the head. But nothing more. Infatuation was tolerable on occasion. It wasn't as base as lust, nor as noble as love, but somewhere in between. Perhaps Bryn was even savvy enough to understand that. Maybe she was infatuated, too, and knew the difference. He might have been watching her from the shadows, taking in every delectable inch of her in that tight-fighting aquamarine silk, but she'd been looking for him, too. He didn't imagine the way her pulse had jumped when he'd joined her. How interesting, they were both *infatuated* with each other.

Her father chimed a fork against a goblet, calling for attention. A small dais had been set up for the occasion and Rutherford stood on it now with Bryn on one side and Selby on the other. The lantern light loved her, bouncing off the discreet *brillants* in her hair and the tasteful diamond choker about her neck. Virgin or not, she was indisputably a lady of quality.

Kitt's eyes drifted to Selby and something twisted in his gut. Selby looked well in his evening clothes, every inch an earl's grandson. He was just the sort of man for Bryn: young, attractive, respectable. He would never put her in danger—then again, he'd never excite her either.

On the dais, Rutherford raised his glass and began his speech. Kitt forced himself to listen, dragging his thoughts away from Selby and Bryn. 'Thank you, everyone, for coming tonight. This is the beginning of an historic turning point in the history of the island and in the history of the British empire. It also marks the beginning of our partnership, long may it prove prosperous.' There was applause and everyone drank.

'You should be up there with them,' Ren growled at his side. The other investors were clumped together in the front row, congratulating one another.

Kitt shrugged his nonchalance. 'I'm in, that's all that matters.'

'You don't have to keep yourself apart.' Ren's response was fierce. 'You've been safe for years. No one even remotely connects Kitt Sherard with Michael Melford. Surely, there's no harm in—'

Kitt shot him a hard, silencing look. Ren had crossed an invisible line. 'I cannot take that chance. I can never be sure and the risk is too great.' He could not be discovered. His family was counting on it, and now his brother's future bride, whether she knew it or not, was counting on it, too. She and her unborn children. Oh, yes, the risk had grown exponentially.

Ren didn't know when to stop. 'I don't think Miss Rutherford minds. I think she'd be very interested in whatever you had to offer, the way her hips were swinging.'

'She might, but I cannot ask her to risk it.' Although God knew he wanted to. Each time he saw her it was becoming harder to resist acting on the attraction. Who was he fooling? Every time he saw her, he *did* act on the attraction and so did she. Each time things went a little further, became a little more explosive. There would come a time when neither would be able to pull back. Kitt relished it and rued it.

Ren was not cowed by his stare. 'Seems like there might be more than a little infatuation going on.'

'Sod off, you…' The last of his unsavoury comment was lost in the tapping of another goblet. Rutherford wasn't done with his announcements.

'What's this?' Ren asked *sotto voce*, but Kitt shook his head, he didn't know.

'If you would all humour me one more time, I would like to offer a second, more personal toast,' Rutherford announced.

Kitt listened, but his eyes went to Bryn. There'd been a moment's surprise on her face. She had not expected this either.

'Tonight also marks the beginning of my partnership with James Selby as we embark on a new venture at the Sunwood Plantation. May this, too, be the start of new innovations and scientific research into the agriculture of the island.'

Kitt felt Ren stiffen beside him, both of them exchanging quick looks. This was the plantation project he'd heard about on his rounds. He wished he knew more, wished he wasn't so sceptical of Selby. On the dais, Bryn looked out into the crowd, searching for him. He met her gaze, holding it. He would never reach her. People were moving around them, making their way to the long dinner tables laid out under the white canopies.

He could see she was stunned by the news. Something protective inside him wanted to go to her. She hadn't known, which meant one thing: Rutherford hadn't researched it. He had merely taken Selby's word and Selby was a man easily misled. Kitt's gut knotted with suspicion. He needed to know the location of Sunwood Plantation.

'What are you thinking? It's on one of the smaller islands. I can send you the co-ordinates. It's about a day's sail away.' Ren intruded on his thoughts.

Kitt's response was grim. 'I'm thinking it's all happening again.'

Chapter Eleven

It had all happened without her! The thought ran through her head in a repetitive loop. Her father, who was in the habit of telling her everything, hadn't told her this. That was the part that hurt. When had he decided this? Why hadn't he told her? She feared it was because he wasn't sure. Why else would he keep the secret except out of concern that she would argue with him?

In her disappointment, she'd instinctively sought out Kitt in the crowd. He'd been as stunned as she, perhaps even more so. His expression had been grim, as if he knew something she didn't. She was desperate to talk to him, but that would have to wait. Dinner was at round tables of eight and she'd spread the investors across all the tables in the hopes of building interest from others in the bank. She was seated with Selby at her father's request. There'd be no chance to talk to Kitt until much later, if at all.

'He's a poor sport, that one, an absolute loner,' Selby said, his head nodding towards Kitt's table where everyone was laughing. The handsome Earl of Dartmoor was seated there, too, and champagne was flowing freely. They looked as though they were having fun.

'I don't know why you would think that,' Bryn replied in Kitt's defence. This habit of Selby's to malign Kitt was most unbecoming.

'He can't stand the idea that anyone else can make money. I'd wager he's envious over the plantation. He'll probably try to sabotage it at some point. If I were your father, I'd be on the watch for something sly.' Selby shook his head. 'I vow, he'll be difficult to work with. If his pockets weren't so deep, he wouldn't have been asked to join.'

None of you would have been asked to join, Bryn thought rather uncharitably. Did Selby really believe all this nonsense about friendships? This was business, pure and simple. It was about who had money. Even now, the tables reflected that. There were the prime investors her father had gathered, a secondary group, and then there were the connections, all the people who hoped to persuade the investors to invest in them.

'Just think about it—any time an idea comes up, Sherard seems to take issue with it,' James persisted with a huff.

'You are quick to condemn him,' Bryn pointed out a tad more sharply than she meant to.

Selby shot her a hard look. 'You are quick to defend him. There are better gentlemen present who hold you in great regard. I would aim higher if I were you, Miss Rutherford. You've done an admirable job of setting up house for your father. This party is a splendid example of that. The other women like you, too. I would warn you not to throw away all the good you've done by championing a bounder who is best left to the company of men.'

This was a new side, a harder side, of James Selby. Bryn reached for her wine glass. 'I shall certainly con-

sider that.' She smiled to suggest he was forgiven and
trailed a hand along his sleeve. 'Enough about Sherard.
Tell me about the island—where is it exactly? Perhaps I
could get you to write those co-ordinates down?' Bryn
shifted in her seat to better show off the tight bodice of
her dress. James's eyes followed.

She'd been surprised by his outburst. The man did
possess some spine after all. Too bad it was supported
by bile. There was no love lost between Selby and Kitt.
It could create some difficulty on the board if the two
insisted on competing. She could easily see her father
in a bit of a tug of war. Her father liked Kitt, but it was
Selby who'd availed himself of her father's time and
ingratiated himself. Kitt had been aloof and absent,
not the best of recommendations if her father had to
choose between them.

You should apply that same standard for yourself.
Who should you believe? Selby, who tries so very hard
to be all a gentleman should be, who has supported your
father at every turn, or Captain Sherard who takes lib-
erties with you, sails away without notice and shows
up late for dinners, making it clear his priorities do not
lie here, all of which points to the fact that he is hid-
ing something.

Bryn was still considering these competing ideas
when the guests departed shortly after midnight. Kitt
had departed much earlier—at least, she guessed he
had, to her disappointment. He'd not said goodbye to
her. For all she knew, he'd slipped out the garden gate.
Selby and his mother were the last to leave.

Selby clasped her father's hand warmly, congratulating him on a wonderful evening. Not for the first

time she wished she could like him more. Selby was safe, comfortable. He would be a doting husband, all a girl should wish for, and yet he stirred her not one iota, except to irritate her. But she'd stirred his gentleman's blood enough to get the co-ordinates.

'We'll leave for the other parishes, day after tomorrow, early in the morning, before it gets too hot,' James was saying. That got her attention.

'Are we going somewhere?' she enquired politely.

'I hadn't had time to tell you, we've just decided.' Her father smiled broadly. 'Some of the other investors thought it would be a good idea to make a survey of the island and see what's out there to invest in. We'll only be gone a week. James has lined up some people for us to meet with.' Her father was leaving on a trip? One more thing he hadn't told her.

A sense of panic began to well. How had everything got so far out of control without her knowing? It wasn't that her father needed her consent. It was just that she was used to being consulted. The closeness of the last two years was slipping away.

The Selbys left, the door shut behind them, the house quiet after being filled with the noise of guests all evening. She smiled at her father. 'I could make us some tea and we could talk it all over,' she offered. 'It was a grand evening.'

Her father shook his head and started up the stairs. 'I will pass, my dear. I am too tired and I have busy days ahead. James is coming by tomorrow to go over some things about the Sunwood project. They're going to need a little more start-up capital than originally thought to get the new crops in—'

'Yes, about that,' Bryn interrupted. 'Did you research

it? I was surprised by the announcement. I had no idea you were considering it. What do we know of it?'

'James knows of it. He would not lead me astray. It would hardly enhance his reputation to have an investment go foul at this juncture. He knows what he's doing. I have every confidence in him.'

But Kitt had thought otherwise. *It's not that I don't trust Selby, it's that I don't trust his judgement.* Who was she to trust? The gentleman or the rogue? Perhaps Selby was right. She was unduly influenced by Kitt's good looks and flirtatious ways.

With her father gone to bed, there was no sense in staying up. Bryn picked up a lamp and made her way to her own rooms. She didn't expect to sleep, she had too much on her mind: her father's new investment, Selby's comments about Kitt, all the little revelations of the evening. All of which led back to the very point she'd been considering since the day Kitt had taken her out to the rock: did she trust him?

Perhaps she did. She'd certainly been quick enough to seek his opinion tonight and even quicker to question Selby's choices instead of questioning Kitt's. The bigger question was why she trusted him. Was it true? *Did* she defend Kitt because she was drawn to him? Was infatuation influencing her decisions? There was admittedly a lot of him to be infatuated with.

She wasn't naive enough to believe she was the only girl who'd ever been swayed by good looks, or even swayed by *Kitt's* good looks to be specific. But for a woman who'd promised herself freedom, it was hardly something to be proud of. Bryn stepped inside her room and set the lamp on her dressing table, and began to absently pull the pins from her hair, her thoughts trying to sort themselves out. What was she playing at with Kitt? How far could she let it go without compromising her dreams? Her promises?

'Very lovely.' A voice spoke out of the darkness beyond the scope of the lamp and she grabbed up her hairbrush out of reflex, prepared to wield it like a club, although she recognised the voice all too well. Perhaps all the more reason to have a club.

'Speak of the devil!' She gasped. 'What are you doing in here?' Kitt's long form emerged from the shadowy folds of her canopy bed. 'Although I should hardly be surprised. You have a knack for showing up in odd places.'

'I couldn't leave without saying goodbye to the hostess.' He gave an impish grin and walked towards her. He'd taken off his evening jacket. She could see it now, folded at the end of her bed. Without it, his shoulders looked even broader, his waist even narrower, his maleness more prominent. He took the brush from her hand. 'What were you thinking to do with this? I don't recommend it as a weapon of choice.'

'A girl has to use what she has at hand.'

Kitt put the brush down. 'Did you learn anything else about the plantation?'

'Are you planning on investing after all?' She was trying to view this interaction with a level of objective detachment that had nothing to do with the fact a handsome male was in her bedroom after midnight, walking slow, seductive circles around her like a stalking tiger. Instead, she tried to focus on Selby's warning. 'Selby thinks you like to discourage others on purpose.'

'What do you think, Bryn?' His eyes never left hers as he circled.

'I don't know what to think,' she admitted honestly, her voice a little hoarse.

'As it should be. I don't know what to think either. I don't know enough about this to think anything, which is both worrisome and relaxing. Maybe there's nothing to worry about. Maybe there is and that should be a concern to your father. If he's being taken advantage of, the whole bank board will look foolish.'

'The Rutherford coffers can handle a loss,' Bryn said, trying to convince herself Kitt's words didn't raise some alarm.

'It's not about money. It's about reputation. This would be a loss of credibility at the fledgling stages of the bank's formation. It could be devastating.' Kitt's voice was velvet in the darkness, seductive even delivering bad news. *Potentially* bad news, nothing was certain yet. She couldn't jump to rash conclusions.

'What are you going to do?' She was certain he was going to do *something*.

She could almost feel his grin as he came up behind her, hands at her shoulders, his breath at her neck, feathering her ear. 'I am going to find that island.'

'And if you don't?' She was sure he could see the race of her pulse, her body firing so easily at his touch. It was as shameful as it was delicious.

'Either way, we'll know if we have anything to worry about, princess.'

'Do you know where to look?'

'No, but I have some ideas.'

Bryn licked her lips in a slow motion, an idea coming to her. She held up the paper she'd carried in her pocket just out of reach. 'I have the co-ordinates.' She watched Kitt's eyes light up. 'But, I'll want a forfeit for them.' He was leaving, again. Everyone was going somewhere, except her. Maybe she could go, too. Bryn turned in his arms, pressing her hips lightly against his in suggestion. 'When are you going?' She gave him a coy smile, her gaze dropping to his mouth.

'Oh, no, minx, you are not coming along.' Kitt's voice was husky, though. He was not unaffected by her little flirtation.

She flicked her tongue over her lips, her hips moving more strongly against his. 'I didn't say anything about that, did I? Maybe I just want a proper goodbye kiss.'

This time it was her tongue that initiated, her tongue running over the even line of his teeth and the smooth planes of his mouth as it explored. It was her mouth that moved over his, drinking and tasting the full flavour of him, her hands that anchored in his hair, drawing him to her, against her, until she could feel the unmistakable press of his erection.

'What are you doing, princess?' Kitt's voice was no more than a groan.

'Giving you a reason to come back.' She gave his lower lip a final tug with her teeth and stepped away, knowing full well her own breathing was as ragged as his.

It was his cue to depart. There was only so much she was willing to risk with her father just a few doors down and her own thoughts so unsettled. 'You can find your own way out?'

Kitt gave a snort. 'I hear the trellis works pretty well.'

Bryn waited until he'd swung a leg over the balcony railing and disappeared over the edge before she followed him outside, her eyes marking his progress as he jogged through the now-deserted garden and out the gate. The only way to trust him would be to test him. Bryn knew what she had to do. She had a day to get on that boat. Round one might have gone to him, but round two had gone to her, he just didn't know it yet.

Chapter Twelve

She was giving him a reason to come back, all right. That kiss was still on his mind two days later as he sat in his cabin, the *Queen of the Main* heading out to sea once more on the evening tide. He was supposedly charting a course for Selby's island, something his mind was only half-engaged in. The other half kept getting sidetracked by memories of Bryn's warm body pressed up against him, very deliberately. It was the deliberate part he kept going back to.

As enjoyable as the kiss was, he couldn't shake the feeling that she'd done it for a reason. If the reason wasn't to tag along, what was it? He'd replayed the scene over in his mind numerous times, much to his body's chagrin. But nothing stood out. That particular mystery would have to wait until he returned. Perhaps the kiss was nothing more than what she'd suggested—a reason to come back.

But that carried its own set of complications. Beyond their clandestine, rather spontaneous meetings, what more could there be for them? A woman of her quality was meant for a gentleman. *If you were in England, you'd have rank and be more than acceptable.* The thought was shocking in its rarity, although it wasn't shocking in its occurrence, poised as it was on the aftermath of recognising Selby as competition.

The idea was not one he trotted out often. It wasn't something he'd even allowed himself to think of in the years he'd been here. This was a land of self-made men and he'd successfully fit that mould, setting aside his former life. Never once had he regretted that decision, never once had he looked back and missed what he'd left behind.

Not even now, his conscience reprimanded forcefully. *She changes nothing.* Bryn Rutherford was a passing fancy. From a logical standpoint, he knew all the reasons she appealed. He could tick them off on one hand. He'd been celibate too long, his libido was on edge; she was new and different; she was beautiful and fine, intelligent and daring, and, to top it off, they'd been thrown together by business interests, forced to encounter one another. Fancies passed, storms passed. Like a storm, he simply had to ride her out.

Kitt shifted in his chair, trying to subdue a growing sense of arousal. Perhaps riding *her* out was not the best comparison at the moment. He went back to the map, refocusing his thoughts on a less exciting topic. After five more minutes of working he sat back and rubbed his temples. He must be entirely distracted. Usually he was a very good mapper. He picked up Bryn's paper and studied the co-ordinates again. Perhaps Selby had got them wrong? Perhaps Bryn had written them down wrong? Those thoughts did nothing to dislodge the sense of unease that had ridden him since the gala dinner. It couldn't be happening again, but early signs suggested it was. He had to find that island and it had, *absolutely had*, to have a thriving plantation on it.

Kitt was about to give it another go when a loud thump drew his attention to the wardrobe. Nothing. He scanned the room, looking for evidence something had fallen off a shelf. Perhaps it had come from outside. The thump came again and Kitt swore in frustration. Great, now he was hearing things. If this kept up, he'd never get anything done. To assuage his curiosity, he strode over to the wardrobe and flung open the door, only to be proven wrong.

Out tumbled Bryn Rutherford with an 'oomph' and a most unladylike oath on her lips.

Kitt stepped back in time to avoid being trampled. He crossed his arms over his chest. 'Well, at least you can swear like a sailor.'

'Stuff it.' Bryn glared and struggled to her feet. 'Do you have any idea how long I've been in there?'

Long enough to be deliciously rumpled. 'You weren't supposed to be in there at all.' She'd probably have a bruise or two tomorrow on that sweet *derrière* of hers, but it served her right for all the trouble she was going to cause him. He strode to the door, already making calculations for what this delay would cost him.

'Where do you think you're going?' Bryn tried to stagger after him. She hadn't any sea legs to speak of at the moment. Kitt reached out to steady her.

'Out on deck to tell Passemore to turn this ship around. I'm taking you back to Bridgetown, as much as the delay grieves me.' The tide and the breeze would be wasted now, but he was *not* taking her with him.

Bryn chose that moment to throw herself in front of the cabin door, effectively blocking his exit. 'I'm going with you to find that island.' She meant it, too. Her grey eyes stormed with stubbornness and Kitt knew he'd make no headway arguing with her. He'd let her have her moment. He leaned against the wall, arms crossed, and watched her. She was fascinating to watch, all those emotions rolling across her face at once. A lady without her ladylike mask of blandness on. Not for the first time, he thought what a trial London must have been for her and what a trial she must have been for London. Society wouldn't have known what to do with her. Lucifer's balls, *he* barely knew what to do with her. He'd have to try another tactic since reasoning was out of the question.

'You do understand, Bryn, that I am bigger and stronger than you, even when you're in a temper. I can simply throw you over my shoulder, remove you from the door and go about my business.'

'The hell you will.' Her eyes shot bolts of lightning and her hair hung forward over her shoulders. She looked like an avenging Fury. If she had a weapon, she'd be positively dangerous, lethal even.

'What a lovely mouth you've acquired,' Kitt drawled with a touch of indolence. It wouldn't do to show any ounce of weakness. 'Do you talk like that at home? Because I have to tell you that will not impress the likes of James Selby.' She managed to blush, but she didn't move from the door.

'I want to go with you,' Bryn repeated staunchly, ignoring his comment. 'This concerns my father. I deserve the right to go and see his investment.'

Kitt ran a hand through his hair. 'Damn right this concerns your father. What do you think he'll say— better yet, what do you think he'll do if he discovers you've hidden away on my ship?' Did she understand the implications of stowing away?

'He won't know. He's out with Selby visiting the other parishes. He'll be gone all week,' Bryn answered with a tilt to her chin that said, *Ha, take that.*

He sauntered towards her, crowding her a little with the bulk of his body. It was time to remind her that she'd stowed away on *his* boat and the two of them were explosive together. He would ensure she made good on that promise of a kiss she'd given him. 'It's not only that. Have you thought about us and the fact that we'll be alone with no one to stop us?'

She had no ready answer for that except for a blush that crept up her cheeks. He pressed his advantage. 'Or is that the real reason you came aboard? Maybe you want an excuse to exercise those passions of yours.'

Her cheeks flamed. Kitt smiled wickedly. So, she had thought of that, too. His hands rested at her waist, his thumbs pressing lightly on the low bones of her hips intimately, suggestively. 'Make no mistake, princess, if you came here for a taste of me, I am up for it.' More than up for it, actually. He wanted her the way a thirsty man wanted water. He hoped a sip or two would quench that thirst and he could move on.

'All that within the span of a day?' Bryn challenged, holding her own against the onslaught of his rather aggressive flirtation. Well, good for her. He'd see what she'd do with round two.

'A day?' he questioned.

'Selby says the island is only a day away. We'll be there and back before my father returns.'

'That might be a problem, princess. According to Selby's co-ordinates, there's nothing there. But when I reverse them, there's an island three days away. Either Selby wrote them down wrong, or he's been had, and, by extension, so has your father.'

'No, that can't be.' Bryn had paled. She moved away from the door to the table with rapid steps. Her finger drew lines on the map, retracing his trail. 'The plantation managers have written. There was an actual letter. They needed more money for the new crops.'

An absolutely classic move in a classic scheme. This was looking more like land fraud with each revelation.

'That's why you have to go back, Bryn. I don't know what we're going to find out there. It may be dangerous and it may not be a quick a trip.' If the island was a fraud, he would want to hunt down the men behind it and there was still Devore to find. He could be gone indefinitely.

'It's every reason why I need to be there,' Bryn protested. 'Do you think James will believe you if you come back and tell him his island isn't there? He'll see it as another competitive ploy to outwit him. He'll believe me, my father will believe me.' She swayed suddenly on her feet.

Kitt moved swiftly to steady her. This was more than not having sea legs. 'How long has it been since you've eaten?' He helped her to the edge of the bed.

'This morning, but I'm fine.' She insisted although the pallor of her face told a different story. Kitt, tell me what's really going on?' The earnestness in her eyes settled it. He would probably regret this but how could he ask her to stay at home and wait? If it was him, he knew he'd never tolerate such a decision. Why should she? Kitt drew a resigned breath.

'I'm going to get you some food and when I come

back I'm going to tell you the tale of a Scotsman named MacGregor.'

She smiled at him, coy and alluring even in distress 'I'll be right here.'

Yes, she would be, Kitt thought grimly, exiting the cabin. It wasn't until he was in the galley gathering up food that it hit him. The minx had won. She was going to stay and it hadn't even required his consent, it had just happened. One minute he'd been spelling out the concern for her virtue and the next she'd been bent over his map, tracing routes with her finger.

For better or worse, she'd be in his cabin for the next six days. What had he been thinking? That was the problem. He knew what he'd been thinking and what he'd been thinking *with*. The organ of record wasn't the brain in his head.

He was going to let her stay! Elation surged. Bryn had not been sure her stowaway ploy would actually work. There'd been a moment when she'd thought he actually would toss her over his shoulder and personally row her ashore if that was what it took. He'd looked quite formidable standing there, legs apart, arms crossed and quite appealing, too, with his shirt open at the neck, sleeves rolled up, breeches tight, hair loose. Lord, he had glorious hair, glorious *everything*. And he'd wanted her. In spite of his anger, he'd wanted her. That had definitely worked to her advantage.

Yes, you won, you get to stay for six days. Six days alone with the pirate captain himself. It's what you wanted—an adventure. What will you do with it? What would she do with it indeed? Would she act on it or would she play the lady and resist? The reality of what she'd agreed to put a damper on the mental festivities. She'd not bargained on six days, just the one.

One day would be tolerable, surely they could keep their…what…their lust…their desires…in check for that long? But six days? Kitt's parting words rang strong in her head, the memory of his hands on her hips burned like a brand. He'd made it clear he was willing. The risk had doubled exponentially. But so had the reason for taking it: the island wasn't there! She hoped it was just a case of Selby mixing up the co-ordinates. Foolishly, she'd let him write them down. But if Kitt was right? It didn't bear thinking about. It would be a debacle before the bank even got under way, something her father's reputation couldn't afford.

Her father's reputation wasn't the only one to consider. This voyage could ruin hers entirely. She could only hope they'd beat her father back and that Kitt's crew could be sworn to secrecy. But, if the island truly didn't exist and it was discovered she'd gone out with Kitt Sherard for nearly a week unchaperoned, there would be no more attentions from gentlemen like James Selby, even if nothing had happened in truth. Which, ironically, made the case for adventure all the stronger. If she wasn't found out, then no one would know what had transpired. If she was found out, everyone would assume the worst regardless of the truth. If she was dammed either way, she might as well indulge.

Would Kitt follow through or had he been bluffing in an attempt to scare her into returning? What were the odds of *that*? Even if that had been his intention, something *would* happen in truth. He was right about their rather explosive history. The smallness of the cabin would make the conclusion inescapable. The size of the quarters would demand a level of daily intimacy she'd not factored in, but she did now and a shiver of anticipation ran down her spine. This was the adventure she sought.

The door to the cabin opened and her heart pounded at the sight of him. There was something undeniably sexy about a man with food. Kitt moved his maps to the side. He laid out the bread and cheese on the table. He gave her a wicked half-smile, catching her watching him as he poured red wine into a stoneware goblet. Her heart flipped a little when he said, 'Come and eat, your table is laid.'

Just like that, the decision was made. *When* he asked, she'd be his. It wasn't a question of 'if' any longer, but a question of when and how, and where. All very titillating considerations.

Kitt took the seat across from her and helped himself to some cheese. 'Have you ever heard of a place called Poyais?' When she shook her head, he went on. 'Not surprising. The reason you've never heard of it is because it doesn't exist.' He nodded towards his bookshelf. 'I have a book about it. though. That's how far someone went to convince others Poyais existed. I bought the book because it seemed interesting, a cautionary tale about what people will believe.'

'Authors invent places all the time, it's part of fiction,' Bryn said, not quite following.

'This wasn't an author. This was a self-fashioned adventurer, Gregor MacGregor, and this is no tale out of the past. He's still alive, apparently. He called himself the cacique of Poyais, telling people he was the head of a new nation somewhere near Belize. He recruited people to go and settle.'

'But no one did, surely,' Bryn said, disbelieving. 'No one sets off across an ocean to a place they've never seen. They had no proof it was even there.'

Kitt raised an eyebrow, forcing her to consider her words. 'How is Poyais any different than what Selby and your father have done?'

'They have letters from the overseer,' Bryn argued. 'They have scientific reports about the crops Sunwood intends to grow and market projections for profit.'

Kitt rose and strode to his bookshelf, taking down a slim volume. He tossed it on the table. 'Those settlers had a book. Flip through it. They could read about the size of the country. It's slightly larger than Wales, by the way. They could read about its climate, the natives. Anything you could want to know is right there.'

Bryn reluctantly thumbed through pages full of maps and drawings, paragraphs of descriptions about fauna and wildlife, all of it very specific, very detailed. Most unfortunately, she saw Kitt's point. Technically, there was no difference between this book and the reports that had been sent to Selby and her father. 'It doesn't mean the letters to my father are not real, just because Poyais wasn't.' The Poyais book had worked because it successfully mimicked reality after all.

Kitt leaned across the table, his gaze serious. 'You're right. This might be a false alarm on my part. It might be nothing more than Selby's incompetence with the co-ordinates. *But*, keep in mind it wouldn't be the first time someone tried to pass off the imaginary as real. New lands are full of opportunities, just not always the right kind.'

Selby wouldn't know opportunity if it bit him in the arse. It would be too much to hope he'd be able to separate the good ones from the bad. Now, he'd potentially dragged her father down with him.

She eyed Kitt with speculation, a horrible thought occurring to her. 'How is it that you know so much about land swindles?'

The gaze he gave her was equally serious. 'Because I've been involved in one.'

'I see,' she said quietly while her stomach churned over the bread and cheese. It was as bad as she thought. Kitt might be right about the island, but Selby was right, too. Kitt Sherard was not to be trusted. What fools they'd all been. What a fool she had been. She hated that realization the most. She'd been willing to trust him with more than money. She'd been willing to give him her body and quite possibly her heart.

Chapter Thirteen

Bryn tried to muster a sophisticated tone that betrayed none of the hurt she felt. 'You're concerned now because you're on the other end. Is that it? It's your money being swindled instead of the other way around.' Perhaps he'd used the Poyais book to run a swindle of his own.

Kitt's eyes darkened and he drew back as if she'd struck him with a physical blow. He pushed back from the table and rose, striding to the window. 'No, it isn't that way at all. Quite the opposite, in fact.'

'Really?' she prompted, her voice doubtful. But nothing more was forthcoming.

'Really.' Kitt's tone carried a finality with it. 'That's all you need to know, Bryn. You'll have to trust me on this one.'

She wanted to be disgusted with him, but the look on his face when she'd accused him had made *her* feel guilty instead. Maybe it was unfair to hold his past against him. Doing so made her no better than Martha Selby. Who was she to deny him a new start? Wasn't that what she was after herself? Perhaps she had no business condemning him. Her tongue had run ahead of her thoughts.

Now they were back in limbo, in the same place they'd been in the garden. Could she trust him? It all returned to that. In truth, he'd given her no reason not to even though he managed to always leave her with more questions than answers.

Kitt turned from the window and held out a hand. 'Come out on deck, I want to show you something.' It was a peace offering. He was sorry for snapping, for being mysterious, and she was forgiven for her accusation.

Bryn glanced outside the window. There wasn't much to see. 'In the dark?'

Kitt gave an exaggerated nod. 'Most definitely in the dark.'

She followed him out on deck, but once they got there, he stepped behind her, covering her eyes with his hands. 'You cannot look until I tell you. Do you trust me?' He'd understood her dilemma in the cabin, his words echoed it. This was to be a trial of sorts. If there was to be anything between them, there had to first be this. Her pride left her no choice in the matter. It was quite the experience walking the short distance to the railing with Kitt behind her, her body entirely dependent on him. It was erotic, too, her other senses heightened by her blindness. She could smell him, could smell the salt of the sea, could feel the breeze against her face.

He turned her around so that her back was against the rail and, she was facing the centre of the ship. At least she supposed that was the direction. His mouth was at her ear, low and pleasing. 'All right, now…look!' He took his hands away and she gasped.

Above the centre of the ship was the largest, fullest, gold moon Bryn had ever seen, hanging so close to the boat it looked as if the mainsail could pierce its rim.

'It's beautiful.' Her voice was no more than a whisper of awe. Kitt's hands had moved to her waist, wrapping about her. It was hard to remember the quarrel and her disappointment in the wake of his touch. All she could remember were the reasons to like him, to want him. She could feel the beat of his heart, slow and steady against her back, life surging through him, through her. The night had become profound as she stared at the moon.

Perhaps this was what she'd travelled across the world to see, to feel, these unbridled moments when nothing mattered but this oneness with herself, this primal thrill. There were no rules, no expectations, no past, only the present, only this moon, only this man and the knowledge that in this moment, nothing could hurt her except hesitation.

'I can hardly believe this is the same one we see in London,' Bryn breathed. She'd seen harvest moons, of course, and perhaps they rivalled this giant glowing orb in some way, but this was a moon nonpareil. 'I want to touch it.' She wanted to do more than touch it. She wanted to dance, wanted to shout her thrill to the skies, wanted to set aside her doubts. This was living life at its finest.

She turned in Kitt's arms, her own arms twining about his neck. 'Thank you for not sending me back. Thank you for this.' His hips were hard against hers where their bodies met, his need for her evident against her stomach.

'Don't ask me to play the gentleman, Bryn,' Kitt growled, his voice husky as he wet his lips, his gaze a sapphire smoulder when it locked with hers in silent communication. If he kissed her tonight, there would be nothing to stop them. And afterwards, there would be nothing permanent, there would be no promises.

'Understood,' she whispered. Absolutely, and completely, understood. After all, it was really the only way she could have him and her promises, too.

Her mouth lifted to his, opening eagerly to him, the fire beginning to ignite in her veins once more. She let it come, slow and steady like a flame running along a fuse. These long kisses were a well-worn trail now. She knew the taste of him, the feel of him, but passion's edge was no less keen for the familiarity. Tonight, they would get to the other side of those kisses, they would take the trail further than they'd ever been, perhaps even depart from it altogether.

Her body was primed for the adventure; heat gathered low in her belly, the place between her legs pleasantly damp in anticipation. Kitt danced her backwards to a large crate, lifting her to its lid. His hand ran warm and firm up her leg, pushing her skirts up until he palmed her mons. 'No pantalettes, again? Tsk-tsk, my naughty girl,' Kitt murmured between kisses, kneading her mound with a stroke that matched the motions of his mouth.

This was a new fire he stirred in her, a slow burn that grew until she ached with it. His hand pressed downward, finding a sensitive spot and she moaned at the sharp, sweet stab of unexpected pleasure. 'Do that again,' came her breathless request.

'Like that, do you?' Kitt's teeth pulled at the soft flesh of her lip, his hand pressing once more.

'Ohhh!' This time the cry was one of anguished pleasure. She was sure now once more was clearly not going to be enough. Bryn arched against him, her body clamouring for more, for surely, instinct told her, there must be more. This new pleasure was merely a prelude to grander things as his kisses had been a prelude to this.

'If it's more you're wanting, you'll have to brace yourself.' Kitt's eyes smouldered, two coals mirroring the fire raging in her. She wanted more and he wanted to give it to her. He lifted her arms and she watched him loop them through a skein of rope hanging above her head. Kitt gave a satisfied tug. 'Do you know what I mean to do?'

Bryn shook her head, the ache in her obliterating all ability to speak. She didn't much care what it was only that it filled her, only that it satisfied the throbbing pulse at her core. He knelt between her legs, his hot eyes locked on hers from his crouch. 'I mean to give you pleasure, Bryn.'

She felt his fingers on her as they parted the lips of her private flesh, then came the press of his mouth, the decadent flick of his tongue over the place where the pleasure had started and she was lost. Bryn sagged against her rope bonds, letting them take her weight, her eyes closed as she let the ecstasy of his wicked caress wash over her. She lost herself in the sensations, each one building upon the other until the pleasure could not be separated from the ache, until her body vibrated with it, warning her the end was near, and it was, falling upon her swiftly in an intense, shattering wave as she arched hard into Kitt's mouth.

She was boneless afterwards. She let Kitt untie the rope, let Kitt rub her wrists where the rough hemp had chafed, let Kitt wrap an arm about her and draw her close as they sat on the crate. 'So that was pleasure, *real* pleasure?' Bryn mused drowsily, her head lolling against Kitt's shoulder.

'Aye, it's a form of it, an uncompromising form of it anyway.'

Bryn wanted to protest. There'd been nothing uncompromising about it, nothing held back, everything physically, emotionally exposed, for her at least. But she knew what he meant. The act left her untouched in the ways that mattered to the Church and to society. A chivalrous pleasure indeed. She smiled against his shoulder. 'You said you wouldn't play the gentleman.'

'Do you know a lot of gentlemen who do *that*?' Kitt's voice contained a trace of humour. He was playing with her again in that bold way of his.

'No,' she said quietly. She knew intuitively there would never be a comparison for the roguish Kitt Sherard, who did not hesitate to pleasure a woman beneath a full moon, yet took care not to let the pleasure leave her spoiled. It made for an odd juxtaposition. What did that say about him? Rake or gentleman? Heaven knew what it said about her. Ladies did not enjoy being tied up by rough ropes and pleasured even more roughly.

Kitt rose suddenly, dislodging her from his very comfortable shoulder. When she was slow to rise, he bent down and scooped her up in his arms. 'Off to bed with you. We have an island to find in the morning.'

'What about you?' The fog of pleasure had lifted and she was starting to think more clearly. It occurred to her belatedly that he had not had his own release, or rather that she had not provided him any satisfaction in return. Robin had taught her that much at least in theory, if not in practice.

'It's a hammock for me. I'll bunk with the crew.' Kitt gave the door to his cabin a gentle kick and pivoted inside, careful not to bang her legs against the frame. He dumped her on the bed quite unceremoniously, making it clear there would not be another romantic overture.

Bryn raised up on her elbows. 'That's not what I meant.' She let her eyes rest meaningfully on his trousers where they pulled at his hips, a certain sign the evening had not been complete for one of them. She remembered the feel of him, the hard length of him the day she'd held him on the rock.

Kitt's eyes narrowed. 'I'll take care of it. I think you've had enough pleasure for one night.'

But just for one night, she thought as Kitt shut the door behind him. She sank back against her pillow with a sigh. Satisfaction now would lead to craving later. How could she *not* want more? Kitt had shown her pleasure existed. It had been so entirely different than what she'd experienced with any of her London bucks and their chaste kisses.

Bryn blushed guiltily in the dark. Should she even compare? Did a lady do such a thing as measure lovers against one another's performance? Love was supposed to transcend such crass consideration. But they hadn't loved her. They'd wanted her name, her fortune, the prestige of being connected to the Rutherfords. Kitt wanted nothing more than the moment. Could she settle for that? Would the pleasures of the moment be enough?

Bryn stared at the ceiling in the dark, letting the rhythm of the boat rock her towards sleep, rock her towards dreams of Kitt Sherard with his blue eyes, his flirtatious ways, his dares, his bold conversation, his unique way of looking at the world. A cynic's way, to be sure, but there was independence and strength, too. He was his own man, he answered to his own code. It was an intoxicating way to live.

He was daring her even now to follow him down that path. For her own sake, not his. This was not because he wanted a partner on that journey. She had no illusions there. Kitt Sherard was too wild. The woman who attempted to tame him would lose him. She could run wild alongside him for a while, but that was all. He'd made it clear tonight he would not share his past. There was a limit to what he was willing to give, a sure sign he had something unpleasant to hide. Perhaps even something criminal. Such a supposition made sense. Why else would he try too hard to be the impossible; a man from nowhere, unless there was something terrible to hide?

This was not new to her. She had known this all along. Men who climbed trellises and all that. This was where her promises collided with her father's. Enjoying Kitt for the moment was not the new start her father had envisioned. He'd envisaged remaking London for her, finding her a nice gentleman like Selby, setting up a house and starting a family of her own just as she would have in England, only now it would be somewhere warmer where they could escape memories of death and fading life.

What happened when fathers and daughters disagreed on their destinies? It wasn't as if this was a choice between Kitt and her father. For one, Kitt wasn't offering. For another, it was bigger than that. This was a choice between living the life she wanted for herself and the life her father wanted for her. It was a lot to think about, especially when she wasn't entirely sure what sort of life she wanted for herself, only that it wasn't raising James Selby's children under his mother's watchful eye.

Kitt, on the other hand, would have beautiful, wild children and no mother-in-law. The thought came out of nowhere and it made her laugh at the sheer ridiculousness of it. Being with Kitt wasn't about the future and it certainly wasn't about a pattern-card future. It was rather ironic that she was envisioning a traditional future with a non-traditional man. Still, one could not dispute the fact that it was a pleasant image to fall to sleep by even if it was a most improbable one.

Kitt had more than one image to fall asleep by as he lay in his hammock among the snores of his crew. Bryn continued to surprise him with the depths of her tenacity, her devotion. He'd known tenacious women before. Women were usually tenacious when they wanted something. It was a selfish tenacity at best, something that bordered on being spoiled. But Bryn's tenacity was of a purer sort. She was tenacious on behalf of others. This current task was proof enough. She was driven by devotion to her father, even though it placed her at considerable risk.

That kind of devotion was unique. Everyone had families, but not all chose to dedicate themselves to those families. Growing up, he'd been surprised to learn his family was the anomaly. His parents were the unusual ones who had not shuffled their twin boys off to the nursery without a second thought until they were old enough to be shuffled off to boarding school.

True devotion, because of its rarity, stood out. The Drydens had it. It was what had appealed to him most about Ren. Bryn had it, too. He'd seen it in her eyes at the gala dinner. She'd been proud of her father. For all her cool demeanour and clever words, she had a soft side. She would love deeply, intensely when she decided to. The recipient of that love would be a lucky man. But she would not give it idly. There was a reserve about her that he recognised and understood all too well, in part because he possessed it himself. It was one thing to play at physical pleasure, it was another to attach any deep emotion to it for the sole reason that while devotion was rare, it was also quite expensive. He knew what devotion had cost him. What had it or what *would* it cost Bryn?

Tonight had pushed things to that most dangerous edge, the edge he was always so careful to avoid. They skated close to the two things he avoided: his past and emotionally driven pleasure.

Even now, with time and space between himself and the pleasure he'd given her, his body demanded its own release, insisted upon it, the image of Bryn claiming hers fresh in his memory.

Kitt's hand slid along the hard length of his cock. She'd been magnificent; a wild creature come to life, sprung from her cage. He'd nearly come undone when she'd whispered those three heady words against his mouth, 'Do that again.' He'd gone one better and done more, knowing exactly what she wanted, what she needed. She'd leaned into the ropes, eyes shut, letting the fantasy take her and in doing so, becoming a fantasy herself, bucking against his hand, crying out her pleasure, pleasure he provided.

His hand began to pump in harder, shorter jerks. There was a manly intoxication in being able to bring a woman to completion so thoroughly. That Bryn Rutherford trusted him to provide her that completion created a whole other level of intoxication. It created complications, too, because, damn it, it wasn't going to be enough. They were physically explosive together. He knew they wouldn't stop with the pleasure tonight. She'd already offered more, offered to be a partner in that pleasure. The male in him would take that offer. He couldn't resist her.

His rhythm surged a final time, his body reliving the feel of her coming against him, his own release following at last. Now he could sleep. There would be time to think about complications tomorrow.

Passemore woke him all too soon. 'Captain, we've reached the co-ordinates! You'll want to be on deck. Come and see.'

Kitt rolled out of the hammock, pulling on his shirt and forgoing boots. This was it, the moment of truth. Sleep faded in the wake of urgency as he followed Passemore up the ladder to the deck. Someone handed him his spyglass. He surveyed the blue expanse, hoping against hope he was wrong, that James Selby had for once done something right. After a minute he collapsed his spyglass and let out a sigh. 'Passemore, can you wake Miss Rutherford and have her come up?'

He was going to have to tell her the news. The island wasn't there.

Chapter Fourteen

'What do you want to do?' Kitt leaned on the rail beside her, the morning breeze in his hair as he looked out over the water. There was a grimness to his features she'd not seen before, yet one more side of this multi-faceted man. It was a deeper side, too, than the mischievous charmer he so readily displayed to the public. The ladies who vacillated between being charmed by his manners and dismayed by his boldness would hardly recognise the man beside her on the rail.

'You can't turn back now,' Bryn answered slowly. She'd been weighing her options ever since he'd called her up on deck to show her the blue expanse where the island should have been. He would turn back though, for her sake. She'd not bargained on six days away from home and all it entailed. They both knew it.

Kitt shrugged. 'We can. We can tell your father the island isn't there.'

Bryn shook her head. She would not fail her father. 'All that proves is Selby gave me the wrong co-ordinates. It doesn't mean the island isn't out there. You said so yourself. You think the co-ordinates direct us to a different island further out.'

'I think there are other considerations besides Selby's intelligence,' Kitt said sternly. He would protect her from herself if nothing else. 'Last night should have proven to you there is more at work than simply hunting down an island.'

Bryn turned so that her back was against the rail. She could look him directly in the face from this position. Her suspicions were growing. 'You're trying very hard to get rid of me. You want me off this ship so badly you're willing to sacrifice a day's worth of travel.' She paused, studying his features. 'What did last night prove to *you*?'

'To be honest? It proved to me I can't protect you, not from me, not from what might be out there.' Kitt gave a sweep of his hand to indicate the ocean. 'Who knows what we might find at the island?'

And who knew how far they'd go the next time passion swept them away? But they did know. The next time there would be no holding back. He'd already warned her and she'd already decided what she wanted. 'I can take care of myself, Kitt. Nothing will happen that I don't want to happen.'

His eyes told a different story. She had to remember he liked being in control, too. It wasn't only up to her. But that wasn't entirely it. The passion wasn't the whole story. He wasn't solely concerned about what lay between them. 'You don't think Selby mixed up the co-ordinates, do you?' she supposed quietly, having to shield her face from the sun with her hand as she looked up at him.

'No. I think there's someone out there running their version of the Poyais swindle.' Because he'd been there in some form or other. He was reliving his past through this. She could see that more clearly this morning than she'd seen it last night.

If Kitt was right, her father was caught in the middle of it. Bryn's heart sank. 'We won't know for sure until we reach the island.' But the island was two long days away and patience had never been her strong suit. If she didn't keep herself busy, she'd go mad in the interim with worry. She caught sight of Will Passemore climbing the ropes. 'Do you think your first mate might have a spare pair of breeches and a shirt?'

'Oh, no, you are *not* climbing around on anything,' Kitt said quickly. 'I don't want to have to drag you out of the ocean.'

'I don't have to climb, but I have to do something. I can't just sit in your cabin for two days waiting.' When Kitt seemed reluctant, she pushed past him. 'Fine, I'll ask Mr Passemore myself.'

'I'll do it.' Kitt caught up to her. 'Just no climbing, agreed?'

'Agreed.' She grinned.

It wasn't enough to keep her off the ropes. He should have asked for more, Kitt realised at some point in the afternoon, after he'd had a few hours to let the reality sink in. Will's borrowed clothes fit her far too well. She was curvier than Will and that made all the difference when it came to those culottes she was sporting. They showed off a nicely turned ankle, because of course she opted to go barefoot, and they pulled a mite tight across her *derrière*, reminding him acutely of the body beneath. Probably not just him either. He wasn't the only man on board who would notice. He didn't want that to become a problem.

'Will!' Kitt called his first mate to him at the wheel. 'Do you see that?' He jerked his head to where Bryn was swabbing the deck with admirable effort. To her credit, she had made herself useful.

'Yes, Captain.'

'What do you see, Passemore?'

'I see Miss Rutherford washing the deck, sir.'

'Who else do you see?' Kitt prompted.

'I see O'Reilly, sir.' Passemore cleared his throat.

'I see O'Reilly, too, and he seems a little, shall we say, distracted? I don't want any of my men distracted. Do you understand?' Over the past twenty minutes, O'Reilly had been giving Bryn's deck-cleaning skills far more attention than the sails he was supposed to be mending. If O'Reilly put his eyes on her *derrière* one more time, he was going to flatten him.

Passemore gave a curt nod. 'I understand, Captain. I'll make sure the crew is apprised of your attitude on the subject.'

Kitt chuckled. 'Apprised of my attitude, is it? And what exactly is that?' Order on board was important and it was his job to ensure it occurred, but he could still poke some fun even at himself.

Passemore's mouth twitched. 'As you are so fond of telling me, "you need to get laid". Miss Rutherford has you surly as bear after winter, as prickly as a hedgehog in winter, as—'

Kitt laughed and cut him off. 'Despite your rather tired clichés, I get your meaning. I prefer a stag in rut, they're more majestic creatures. A hedgehog , really? That seems like it would be awkward business.'

He felt like a hedgehog, too, with all its quills extended, all prickly and aroused as he went through the motions of doing his job.

By late afternoon, Kitt had had enough. He needed to expend some energy and his crew did, too. 'Passemore! Set a course for that island over there and see if we can sail the ship into the bay on the east side.'

A general whoop went up from the crew as the news carried down the line. Everyone knew what that meant: Free time on a pristine beach. Within the half-hour, the ship was anchored, the dories loaded with his twenty-member crew and Bryn, rowing towards the island.

Kitt had chosen the island well. There was plenty of beach and jungle for his men to explore and a pretty, sheltered cove past the headland for privacy. He gave Passemore instructions and took off with Bryn in tow for the cove.

'I'm sorry,' Bryn said, catching up to his long stride. 'Maybe the breeches weren't such a good idea.'

At least she wasn't oblivious, he'd give her that. It wasn't her fault she was built like a goddess with the kind of beauty that dared a man to claim it, possess it if he could. Goodness knew Kitt wanted to be that man.

'Oh, but maybe it was worth making you angry just to see this place!' Bryn stopped, taking in the white beach and the water. She tossed him a teasing smile. 'This beach might be nicer than yours.'

Kitt felt something in him begin to relent. He'd over-reacted. She'd only been trying to keep busy, she was worried about her father, she was in an entirely new part of the world with no friends to speak of. Except him. He wondered if she realised that, too? She was rather dependent on him at the moment whether she wished it or not. Probably the latter. She was definitely an independent sort. So was he. He wasn't used to people being dependent on him. Oh, there was his crew and there was Ren, but that was different. Or maybe *this* was different.

It struck him that he could make this adventure good for her if he wanted and he did want to. There was so much he could show her. He wasn't a heartless bastard, just a horny one.

'What was that!' Bryn pointed to something in the ocean. 'There it is again.'

Kitt shielded his eyes with his hand and followed her finger. He grinned. In terms of showing her things, he could start with that. 'Dolphins. Do you swim?' A swim was just what he needed to take his mind off things.

She smiled at that. 'Probably better than you do.'

Kitt already had his shirt over his head before the import of what she'd implicitly agreed to sank in. She could not swim in her clothes, or rather Will's clothes. She'd swum naked with Robin, but this was different. Robin had been her friend. Kitt was rather more. Sensuality rolled off of him as naturally as most people breathed.

Kitt tossed a look over his shoulder. 'Well, come on. What are you waiting for?' he prompted. 'We'll be in the water. I'll hardly see anything. Besides, it's not every day you get to swim with dolphins. They're usually not so far in. Unless, of course, you're bluffing me about those swimming skills?'

That did it. He was daring her and she'd be a fool not to go. He'd been far more intimate with her body last night and she had not hesitated. When would she ever have such a chance again? She'd already come this far.

Bryn stripped out of her clothes, leaving on only her chemise. She folded the garments neatly and left them on a warm rock with their towels while Kitt laughed, gloriously flaunting his nakedness. His clothes had been thrown haphazardly on the beach.

He was right, though, it hardly mattered in the water. As soon as she began swimming, Bryn quickly forgot about clothing or the lack of it. There were too many other things to focus on: the warmth of the water, the gentleness of the waves in this protected area away from the open ocean, the powerful feel of her body exerting herself.

Beside her, Kitt was a sleek athlete, cutting through the water with strong, confident strokes. When they reached the dolphins, Kitt motioned that they should dive under the water and swim alongside them.

She could not believe she was doing this! Unmitigated joy bubbled inside her as they dived. This was incredible, almost indescribable. Beneath the surface, they mimicked the dolphins' undulating movements, rising every so often for a breath. After a while, the dolphins seemed to understand they were playing with them. The dolphins starting leaping, showing off their acrobatic skills, much to Bryn's delight. She and Kitt trod water, content to watch the graceful creatures and be among them as welcomed guests.

'We should probably swim back in,' Kitt suggested. The dolphins had settled back down, their leaping done for the afternoon. 'There's more I want to show you.'

Bryn couldn't imagine what more there could be that would rival this, but there was. On the way back, Kitt showed her a small reef full of coral and colourful fish. They swam past the rocks where the sea turtles gathered to sun themselves, their large brown shells gleaming. By the time they regained the beach, Bryn was pleasantly exhausted.

Kitt retrieved their blankets and spread them on the sand. 'This is heaven, everything is so different here.' Bryn stretched out on a blanket, not caring if her chemise was plastered to her skin, not caring what it revealed. She felt full of life at the moment—nothing so trivial as nudity mattered. She was starting to understand Kitt's comfort with it.

Kitt stretched alongside her as they lay face-to-face. He lifted a hand to push a wet strand of hair behind her ear. 'Then you fit in perfectly. You're different, too. I don't know any women like you.' His voice was husky, perhaps evidence that he was caught up in the moment, of the profoundness of what they'd experienced; nature at its finest. Or perhaps, she thought, her heart giving a little leap, it was evidence of what the admission cost him, that the words were more than mere flattery. She knew he found her attractive, his body had told her that in many ways, but to hear the words and to hear them spoken by this sea god, this Poseidon on the beach, went beyond an appreciative look.

He moved into her then, drawing her body along his, his mouth taking hers in a long, slow kiss that asked the question for him. No man, not even Robin, had made her feel this way. No man had ever asked for what he was asking. Her body answered without hesitation: 'Yes, yes, I will be yours in this moment out of time.' There was nothing beyond this. There was no tomorrow, no future, only the present, only this beach, only this man, only now.

Kitt peeled the wet chemise over her head and tossed

it aside. He drew his hand down her breastbone, his touch possessive as his eyes drank in her nakedness like a fine wine; something to be savoured and lingered over, then he bent his head to her breast and sucked, his tongue licking small circles around her peak, slowly, venerating until her back arched, thrusting upward to meet his mouth, clamouring to be part of this reverent experience. This was not a heated, carnal claiming driven by lust. This was *worship*. Instinctively, her hands went to his head, tangling in the wetness of his hair, wanting to touch him, wanting to be part of this intimate communion.

He moved lower, kissing her navel, his hands framing her hips as he held her, taking a more intimate kiss between her legs. Her body pulsed for him, for what she knew could come. But he did not take her with his mouth as he had the night before. Instead, he levered himself up and positioned his whole body between her legs, letting the length of him lay against her mound, announcing, previewing what he intended next.

'Oh, God, yes, Kitt,' she moaned, as if he needed further urging, further confirmation that she wanted this. She was far beyond wanting—at some point it had become a need she would not be complete without. He moved into her then, a slow thrust that filled her, her lips moving in a thousand silent hallelujahs as Kitt claimed her, over and over, invoking the primal rhythm of the ocean in the push and ebb of his thrusts, his phallus stroking a place deep inside her with each pass until the intense friction of his efforts had her moaning incoherent words, her body bucking, her legs wrapped about his hips in an attempt to draw him even closer.

She was not alone in this. Kitt's eyes were riveted on

her, his blue gaze nearly the shade of midnight with desire. The muscles of his arms bulged with the effort of
lovemaking, his body taut as climax loomed. They met
it together; a final thrust, a final cry, and they were falling, blue sky above them, white sand below them and
a universe of pleasure in between. She'd been wrong
earlier. *This* was heaven and this man beside her, within
her, was angel, saint and sinner all in one.

She floated back to earth slowly, confronted by the
realisation that Kitt Sherard was more than the proverbial sum of his parts, manly or otherwise. He'd shown
himself to be both a man who could have sex—that had
been last night, a physical game between two willing
players—but here on the beach, he'd shown himself to
be a man who could make love and *that* man knew the
difference.

'I can see why you love the Caribbean so much,'
Bryn murmured sleepily, her finger tracing idle designs
on his chest. 'Do you ever think of going back to England?' She was already regretting the time when she
and her father would return to cold, dreary England,
their mission accomplished.

'No, I don't think of England as home, not any more,'
Kitt answered. She was almost sorry she'd asked. His
tone had lost some of its usual ease. His body and his
gaze moved away from her. He tucked one arm behind
his head and looked up into the sky. 'My life is here,
with my ship, my men, my business.'

'And your villa?' Bryn interjected.

'Yes, my villa.' Kitt chuckled. 'I'm starting to think
you covet my villa. It seems to come up in your thoughts
on a regular basis.'

'It is rather magnificent,' she teased, knowing he

would hear the innuendo. She wanted to return to their earlier intimacy, wanted him to trust her with part of himself no matter how small. She wanted to know him.

'Now I'm starting to think we're not necessarily talking about my "villa".' They were back to the sexy banter that was second nature to him, the casual nonchalance he wore so easily. Conversation with Kitt carried an edge. It was always a battle of wits. Was it armour, too? She wondered what depths lay beneath all that cleverness. What did he work so hard to hide?

Bryn was loath to let the profundity of their recent moments go. She shot an upward glance at his face, watching him study the clouds, his eyes thoughtful. Those moments were worth fighting for. She would risk it. 'Kitt, tell me something about yourself. What was your life like back in England?'

'You assume I had a life in England,' he challenged, but the question had made him vulnerable. It was there in the way he sat up—a sudden movement that dislodged her from his shoulder and sent her scrambling to sit up as well. They faced one another, eyes duelling.

'You want to know something about your lover, is that it?'

Kitt's tone was dangerously silky. She should take his tone as a warning, but Bryn would not retreat. She met his gaze with the tenacity she'd met his other challenges. He'd not succeeded in scaring her off yet. 'Yes.' She smiled, a tigress to match this lion of a man.

'Very well.' Kitt gave a grin. She wondered if it was meant to distract her. He did that sometimes. Doing it now was a sign of how deeply disturbed he was over her question. 'If I tell you something, you have to answer my question, whatever it is.' He laughed at her hesitation. 'Ah, it's a little different when the shoe's on the other foot, isn't it?'

Her chin went up a fraction and she squared her naked shoulders. 'Fine. One answer of mine for one tale of yours. I have nothing to hide.' Kitt, on the other hand, could make no such claim and they both knew it.

Chapter Fifteen

Kudos to Bryn. She had him cornered. Her request should not have surprised him. A man could not make love to a woman and not expect her to ask questions. It was a woman's nature to seek that attachment. Yet, he'd bolted upright and tried to dare his way out of it. Perhaps not his best reaction. It would only confirm for Bryn what she already suspected—he had a past he would not willingly trot out for just anyone.

He should have known by now Bryn didn't scare. A dare only caused her to entrench further and now here they were, ready to exchange battle stories as it were. It was some consolation to note that while she'd taken the dare it hadn't been without hesitation.

'My life in England was…predictable,' Kitt said. He settled back on his blanket and pulled her to him. Her warm skin felt reassuring against his as he picked his words, trying to weave a suitable truth from the fabric of his tragedy without giving away too much. Perhaps, too, he could use this intimacy for other purposes that would demand more of her attention than this exchange of stories.

'I doubt it.' Bryn's head had found its way again to the notch between his shoulder and his chest where it fit perfectly.

'Well, you can believe what you like. It was predictable.' Inside that predictability he'd had all the security of being raised the son of a peer and all the luxury, too. He had not fully appreciated what that meant until he'd been without the privileges it had provided. He understood now in retrospect it was what had driven him to purchase the villa—a chance to recreate some of that security. He had proven he could recreate the material security, but not the other, the security of knowing people loved you.

'Predictability has its benefits, but I could see the whole of my life laid out before me, the next thirty or forty years unless I died of ennui before that.' That was almost true. He *could* see his whole life laid out; what his parents wanted for him; what life had to offer a second son who was loved or not by his family. The options were minimal. The prospect had not especially bored him, but it had frightened him. Even then he could see the potential for his life to amount to nothing but one entertainment after another. As much as his family cared for him, he wanted more. It had been equally frightening to not know what more might be.

'An opportunity arose to leave and I took it.' He'd been restless in the months leading up to that 'opportunity'. He often wondered if his 'sacrifice' had been selfishly motivated after all. If he hadn't been restless, would he have been so eager to take his brother's place? But that was part of the story he couldn't tell Bryn.

'And you left, just like that?' Bryn snapped her fingers. Kitt thought he heard admiration in her tone. She'd taken the story to the intended conclusion—he'd left because he sought a new challenge. He was doing fairly well with his story. He'd managed to leave out places and people, or any reference that tied him to the aristocracy.

He could answer this latest question without any artifice. 'Yes, I did. Once I decided to leave I went. I took two trunks and whatever money I could lay my hands on.' He didn't want Bryn making him out to be any sort of hero. What had followed had been anything but the stuff of legends. He'd left within the hour of making the decision. It might have been the quickest exit in history. He could still see that last scene with his father, the two of them in the front parlour, his father's drawn face as he gripped his hand and pressed a thick wad of pound notes into it. *'Be gone, don't come back. You can never come back, promise me?'* Words whispered in love, not hatred, a father's desire to protect his son. Kitt knew all about promises. To break that promise meant to die, to be killed, to resurrect a scandal his mother's social expertise would have taxed itself to put to bed. Kitt had given his word and he'd become the prodigal son who could never return.

Bryn snuggled into him. 'I don't believe you. There has to be more to it. What compels a man to give up all he knows and sail into the unknown?'

'Why don't you tell me? I suspect our stories aren't terribly different at their core.' That was probably an outright lie. She wasn't protecting a twin from an unthinkable scandal, but it was time to turn the tables. He couldn't sustain this pseudo-truth telling much longer. 'What compels a lady of your background to leave the comforts of England and throw her virginity away on a pirate rogue she knows little about?' She tensed at that and he chuckled. 'Did you think I wouldn't notice? Tell me, were you bored, too, Bryn?'

He'd not said it meanly, but his words were a direct hit all the same, challenging her on so many levels. Her eyes narrowed, her body stiffened as she pulled away from him.

'I expect nothing from you, Kitt.' She levered herself up on her elbow, her hair hanging in a chestnut sheet over one shoulder. She looked as tempting as Eve in the garden. His body was thinking of things other than questions. It was thinking how he wanted her again, this time on top of him, her hair falling over her breasts, not Eve, but Godiva riding her steed.

Kitt mustered some self-discipline. He wasn't fooled. Virgin or not, she knew how to use her assets to advantage. He'd shifted the conversation to her and she was uncomfortable with it. She was trying to retake the offensive, but the truth was he had her on the run. So be it. She wasn't the only one who wanted something. He wanted answers, too. He felt compromised over the fact she'd not told him she was a virgin, never mind that he'd suspected it. Part of him argued that she should have said something, should have warned him. *Why? Would it have made a difference?* He knew it wouldn't have, not at the critical moment.

'Well, I do expect something. I expect a story. That was our bargain. What are you doing here, Bryn? What are you doing with *me*?' He'd turned on his side, propped on his elbow to match her. 'Who's the man who drove you to the Caribbean?'

Her eyes dropped and he knew he'd hit a target. 'Why does it have to be a man?' She was avoiding a direct answer. It heightened his curiosity. How could it *not* be? 'Because you're beautiful, you're intelligent, you're wealthy, all the things a London gentleman is raised to admire.' He could almost see it written on her face: Of all the questions in the world, he'd had to ask that one.

Bryn shook her head. 'It's complicated. I don't know where to start, really.'

'Take your time.' Kitt gave her a lazy smile, but he did not mock her hesitation. 'I've got all afternoon.' He wanted to know, wanted answers to the puzzle of her. Since he'd met her, there'd been pieces that didn't fit.

When she spoke, her words came slowly. 'My mother wanted me to be a lady, the very finest lady, the sort that was beautiful and polished, who knew all the rules, who could command a room with the nod of her head. It was what I was trained for since I turned fourteen. Eventually, I persuaded myself I could do it, that it would be enough.'

'Why did you need to persuade yourself?' Kitt watched her, waiting patiently. It struck him that she was putting this together in words for the first time although the thoughts were clearly not new to her. He felt a twinge of guilt. She was being entirely forthcoming with him and he had told her a piecemeal truth.

'Time was running out.' She furrowed her brow and ran a finger through the little river of sand separating their blankets while she gathered her thoughts. 'I'd had my debut at eighteen. It was quite the success. I was supposed to follow it up by making a stunning match the following year—after all, I'd been the toast of the Season. Rutherford girls are never out more than two Seasons. But my mother took ill with consumption. We didn't go back to London. Instead, we went to the country, we went to the seaside. We went wherever we thought she'd get well. My father and I devoted the next three years to her, to chasing hopes. '

Bryn looked up, her grey eyes misty. Kitt swallowed, tempted to make her stop. 'London and fashionable marriages lost their appeal in the wake of our family tragedy. My father loved her quite intensely. He would have gone to the moon to save her.'

'And you loved her, too. You wanted to marry for her sake?' Kitt divined in soft tones. If she'd been willing to give up three prime years of her life, it was not surprising Bryn had been willing to risk her reputation by sailing off with him to preserve her father's standing. 'You wanted her to know you were settled and taken care of?'

'I wanted her dream to come true. She'd invested a good part of her life in me. I thought it was only fitting she be rewarded.' He saw Bryn's throat work, trying to fight tears. 'She was running out of time. My young adult life had been devoted to my parents, naturally. It was just the three of us, it had always been just the three of us. We were close.'

He could understand just what those three words meant and the loss they implied. He'd lost that, too, not just with his family, but with his twin. It was something Ren would never understand. Ren might be half a world away from his family, but they were still there, he was still part of them in a way Kitt would never be a part of his family again, the way Bryn's family would never be whole again. It was a blow and a comfort all at once to know someone else understood exactly how that felt and he could never tell her.

She looked again, studying him. He must have looked

bewildered in his private discovery. 'Am I making any sense?'

Kitt reached for her hand. 'Yes, absolutely.' He could see where the story was headed, how very difficult those last years must have been for a girl of Bryn's vibrancy, to be limited to accompanying an invalid from post to post when her heart yearned to be out dancing and *living* and yet her heart was devoted to her family. She would give anything for them.

The truth of his own situation wasn't much different, but he could not tell her what he'd sacrificed for his family without the risk of making that sacrifice useless. 'But her dream came at the expense of your own?' Kitt understood that side of the coin, too. Saving his family had come at a high personal price: guilt and anonymity.

She looked at him, surprised perhaps at the insight. 'Yes. I was far more wild than she knew and far wilder than I truly understood at the time.' Bryn smiled. 'I had a friend, Robin. He and I were wild together. We grew up best friends and we stayed that way. But my mother saw trouble on that particular horizon. She was probably right. I would have married Robin, but she aimed higher for me and our mothers conspired to politely separate us. They understood our relationship was no longer proper. He was a squire's son, you see, not quite on the same level except in wildness.'

Kitt nodded. 'Your mother wouldn't approve of me.' He had some answers, but he wanted more. What was she doing with him?

Bryn shook her head. 'I think in her younger days she might have. In my heart, I believe she was wild once, too, although I have no proof for it. That's the part I never understood. What I remember of her was that she was so perfect, so proper, yet that didn't match the stories in the village. My parents were something of a local legend. He was the reserved youngest son of the earl who had won the heart of the beautiful Esme Hatfield, a woman who was as high flying as she was lovely. The villagers said she could have had any man, even my father's sophisticated cousin who was in line for a marquisate. But in the end, true love triumphed. I could never reconcile my mother with that vision of unbridled *joie de vivre* and it makes me wonder if "true love" exists or if it's an illusion.'

Kitt threaded his fingers through hers in the sand. 'Are you a romantic or a cynic, Bryn Rutherford?' It was hard to tell.

She looked down at where their hands joined. 'I've come to believe that there are no happy-ever-afters for ever, Kitt, just happy-ever-after moments. We should do our best to collect them and enjoy them for what they are and not worry about what happens next. That's what I'm doing with you. I think you understand that.'

'I'm not sure if that is a beautifully expressed sentiment or extraordinary cynicism,' Kitt replied. Whichever, though, it explained much about her, about the source of her passion, her willingness to give it free rein. 'Would today qualify as one of those moments?' Kitt asked softly, aware that the sun was starting to go down on the horizon. They, too, were running out of time. There was an hour at most before they had to return to the boat.

'Yes.' Her reply was breathless, her desire shifting her focus from the conversation to other things.

'Then let's send it out in style.' Kitt kissed her hard and dragged her up over his body, ready to do battle with the ghosts of her past. 'Come ride me, Bryn, I want you.' This would not be a languorous coupling, there would be no reverence. It would be rough and exciting, an exorcism of the past. He knew what she was doing with him. It was time for her dreams now. She wanted to fly...*with him*. He could set her free. He only hoped when she came back to earth the landing wouldn't be too hard.

He wanted her. The knowledge made her blood fire, made her adventurous as she straddled him, her body poised just above his straining phallus so that its tip could touch her private furrow with the lightest of caresses, creating an exquisite torture for them both as she moved across his tender tip. Her hands splayed on his chest, her thumbs teasing his flat nipples into erectness as he'd teased hers. But Kitt wouldn't let her play alone for long. His hands slid beneath the long coils of hair hanging over her shoulders to cup the breasts hidden beneath the chestnut curtain.

'You fit in my hands like you were made for them.' Kitt groaned, his eyes dilated with the potency of intimate touch. 'Slide down on me and show this man some mercy, my Godiva.'

She sheathed herself on him, feeling her body stretch, welcoming the strength of his erection. This was glorious and new, to have him deep inside her at her request. This time, she'd taken him and there was power in knowing the journey to pleasure was up to her.

Bryn began to move, slowly at first, exploring the possibilities of this new position. Her muscles contracted and released around him as she slid up and down his length, shuddering each time his phallus passed over the secret place it had found before. Once, twice, three times—the more it passed, the more she wanted it.

She moved on him faster, increasing their pleasure. She was gasping her delight now, Kitt's head thrown back, his body tight in ecstatic agony as he arched into her, his hands digging into her hips as they surged towards release. When it came, it was explosive and consuming, leaving no doubt this was indeed a moment she would not forget, a thousand sensations to live on for a lifetime.

Chapter Sixteen

Eventually there would be hell to pay for this heaven. She was no fool. But not yet.

She knew what happened to virgins who gave away their virtue. *If they were caught.* The size of Bryn's world had shrunk to this ship, this man, this journey. Nothing outside of that mattered. She had everything she needed right here in this cabin, in this bed.

Kitt laughed when she told him, his chest rumbling beneath her ear where she lay against him. 'The Caribbean does that to a person. It reminds you what matters, what's truly important. It's not big houses, or piles of money.'

'You have both,' Bryn argued, but not too heatedly. She was content, lulled into drowsiness by the rocking of the boat and the heat of Kitt's body beside her in the captain's bed. It was easier to think of here and now than it was to think beyond that. She didn't want to think of the missing island and what it might mean or what it might mean if she were caught with Kitt. Even if she wasn't caught, what would happen between the two of them once they returned home? There were to be no expectations, it was what they'd both agreed upon and yet she wouldn't mind if there were.

'Yes, I have both, but with the understanding that nature could take both away at any moment. The Caribbean is beautiful and deadly, kind of like a woman,' Kitt teased. 'One hurricane, one tidal wave, one disaster and it's all gone. Talk to any of the natives and they'll tell you the only way to survive is to live for the present. The future offers no guarantees.'

Was this a carefully veiled warning not to question him about the future? 'And yet the British have come and planned for a future,' Bryn said thoughtfully, wondering if she dared risk the question his comment provoked. 'It's hard to say who has the right of it.'

It was on the tip of her tongue to want to ask him if he planned for the future or if he counted himself among the natives in that philosophy. It was hard to tell with Kitt. He had forsaken any acknowledgement of the past. Had he done that with the future as well? On the surface, he retained some of the trappings of a future-minded British man—the villa, the investments, the ship, the business—but then he'd make comments indicating he lived his life in a more present-focused fashion. Where did a relationship fit? Did he even have 'relationships' the way she and the rest of the world understood them?

'You've gone quiet,' Kitt prompted. 'What are you thinking?'

'You don't want to know.' She could hear the drowsiness creeping into his voice. This was not a subject to fall asleep by. Talking about relationships would likely queer the pitch prematurely. The last thing Bryn wanted was for Kitt to become aloof and he most surely would if he thought she had any of those expectations she said didn't matter.

She let him drift off, content to be in his arms, content to be with her thoughts, to sift through the dazzling events of the day. She'd swum with dolphins and made love to a man on a beach. The next few days promised to be filled with more of the same. But then came the reality. They would go home to Bridgetown and it would be over.

Kitt had made it plain since the beginning he would not play the gentleman. He would not 'do the right thing' by her at the end of the voyage, brought up to scratch by feelings of guilt. If he thought she entertained such notions, he'd withdraw entirely and go back to his hammock in the crew quarters. That would be intolerable. There *would* be an end, but she'd think about that later, much later, and heaven forbid she do anything in the interim to hasten that end. She wanted to hold on to Kitt, to this newly discovered magic, as long as she could.

They'd come back to the boat and eaten a dinner of shellfish and bread in his cabin by the light of a lantern. They'd strolled the deck hand in hand, the crew making themselves absent to give them privacy. Back in the cabin, Kitt had made love to her in his bed, for the third time that day, his stamina for passion meeting the demands of their bodies. He'd warned her she'd be stiff tomorrow and he'd given her a chance to beg off, but she would not hear of it. If there was no guarantee how long this would last, she didn't want to waste a minute.

She'd not guessed it could be like this. She'd thought passion, once satisfied, would diminish. But with Kitt, she was hungry for more. For the next few days, she could have all she wanted. But what then? That was a dangerous path to travel down. She'd take her moments and leave it at that. She would not think about it. This was a chance to live the philosophy she'd so bravely spouted to Kitt on the beach, to reach for the blithe promises she'd made herself. She would seek moments and not create expectations beyond them. Kitt was the perfect man with whom to explore the efficacy of that new criterion. He had told her bluntly expectations would be useless.

That was fine with her, she'd had enough of gentlemen.

The experience he offered was ideal—meaningful lovemaking without creating those expectations he was so keen to avoid. Bryn looked at the man sleeping beside her, a thought coming to her. He'd got the better part of the deal today. She'd told him more than he'd told her. How much of his desire to avoid expectations rose from his desire to avoid the past? One could hardly build a future without it. The present was different. It didn't require a past or anything else. The present could sustain the unsustainable: perfection. The very reason for perfection's success lay in its temporary condition. But it provoked the question: how did one make a dream last? It was a heady question to fall asleep by. She couldn't help but feel if she knew the answer to that, she'd know the answer to everything.

Bryn slept late the next morning, awaking to find the bed empty and her body sore. Not unpleasantly so, it had been well used on sand and sea. She dressed in one of the plain skirts she'd packed, regretfully eschewing the borrowed breeches after the turmoil she'd caused yesterday. She'd miss the freedom of those clothes but she didn't want to make things difficult for Kitt, even by accident. She borrowed Kitt's brush and plaited her hair into a thick braid before going out on deck to greet the day and whatever it brought.

That sentiment turned out to be quite optimistic. A man she didn't know by name was at the helm, Kitt was at the rail with his spyglass, Will Passemore beside him. The snatch of conversation she overheard didn't sound promising.

'They picked us up again last night, Captain,' Passemore was saying. 'I don't know if they're following us or if they're just sailing in this general direction. The ocean's free country. It doesn't have to mean anything.'

'Given our circumstances, I wouldn't back that bet.' Kitt sounded surly.

'Who's following us?' Bryn said brightly, causing both men to turn and face her. Kitt slammed the articulated spyglass closed, not amused by her intrusion, a sure sign he was hiding something.

'Maybe no one,' Kitt said, shooting Passemore a look that clearly indicated he was not to tell her anything.

Bryn pretended not to notice. She came at the question from another angle. 'Why would anyone be following us at all?'

Kitt smiled. 'Exactly. It seems unlikely, we're just being cautious.' He put an arm about her shoulders to steer her away from the rail. 'Have you had breakfast? Let's get you some food.'

Something was definitely wrong. She'd give him five minutes to confess before she demanded an answer.

'Are you going to tell me?' Bryn asked between bites of sweet breakfast ham and toast. The five minutes had come and gone. Kitt had said nothing, trying to reroute her curiosity with food. Kitt's cook was more than competent and his larder was far better stocked, she suspected, than the standard ship's, but it would not be enough to distract her from the business at hand.

'It's not your concern.' Kitt's voice contained a quiet force that heavily suggested the conversation was to go no further. There was something he wasn't telling her, yet another sign the trouble was beyond trifling. She worried more when people didn't tell than when they did. Her parents had kept her mother's illness from her until it simply couldn't be denied. While she'd understood their reasoning, she didn't agree with it any more than she agreed with Kitt's choice now.

'Ignorance does not protect.' Bryn pushed her plate away and met him with a hard gaze over the wooden table. 'If there is danger posed to a ship I'm on, it is definitely my concern. Peril to my person is always my concern.'

Lucifer's balls! She wasn't going to let it go. 'It could be nothing.' Kitt blew out an exasperated breath. How was he to tell her that he hadn't come out here just to look for an island? How did he tell her he had men out to kill him quite possibly in retribution for an altercation last year? Keeping such company hardly recommended him. He'd asked her to trust him and yet there was so much he needed to hide from her.

It most certainly was a stain on his credibility, too, when it came to her father. He needed the board to believe his opinions, to be swayed by his advice rather than Selby's at this juncture. It was bad enough that she suspected him of some involvement in a previous land swindle, even if she didn't understand what that involvement had been.

That rationale sounded a bit thin even to him. *Perhaps that's not all*, a little voice inside him spoke up. *Perhaps it's not the bank you're worried about so much as her. What would she think to see your roguish life up close? It's one thing to know about it, another to see it in action.*

He wanted her safe, that was all, just as he would want any passenger on his ship safe. This had *nothing* to do with the fact that his body craved her, that he knew when she was in a room, that she permeated far too many of his thoughts these days.

'Kitt? I demand an answer. If our positions were reversed, you would, too. The only difference is that *I* would give you one. Yesterday was proof enough of it. I told you more than you told me. You owe me.' Her tone was sharp, her gaze challenging. She believed her words for now because it suited her purpose. Kitt doubted she'd feel that way if the shoe was truly on the other foot, if she risked his good opinion. *And yet, she's risked her virtue, something far more valuable. What more does a woman have to risk when it comes to her reputation?*

'We don't know it's anything at all, just another boat out sailing.' Kitt tried his last line of defence, but it was weak and she laid siege to it with devastating ferocity.

'Yes, I heard that part on deck. I also heard your response to it. You don't believe it's nothing, ergo, you believe it is something *and* you have an idea of what it is.'

Kitt rose from the table. 'Come walk with me. I don't want to discuss it here.' He wanted to be back on deck to check the ship's progress and to gain a measure of privacy. The next shift would be getting ready to go on and men would be drifting down for food.

Outside, the intruding ship had made no move to sail closer, keeping its distance and giving every appearance it was going about its own business. Bryn leaned against the rail, her face showing the glorious effects of a hatless day in the sun. A small trail of freckles brushed the arch of her nose. She looked fresh and vibrant, except for the shrewd look in her eyes, a reminder to Kitt that he was up against a most enticing equal.

'Are you concerned the ship might be some of your enemies?' Bryn asked, cutting right to the heart of the matter. 'I know your business is sometimes dangerous, although if it's simply the matter of trading I don't pretend to understand why.' There was a scold in there for him, that he'd somehow not been forthcoming when he should have been.

'Rum is not my only cargo,' Kitt answered. 'Last year I ferried four men into exile after they tried to burn down a plantation and force a cartel in order to leverage sugar prices. Two of them took the situation poorly. I would not put it past them to have revenge on their minds and designs on my person.' Although he wished they'd picked a better time to come after him than when he had Mr Bailey Rutherford's daughter on board. But perhaps they knew and had done it for just that reason. Bryn would certainly limit his options for dealing with them if they made a move.

He watched Bryn cock her head to one side, a habit she had when she was thinking. He could nearly see her mind fitting all the pieces together. It was only a matter of time now. 'Is that why you climbed my balcony? You never did tell me.'

Kitt nodded. 'They were waiting for me when I stepped ashore.' Perhaps knowing would be for the better, a very real reminder that the life he lived was unsuitable for her, just in case she was entertaining ideas to the contrary. Now she knew. He must always be vigilant in his line of work; vigilant for opportunity, vigilant against danger.

'Now you are paying for having done your civic duty and rid the parish of rotten scoundrels,' Bryn surmised with an arch of her dark brow. 'Assuming you're right about the nature of that ship, of course. It was quite selfless of you, knowing you'd be the one to draw their fire eventually.'

That set off alarm bells. 'Oh, no, you don't, Bryn. Do not make me into a hero.' That was the last thing he wanted. What he *needed* was for her to understand the danger in associating with him. 'It can't change anything.'

Bryn's voice was dangerously quiet. 'I don't want to change anything, I just want to understand it.'

'For your father's sake?' Kitt asked sharply, feeling as if he was about to be in over his head. The moment she acknowledged this inquest had stopped being about her father's banking and had become more personal, he would be.

'No, for mine.' Bryn speared him with her stormy eyes, her gaze pinning him to the rail with their intensity. 'Is it so wrong to want to *know* you, Kitt Sherard?' There it was, the admission that proved it.

He did not hesitate to answer. Better to say it now than to say it later. 'Yes, it is if it leads you to think differently about our situation. When we get back to Bridgetown, this will be over.'

'If that's what you want.' Bryn looked out over the water, her jaw tight in the wake of his harsh words. She refused to meet his gaze, perhaps realising she'd gone too far, maybe even further than she'd meant to go. Goodness knew he had. He had not meant to be so blunt.

'It's what I want. It's what has to be.' He wanted to add that she'd agree if she really knew him, but that would give her an opening he couldn't afford. He could not let her know him.

She had no response for that. In the distance they watched the worrisome ship veer off, sailing away from them. 'Too bad it didn't sheer off a few minutes earlier. You could have saved yourself a lot of trouble,' Bryn said drily. 'I guess there was nothing to worry about after all.'

'Bryn, you knew when we started this—' Kitt began, only to be interrupted by a cry of 'land ho' coming down from the crow's nest, a reminder that their second island loomed. He didn't hold much hope for this discovery. The island was too remote. It would be too difficult to populate it, to support it. Great, the morning was just full of fraud. 'Get a towel and whatever you need, we're going ashore.' Kitt pushed off the rail and went to join Passemore at the helm.

Other than not being the home of an innovative, new plantation, the island held promise in other ways. With luck, maybe he and Bryn could get back to what they did best: sex on a beach one more time before he had to pull away from her entirely for her own good.

Chapter Seventeen

'Why did we pull away? We could have taken them on that island!' Hugh Devore's fist came down on the captain's desk, rattling the inkwell and other accoutrements. 'What's the point of following them out here only to turn back?' When he'd decided to follow Sherard's ship out of the harbour, he'd not bargained on being gone so long. Three days out and he was growing impatient. He had other business that demanded his attention.

'It's called protecting my ship,' the captain, a big burly Jamaican he'd hired because the man's size and temperament matched his, growled, unfazed by his surly manner. 'Besides, it's what Sherard wanted. He was too ready for us. His crew has been watching us all morning. They'll see us coming, they'll be prepared. I won't wreck my ship for your vengeance.'

Devore had to admit to the merit of the captain's thinking and tried to shape it to his advantage. 'We know where they are and where they'll be. Let's lull them into complacency first, let them think we were nothing but another trading ship. We can take them when they leave.'

'We'll see about that,' the captain argued. 'The *Queen of the Main* is a fast ship and Sherard's a canny one.'

Devore sat down and stretched his leg. His knee was starting to ache from the exertion of being at sea. Sherard had done this to him, caused this pain. He'd shot him in the knee as a show of power. He would extract pain in return from Sherard ounce by ounce until Sherard wished he had killed him outright when he'd had the chance. 'Nonsense, it's the perfect set up,' Devore insisted, helping himself to the captain's brandy. A battle at sea would have no witnesses. He would have preferred to have stormed the beach and killed Sherard, crew and all, on land. But perhaps the captain was right and it was better to wait.

It probably didn't much matter where it happened as long as it did happen. It was perfect *and* necessary not just for his personal vendetta, but for the security of his other business ventures. He wasn't certain what Sherard was doing out here, but it seemed ominous that the man had sailed with the banker's daughter on board just days after Rutherford and Selby had invested in Sunwood Plantation.

'I told you this would happen.' Elias Blakely spoke up from his corner where he'd watched the whole exchange. Usually, he was a quiet mouse of a man, sharp with numbers, but not much else unless his profit was threatened. Then, Blakely could be as lethal as the next person.

Devore shot Elias a hard look intended to make the man squirm, but Elias didn't back down. 'We should have let the plantation scheme go when Rutherford showed up. The situation was too hot. But you had to go and overreach yourself, taking money from men who were bound to ask questions.'

'Selby didn't ask questions,' Devore ground out defensively. They'd decided last year it was much more lucrative to run imaginary plantations than to run real ones. But the money was real enough. Men were eager enough to invest for a quick profit. They paid them, too, a nice sum within the first month to inspire trust and to foster future investment, which of course would be much more than the initial outlay. Men like James Selby were happy to donate to 'the cause', never guessing the only thing they made back was money they'd already given. But men like Kitt Sherard were dangerous. They and their questions were avoided at all costs.

'You think he was looking for the island,' Elias continued. 'We're sunk if he tells anyone. He'll come after us.'

'Yes, you nodcock!' Devore snapped. 'That's why we have to take him before he gets back to Bridgetown.' There were other reasons, too. He and Blakely weren't exactly welcome in Bridgetown after the debacle last year. Dryden and Sherard had made sure their presence would not be tolerated. Once Sherard reached Bridgetown, Devore could only rely on hired men to get to Sherard.

'What about the girl?' Elias asked.

'Sherard owes me a woman, by my count.' After he'd lost everything at Sherard's hand, his wife had sailed for England and her family, refusing to follow him into exile and poverty. 'She'll have to die, too,' Devore replied grimly. He'd kill the girl first and make Sherard watch on the off chance the girl mattered to him. She was the banker's daughter—it was entirely possible Sherard was simply using her to lever his way into respectability. Although, what he'd seen through the spyglass on deck a few nights ago hadn't looked like play-acting. Perhaps he'd have that chestnut vixen spread for him—a nice consolation prize for all the upset Sherard had caused. Maybe he'd make Sherard watch. That was a better idea yet.

Who would have guessed one of the plantation investors would actually have known Kitt Sherard, who was in turn carrying on with another investor's daughter? Fate and coincidence had conspired quite cruelly against him just when he was back on his feet and making money. Devore squeezed the stem of the brandy snifter with such force it snapped in his hand. Having Sherard's woman would be small consolation for all the upset the man had caused. Damn it! Devore pulled out a handkerchief and wrapped his bleeding hand where the glass shards had bit into his palm. It wasn't supposed to be this way.

It wasn't supposed to be this way! Kitt's primal instincts were barely leashed as he thrust hard into Bryn's welcoming wet core, the waterfall sluicing over them both, Bryn's cries swallowed up by the pounding cascade. He wasn't supposed to want her, to keep her. She was supposed to be merely another lover, one of many and one of more to come.

Her legs were wrapped tight around him, her body balanced between him and the water-smoothed surface of rock wall under the falls. Her neck arched back, her body bucked. Perhaps she, too, felt the wrong rightness of this, perhaps she knew as he did that this had to be the last time. Practical realities demanded it.

He buried his mouth against Bryn's neck, his climax fierce and powerful as he pumped into her one final time. Kitt let the climax claim them both, giving himself over to these last minutes of peace. He knew full well in the clarity that accompanied the intensity of release, his mind would be swamped with all that needed doing in the aftermath of this journey.

There would be a new voyage to plan, one full of danger and without Bryn. He would find the bastards who had set up the land scheme and bring them to justice before they could ruin any more bank accounts and reputations. He'd seen first-hand how families suffered from schemes such as this. It was clear now that the plantation was a swindle. There was nothing on this island except jungle and falls. It was beautiful and lush, like the woman in his arms, but it was not home to an investment property. The best they could do now was set a fast course for Bridgetown before her father returned and be there to prevent him from investing any more money.

Against his skin, he could hear the pounding of Bryn's heart starting to slow into its usual rhythm. These last moments of intimacy would have to do, would have to last. Even if he hadn't proven it to her, this trip had proven to him what he'd already guessed in theory: there was no place in his life for a woman like Bryn—a woman he could easily become attached to, a forever woman. His life was far too unpredictable, too dangerous. *And he liked it that way*, Kitt reminded himself. He'd made this choice long ago. He wasn't going to give it up, risk it all for a woman. He'd have to give up the woman, this beautiful, vibrant woman.

Separating himself from Bryn would be tricky. There would be her father and the bank, a partnership that would potentially put him in contact with her from time to time. Much of that business could be conducted by letter. Eventually the bank would set up formal offices on Bay Street and there would no longer be a reason to call at Rutherford's house, a situation Kitt thought he could help along when he returned. He had a currently vacant property that would do well for the office, something he'd acquired in a card game a few months back.

'Come back to me,' Bryn whispered at his ear, her hands combing back his tangled hair. 'You're a million miles away.' She held his face between her hands, her eyes meeting his. 'Don't worry. We'll find the people responsible and make things right. For a man who says he cares about nothing, you take too much on yourself.'

'It does me no good to see the bank's reputation tarnished before it even opens.' Kitt stepped out of the falls and reached for a towel. Perhaps waiting to put distance between them was a bad idea, perhaps he needed to start that process now. It would be easy enough. A swift journey home would demand his attention on deck. He'd not have time to worry about the chestnut beauty lying in his bed. He wasn't comfortable with this version of Bryn Rutherford who saw too much. It was simpler when he was just a rogue on a balcony with no history. That was the problem with relationships. You got to know someone, façades were stripped away until all you were left with were truths.

Bryn would not like those truths when she came to

them. Right now she saw a hero, but soon she'd see a man who had broken with his family, a man who was loyal to a few rare friends, but mostly loyal just to himself. In short, she'd see in him all that she wasn't and she'd abhor him for it. All he would be able to say for himself was that he'd been honest about it, he'd warned her.

Kitt watched her wrap the towel around her hair and reach for her clothes. He watched her glorious nakedness disappear beneath the fabric, memorising each curve, each line. He was going to miss this. He slipped on a pair of loose culottes and held out his hand to her. Best to get it over with. 'Are you ready? It's time to go.'

Time to go *home*. Bryn reluctantly took Kitt's hand and let him help her over the rocks. The idea did not appeal at all. Time to go home meant the end of this adventure, it meant confronting her father about Selby's mistake. Most of all, it meant the end of this interlude with Kitt. Everything would change when they reached Bridgetown. It was changing already. She wasn't entirely convinced Kitt's thoughts had only been about the land swindle, but about them, about *her*. He was already leaving, trying to distance himself from her.

It was probably for the best. How would they keep this affair up in Bridgetown? He certainly couldn't keep sneaking into her bedroom and one too many trips out to a garden would eventually be noticed. But those were just practical reasons for ending it. If they kept this up, it was bound to reach a point where it meant something, at least to her. In fact, that point might have already been reached, promises to the contrary notwithstanding.

It had become readily apparent to her over the last

few days that she could make all the vows she wanted about not falling for a man, about not leaving herself vulnerable to the emotions that came with physical contact, but those vows could only serve as warnings, they could not actually force her to take their advice, nor could they stop it from happening.

On board the *Queen*, the crew was a unified mass of moving energy, everyone busy with their tasks. Kitt's orders had been plain: make Bridgetown with all speed possible. This would be no leisurely sail home. There would be no side sojourns to swim with dolphins, no waterfalls to bathe under, no languorous afternoons spent on sunny beaches. In short, no time for her.

Bryn took up an unobtrusive post at the rail where she could watch Kitt and stay out of the way, of which the latter was clearly what he wanted. The sting of separation hurt, there was no doubt about it. Even now, with the feel of his body still imprinted on hers, her hand still warm from his grip, she felt bereft—something she had no right to feel, she reminded herself sternly. She had no right to feel abandoned, no right to wallow in self-pity like a jilted miss, no right to feel anything. They'd implicitly agreed it would be this way.

Apparently she wanted to rub salt in her emotional wounds. She couldn't stop staring at him. Her eyes followed him around the deck, watching him work. He remained shirtless, putting his muscles on display as he heaved ropes and raised the sails, his culottes riding scandalously low on his hips, reminding her she knew precisely what lay beneath them.

Overhead, the sky started to cloud, the wind rising.

'It'll make for good speed!' Kitt called to Passemore, who questioned the weather.

'Are you sure we shouldn't stay in the cove and shelter until it passes?' the first mate called back.

Kitt shook his head, shouting to be heard. 'We cannot delay in reaching Bridgetown. With a wind like this, we'll make excellent time, perhaps even outrun the worst of the squall.'

Bryn turned her gaze skyward. Grey clouds gathered, blocking out the setting sun. The peaceful blue-skied day was gone, replaced by an ominous dusky light. The island was still visible behind them. She much preferred Passemore's suggestion to Kitt's idea of a fair race between them and nature. Overhead, a fork of lightning lit the sky in the distance, at once both terrible and beautiful in its power. Passemore gave Kitt a final challenging look, but the rest of the crew seemed oblivious.

'We've sailed through far worse.' She heard Kitt laugh and clap Passemore on the shoulder. 'You take the helm and I'll finish with the sails.' He disappeared to the far end of the ship.

Bryn turned her gaze outward to sea. They were definitely picking up speed. The serene blue waters had turned the colour charcoal, no longer a flat, peaceful sheet of ocean, but an erratic collection of choppy, white-topped peaks as the *Queen* cut through them. She could feel the ship roll beneath her feet. She hoped Kitt was right and they would outrun the weather. Otherwise, it might be a very long night. It was going to be a long night anyway in an empty bed.

The first raindrop caught her on the nose, a fat, wet

splat. She blinked, wiped it away and blinked again, her eyes catching a shape on the horizon that had not been there before. There was a ship under full sail and it gave every appearance of closing fast.

Chapter Eighteen

Hell and damnation! Kitt swung down from the rigging, calling for his spyglass. Passemore had it waiting before his feet hit the deck. 'Is it the same one?' Kitt asked, putting the scope to his eye. This was disastrous. He needed clear sailing to Bridgetown, but fate and nature seemed determined to conspire against him, first with the storm and now with this mystery ship reappearing out of nowhere.

'I think it is, Captain,' Passemore affirmed. 'But the ship is unmarked so it's hard to tell.'

Kitt gave a grim nod and handed the glass back to Passemore. It was his belief, too, that it was the same ship. 'Run up the quarantine flag and let's see what she does.' A ship meaning no harm would respect the warning and leave them in peace with their sick. Only a ship bent on menace would ignore the quarantine, or even suspect the quarantine was a lie.

Another fear began to surface. If it was the same ship, it had picked them up fairly quickly after they'd left the island, suggesting to Kitt it had deliberately lain in wait for them. He looked up at the white sails filling with the full force of the wind. The *Queen* was fast. This would not be the first time he'd outrun storms and villains. Now that the *Queen* was under full sail, the other ship would be hard pressed to keep closing. He made a decision. 'Passemore, let her run. If these bastards want us, they'll have to catch us.'

Passemore grinned with far more enthusiasm than Kitt felt. 'Aye, aye, Captain.'

Kitt risked a glance to where Bryn stood at the rail looking out over the sea, soaking in the rain. The silly woman, she should be off the deck. Didn't she know she was in danger up here? Of course she didn't. He hadn't told her, not explicitly. He grabbed up an oilskin from the storage trunk they kept on deck and strode towards her. His tone was gruff and sharp when he spoke, anger disguising his concern. 'You should have gone to the cabin the moment it began to rain. I don't need you sick with a chill.'

'We had a squall or two on the crossing, I can manage bad weather,' Bryn said confidently, but she didn't shrug him off when he draped the oilskin about her.

Kitt had every intention of ushering her to the cabin, but she twisted out of his grip, refusing to be mandhandled. 'Will they catch us?' Bryn asked, her gaze riveted on the dark shape of the ship trailing behind them.

'They may not want to. I've run up the quarantine flag. We'll know soon enough if they mean business. Now, let's get you somewhere warm and dry.' This time, she let him lead her away from the rail and he knew relief as they gained the shelter of the cabin, not just because it afforded her protection from the elements, but also because it afforded her safety.

If this boat behind them meant menace, Kitt would

prefer it not know a woman was on board. He wanted a fair fight if it came to that. He'd match his men man for man and the *Queen*, too, against any roguish frigate's crew in the Caribbean. But he absolutely didn't want a fight where Bryn was used as leverage against him. There would be nothing fair about that.

Bryn was no fool and his gruff tones hadn't masked his concern. She reached for him as he turned to go, a firm hand on his arm. 'I have two pistols in my valise and I know how to use them.'

Kitt gave her a curt nod, understanding her implicit message. *If the worst happens, I'll be fine. You needn't be distracted by worry for me.* It was a gesture entirely her, selfless Bryn thinking of others before herself even in a potential crisis and it was the undoing of him. His mind screamed a desperate warning: *Not now, not now!*

'The *Queen* is fast,' he assured her, trying hard to betray none of the emotions rocketing through him as he stared into those eyes of hers, so hard and determined. His insides were chaos. He'd not imagined it would happen this way. He'd always thought if, on the remote chance, it ever *did* happen to him, it would happen in bed, a beautiful woman staring up at him with soft, dreamy eyes. It most definitely wouldn't happen in the midst of a crisis with a woman telling him she was priming her pistols. That was when he knew. Love had found him and at the worst of all possible times. It was a hell of a time to realise he'd fallen for Bryn Rutherford. But it didn't matter. It couldn't change anything, it could only hurt more. He would get over it. He'd hurt before and he'd survived.

'You won't need them,' Kitt repeated with a final grim nod before stepping out into the rain, shutting the door firmly behind him and wishing he could leave his emotions behind as easily.

She won't need them, he silently vowed, pulling his arms through an oilskin slicker and joining Passemore at the helm. The rain had picked up substantially, but that was expected. The storm was bound to get worse before it got better. Beyond the rail the dark ship was keeping its distance.

That was expected, too, either because the storm and the *Queen*'s speed had not allowed any further gains or because the quarantine flag had done its job. The distance was reassuring, but Kitt suspected it was for the former reasons and not the latter. If the flag had worked, the ship would have probably charted a different course. Even small-time pirates would not have made the effort to go after a quarantined ship. Still, it would be difficult to overtake them. Byrn could put her pistols away.

If it wasn't for Bryn, Kitt would have opted to turn and fight, the only sure way to end this guessing game once and for all: who was indeed behind these attacks on his person. Outrunning the ship simply delayed that particular resolution for another day. It was clear to him that he was the target of this chase. At least that gave him something to bargain with if it came to protecting his ship and protecting Bryn: himself. But he would not go easy. He would put his faith in the *Queen*'s speed.

'I thought you said this ship was fast!' Devore fumed, water dripping in his face in a cold, steady stream. The rain was miserable and they were making no headway in catching Sherard's ship. The storm was working to Sherard's favour, but not theirs. Every time Devore looked up, it seemed they were falling further behind.

'The *Queen*'s a fast ship, I'm doing all I can!' the captain yelled over the wind, as surly as Devore. Devore swore and turned away, kicking a foot at a coil of rope in frustration. Dammit all! This was supposed to have been easy. They'd lain in wait, sails at the ready to take the *Queen* swiftly before Sherard could get it under full sail.

Even then, they'd been outplayed by the rising wind, but not before Devore had caught sight of something of interest in the spyglass; Sherard had gone to the woman at the rail, his hands lingering at her shoulders as he'd wrapped an oilskin jacket around her. It was definitely not a neutral act. He could have sent someone else with the jacket, he could have simply handed one to her. Sherard's gesture spoke of a caring that went beyond politeness. It confirmed what he'd seen through the telescope earlier. Sherard had developed feelings for Miss Rutherford. Devore almost rubbed his cold hands together in glee. Before, he'd counted on deep-seated honour to make Sherard accountable. He didn't think Sherard was callous enough to stand by and watch any woman under his protection suffer regardless of his attachment to her. But now, this was different, this was better. A woman Sherard *cared* about would be exquisite leverage indeed. It guaranteed Sherard's capitulation if they could just capture the ship.

'We need more drastic measures.' Devore returned to the captain at the helm. 'We've got to slow him down, make him turn and fight. You have cannons. It's time to use them. Shoot to disable the ship only. I don't want to sink it.' Not yet anyway. He wanted to do that when

Sherard could watch. Oh, this was perfect. With the limited visibility of the rain, Kitt Sherard would never see it coming, not until it was too late.

The first shot shook the cabin, sounding like a clap of thunder had occurred directly overhead. Bryn screamed in abject shock, the force of the sudden explosion sending her reeling on to the bed. Outside the cabin door, footsteps pounded across the deck, the air filled with the abrupt shouts of men racing to do a task. Bryn picked herself up off the bed, a terrible thought occurring. It hadn't been thunder, but something worse.

Bryn scrambled for her valise tucked away at the bottom of the wardrobe. Now seemed like a good time to retrieve those pistols she'd boasted of to Kitt. Her heart was racing and she took a few breaths. A shaky hand didn't do anyone any good, nor did a shaky mind. She needed to be calm, she needed to think with cool detachment.

Her hands closed around the smooth butt of one pistol, then the other. The feel of the familiar grip offered some measure of comfort. She'd bought them before she'd left England and had taught herself to shoot. She was by no means an extraordinary marksman, but she'd find her target in close quarters. She hoped she wouldn't have to prove it.

Bryn checked to make sure the safety was on and returned to the bed just in time. The ship made a sudden lurch. They were turning back! There was a low rumble and the clank of chains from under the deck somewhere. It sounded as if cannons were being rolled out. That meant engagement. Someone had fired on them. Worse, it likely meant Kitt couldn't outrun them.

Oh, the curiosity was killing her! Bryn fought the urge to go out on deck and demand information. She wanted to see the damage first-hand, wanted to know what was going on. Most of all, she wanted to see with her own eyes that Kitt was unharmed. But she was practical, too. She understood on deck she was a liability: a distraction to Kitt and a danger to the crew. If she were taken, their lives could be forfeit to save hers. Kitt would be forced to bargain, to choose whose lives mattered. It would be an intolerable situation. So she did the right thing, the hard thing. She sat on the bed with guns primed and aimed at the door in case the worst happened, occasionally risking a glance out the window, but since it was in the bow and they were turned sideways to face the oncoming ship, the window could tell her little of the action.

The volley of cannon fire rattled the cabin, this time from the *Queen*'s own. It was returned. Outside, men yelled, items shattered and crashed. She thought she heard Kitt's voice calling to reload the cannons. It was comforting to know he would fight to the end, but what would that end look like? Would Kitt and the *Queen* prevail? Bryn thought not. A ship would not fire and demand a battle if it didn't think it could win.

The *Queen* was a merchant ship, and its prime weapon was speed. Its cannons were primarily for protection, not for deliberately provoking other ships into a fight. It was quite likely only a matter of time. Kitt could not hold them off indefinitely. That decided it. She would not meet her fate quietly sitting in a cabin waiting for it. Bryn cocked her pistols and stepped out the door.

The deck was a ghastly scene straight from a pirate novel, exacerbated no doubt by the dark weather.

Wind whipped at her hair, the slanting rain pelted her newly dried skirts. Debris lay strewn about. She could see where the first shot had severed part of a mast and ripped through a sail. The jagged mast piece lay on the ground, looking much larger at her feet than it had up in the air.

It was all she had time to see. A body barrelled out of nowhere with a yell, taking her to the wet deck with a bone-jarring thud just as something whizzed overhead, ripping the air. 'You are supposed to be in the cabin.'

Kitt! She pushed at his heavy form, trying to regain her breath after the sudden impact. But Kitt would not let her up. His voice came low and fast at her ear. 'How can I protect you if I don't know where you are? If you don't follow instructions? Cannon balls are indiscriminate things, Bryn. They don't care who or what they hit.'

'They're coming, Captain!' Passemore scrambled across the deck towards them. Kitt rose. 'They just launched the longboats. Shall we fire again?'

'Fire as long as you can,' Kitt barked out for everyone to hear. 'Cannons are our best chance. We want to keep them at a distance. Do not let them board this ship!' His voice was full of authority. Men ran to obey, but Bryn saw the futility of it in his eyes. She grabbed his arm, forcing him to look at her.

'It's not going to work, is it?' She willed him not to lie to her. She was too smart. She knew the numbers. Kitt had a crew of thirty. It appeared the numbers were against them, three to one.

'Don't worry, they won't sink the ship, Bryn. They don't want the *Queen*, not right away at least.'

She searched the grim lines of his face. 'What do they want?'

'They want me.' His eyes moved beyond her, look-ing at a point past her shoulder, his mind already cal-culating options and discarding choices of which she knew there weren't many. The question now was not if they'd surrender, but when and how.

'No, Kitt. You can't.' Bryn's grip tightened on his arm as if she could hold him there with her strength.

'If anything happens to me, Passemore will see you to safety. Get to your father. Tell him what we found.' He shook his head, his tone softening for a moment, his eyes caressing her face with their gaze. 'I am sorry, Bryn, for dragging you into this.' He kissed her on the forehead, a quick hurried gesture. 'Stay in the cabin. Hide, defend yourself. I'll have men posted outside the door, good men, it will be hard for anyone to get through. You will not be alone.'

But not with him. Bryn understood that message and worry ripped through her. What was he going to do? He simply couldn't turn himself over. Of course he couldn't be with her. It would be tantamount to suicide for them both to be caught together. Strategically, she understood that. Emotionally, though, it was all she wanted. If she could see him, she would know he was safe, she would have a chance perhaps to protect him. Out of sight, she could control nothing.

'No, that option is unacceptable,' Bryn said, her chal-lenge taking Kitt by surprise. She was *not* going back there to sit and wait. It was the very thing she'd come out here to avoid. If she went back and sat on the bed with her pistols, fate would just outwait her. The end to this adventure would be inevitable and obvious. 'There has to be another way.'

Kitt stepped close, frustration evident in his eyes.

She involuntarily backed up a step. She'd crossed a line with her latest bit of defiance, but she'd not give in. In her gut, Bryn knew she had to win this argument for both their sakes. Kitt was worried for her and that had limited his perception of the options. 'Bryn, I need you to follow directions. How can I keep you safe?' he ground out the old argument.

'No.' She shook her head, an idea forming. She spoke quickly, the words coming rapidly, racing against time. 'You're only saying this, only acting like this, because I'm a woman. What if I wasn't?'

Kitt gave a wide grin, some of the grimness receding from his eyes, his voice full of mischief the way it usually was. 'Now that would be *very* disappointing.'

Chapter Nineteen

If Bryn didn't have to be a woman, he didn't have to
be the captain. Of course, in his case, success was less
assured. Depending who was on that ship, someone
might recognise him regardless of disguise. If it was
Devore, as he suspected, Devore would know him. *But*
if it was someone else entirely, or if Devore didn't board
the ship, he stood a chance of escaping detection. Not
that it mattered as much for him as it did for Bryn.
Bryn's disguise took away leverage that could be used
against him. It ensured her safety. His disguise simply
enhanced the element of surprise.

Kitt rummaged through O'Reilly's things in the crew
quarters, looking for a knit cap. His own soaked and
worn culottes would certainly pass muster as crew attire, but he'd been bareheaded and a cap would go far
in hiding his hair. Any distraction would help. He had
no illusion that pretending not to be himself would resolve this ambush favourably. But it would be a start.
There was still the issue of keeping his ship and crew
intact and being able to sail away when this was over.
For that, he'd need a knife, a nice long sharp one.

Back up on deck, he gave Passemore a wink and instructions to wave the white flag. 'We want to be able to sail away when this is done.' He'd not lied to Bryn. He wasn't worried about being sunk. But he did worry another volley might render the *Queen* too incapacitated to sail away in a timely manner and it would be better to get this ruse under way sooner than later.

His men assembled, waiting in an orderly but dangerous line, for the longboat of invaders to reach them. They knew without being told this was no textbook surrender. They were to be vigilant and wait for their moment. He almost missed Bryn entirely, his eyes picking her out at the last moment. His optimism rose. This just might work.

A beefy Jamaican was the first on board, a mean, wicked-looking man. The captain no doubt. Kitt narrowed his eyes, keeping his attention on the man who would be his opponent. The Jamaican walked down the line, his voice deep and barking, carrying over the wind. 'Where is Captain Sherard?'

Come on, come a little closer. Kitt's hand closed around the handle of his hidden knife. He wanted to be the one to answer that question, but only when the brute was close enough to seize. Kitt didn't want the gambit working the other way. He didn't want one of his men pulled out of line and forced at knifepoint to reveal his identity. He wanted to do all the revealing, all the knife work. Nobody took what was his. This audacious bastard needed a lesson in that.

When no one answered, the captain stopped by Bryn five men down the line from him. Kitt swallowed. *Move away from her.* He wondered if he could reach her in time. There would be a mêlée. The captain had not come alone. Kitt counted twenty men in the longboat with him and another twenty were probably on the way. He wasn't looking for a fight. He was looking for leverage.

'Will no one tell me?' the captain yelled again, starting to move forward once more. 'Shall I select one of you to tell me?' He halted by Passemore standing beside Kitt. The captain turned to call back down the line. 'I shall start slitting throats, beginning with this one.' That was his fatal mistake.

Kitt knew he wouldn't get a better chance. He grabbed the man from behind, knife at the man's neck. Anger and rage pulsed through him as Kitt hauled the brute to the rail, his men leaping into instant action, weapons drawn from secret locations on their persons to minimise any heroics on the part of the Jamaican's crew.

'One move and he dies!' Kitt bellowed, making sure the other ship could see him. He was betting whoever was left over there wasn't fool enough to fire on the *Queen* with so many of their own men on board. He was relieved to see the oncoming longboat turn back. There'd be no reinforcements. Cowards and mercenaries, then. Kitt thought. Not a crew like his who had been together, who could rely on one another. He raised a bead of blood to make sure the other ship knew he meant business. He could not afford to bluff, not with Bryn, his crew and his ship depending on him. Truth was, this captain was dead regardless. To let him go gave him a second chance to blow them out of the water.

'You surrendered!' the captain ground out, starting to sweat. He'd probably just come to the same realisation. 'You are not respecting the rules of the game!' It was a desperate plea, one captain to another.

'*I* ran up a quarantine flag and *you* did not respect

that,' Kitt growled, pressing his knife tip. 'The rules had been broken long before now.' Whatever he did, he'd have to do it soon. It was a dangerous guessing game now. If his men released the crew and allowed them to return to their ship, would they fire on the *Queen*, sacrificing their captain, or would the captain's presence be enough to prevent it? Maybe it didn't matter if the captain lived or died. It was hard to know in what capacity the captain was most valuable.

'Passemore!' Kitt made his decision. 'Round up the men who don't wish to be shot. Take them below to the hold as our prisoners! They will be dealt with in Bridgetown.' Short twenty men, the ship would be hard pressed to follow them at full speed. 'Except that one.' Kitt pointed to a smaller, younger fellow. 'Have him take a message back. If they aren't under way in ten minutes, I will execute the captain.' He hoped it wouldn't come to that. He hoped whoever was on board would understand they were beaten for the day and retreat.

It was the most important question of the day. One look at the captain's face told him the man didn't know the answer any more than he did.

He had eight minutes left to answer and the first mate—the captain's brother as it turned out—was staring him down. Devore cursed and kicked the table leg with his good foot. Damn and double damn. Sherard had him in a bind. Did he risk firing on the *Queen* and sacrificing a third of the crew for the sake of a second try? Even then, at such close range, the *Queen* would be able to fire again. The damage Sherard had already done to the boat was going to cost him. Would the remaining crew follow his orders? He wasn't the one in charge, just the one paying the bills. If he did let Sherard have his captain, where would he find another one? Captains without scruples were expensive. He'd have to start all over and that would definitely put him behind.

On the other hand, Sherard's ship was limping, too. This might be his only chance to take Sherard. It was frustrating to have the man at such close range only to let him slip away. The captain was only one man. If he let Sherard make it back to Bridgetown, the stakes rose substantially. This went from being a personal vendetta to taking on the crown's banking and legal system. He'd be wanted for fraud.

'What will it be, mon?' The first mate glared, fingering a wicked blade with feigned idleness. 'A short life or a longer one? If they do my brother over there, I will do you a minute later.'

Devore unconsciously fingered his throat. That made the decision a bit easier. 'We'll pull away, of course.' He smiled. 'A fine captain like your brother would be too hard to replace. Tell the crew to make ready to depart.'

The first mate gave a cold smile. 'A very good decision, mon.'

Maybe not a good decision, but the only decision. Devore helped himself to a hefty serving of the captain's rum. After all, fraud was fairly difficult to prosecute and they'd have to catch him first. Sherard would understand today hadn't been a victory, it had been a draw. Sherard would have to live with the knowledge that he was still out there, still coming for him and that kind of knowledge made it hard for a man to sleep at night. Oh, no, this was definitely not a victory for Kitt Sherard, but perhaps it was a tiny victory for *him*.

* * *

Kitt's crew gave a victory cry as the dark ship moved off into the rain. The movement was slow—the *Queen*'s cannons had done some damage, giving as good as it had got. They were safe now. They could look to mending their own hurts. It would be wet, messy business in the rain. The weather was not pleasant, but thankfully it hadn'tworsened. By morning, the sun would be out, but Kitt didn't want to wait until then to get under way with twenty prisoners and the enemy's captain on board. Any sign of weakness could be an incentive for them to attempt a mutiny.

He put Passemore in charge of repairs and gestured for O'Reilly to join him. It was time to get some answers. He allowed himself to seek out Bryn with his eyes. She'd dedicated herself to cleaning up the deck. Her face was white, but stoic, as she worked. He wished she was in the cabin, getting warm and dry, but he understood why she wasn't: too much adrenaline. He could no more expect her to sit than he could expect it of anyone else right now. Men needed to work after a battle, needed to have purpose. He wanted to go to her, but there was no time and this was not the place. He had to be the captain first and there was still a job that needed doing, further testament Bryn could not be part of his life.

He drew a breath for fortitude. 'Come on, O'Reilly, let's go see our guests.' But O'Reilly had seen the direction of his thoughts. The big man clapped a hand on his shoulder.

'Your woman did well today.' O'Reilly's face split into a grin. 'I doubt many women could have pulled it off. She didn't flinch when the captain stopped right in front of her. Of course, I was next to her and I wouldn't have let the captain touch a hair on her head.'

'Thankfully it didn't come to that.' Kitt smiled politely. O'Reilly meant well, but that was the problem. Bryn made men feel chivalrous. Men would fight for her, die for her whether she wanted them to or not.

He could not have that, not for himself or his crew. Today had gone right by luck. There was only so much he could control. He couldn't control where the captain stopped along the line. He couldn't control who the captain picked as a first victim. If O'Reilly had been forced to protect Bryn, there would have been blood spilt and quite a lot of it. Bryn stripped away all objectivity from a situation. He couldn't have it, he simply couldn't have it.

Down in the hold, Kitt gave O'Reilly his instructions. 'I want to know who was behind this ambush today. Remember, you're the ship's doctor. You're supposed to patch people up, not rip them open,' he cautioned O'Reilly when the big man cracked his knuckles with a bit more glee than Kitt would recommend from a physician. 'We're going to play nice.'

'Of course, Captain,' O'Reilly said respectfully. 'And if that fails, we have plan B.'

Her plan had worked brilliantly—so brilliantly, in fact, that she'd never been so scared in her entire life! Bryn slipped out of the oilskin slicker, having finally allowed herself to seek the sanctuary of Kitt's cabin. She was cold, something she'd thought she'd never be in the Caribbean with its sticky, underwear-forgoing heat. Her teeth were even chattering.

Bryn carefully peeled the wet clothes from her skin.

She'd borrowed some of Kitt's since Passemore's had obviously done little to hide her more feminine assets. Kitt's clothes had been far larger, though, and she'd had to make liberal use of rope to tie up his pants. Now, all that extra cloth was haunting her. Her cold fingers fumbled on the extra fabric, her tired legs threatened to tangle in the legs of his culottes. At least, the effort kept her mind from wandering down less pleasant paths.

Finally, she was free of the wet clothes. She wrapped a blanket about her, letting warmth start to creep into her skin, but thoughts began to creep in, too, images of the day and with them came the horrible 'what ifs' she'd not dared to dwell on as the events had unfolded for fear they would steal her courage. But now, there was nothing left to restrain them, nothing left to keep them at bay and they came, in floods and in torrents.

Always Kitt was at the centre of those images. The desire to see him, to assure herself he was safe, or maybe it had been the desire to assure herself *she* was safe, had driven her on deck. Her eyes had known where to look for him. He'd been everywhere, shouting orders, lending a hand where it was needed and he'd saved her from her own careless foolishness when the cannon ball had whined overhead. He'd been vibrant and alive in those moments. But that man had also been a stranger.

She did not know the grim captain who had argued with her to seek the safety of the cabin. He was so different than the laughing, cocksure Kitt she knew, to whom everything was a game, even life itself. That had not been the case today. Today had been serious business.

She understood why. This ambush had not been a game to the captain who'd boarded them. When he'd stopped in front of her, it had taken every ounce of her bravery to see those moments through. He could hardly have stood there more than a few seconds, but it had seemed an eternity. The only thought she'd been capable of thinking in the interim was that he'd not been bluffing. He would have killed to get his answers. He was a brute. But when Kitt had drawn his knife, she'd known Kitt would have, too. She'd hardly recognised the ferocious man who'd leapt into action five men down from her.

There were people who claimed they'd kill for something, but those were just words. Worse, in her own bloodlust, in her own desire for safety, she'd wanted him to do it. She'd wanted him to kill the man and put an end to her fear. Kitt had proven better than that, though. He'd seen the long-term advantages to keeping the captain alive. He was below deck even now, interrogating the captain for information. What did that make *him*? Was Kitt a brute just with better looks? No, that was unfair and she knew better. She'd made quite a discovery today. Deep down, hidden away beneath the armour of his carefree nonchalance, Kitt was loyal to the bone.

Today, Kitt had protected his crew, his ship and her by any means possible. He'd not hesitated to draw blood to see it done. All of which pointed to the reality that this, or things like this, had happened before. She'd not missed the fact that his crew had taken each progression of the battle in stride. They'd fired cannons with efficiency, they'd been prepared to flawlessly enact the mock surrender without giving away their captain's identity. Flawlessness required practice. Proof enough, these things not only happened, but they happened with *frequent regularity*. Today, she'd had a glimpse into the real life of Kitt Sherard. This is what he spent his days doing, this was how he'd built his fortune.

It was, admittedly, quite a lot for a girl to take in. Although, why she should find it shocking escaped her. *You knew. You've known from the start. Good men don't climb balconies. Good men don't roam beaches in bedsheets. Good men don't make love as if they won't see tomorrow.* She *had* known. She really had. But as the saying went, seeing was believing.

The door to the cabin flew open, helped by the wind. Kitt stepped inside, all dripping, soaking, six feet of him. Every inch of him a man against all, a man who had won. Bryn's pulse raced, her eyes unable to look away from the sheer attractiveness of raw, potent male on display, a man fresh come from battle.

'Bryn!' The hoarse word ripped from Kitt's throat as he crossed the room.

She rose, dropping the blanket, meeting him halfway. She was seeing, and heaven help her, she was believing.

Chapter Twenty

Heaven help him, he could not be gentle. Kitt pulled
her to him in a rough embrace, his mouth ravaging hers
in his need, his wet, soaking body pressed to her naked
one, selfishly drinking in her heat, her life. How he'd
wanted to do this for hours! How he'd wanted to wrap
his body around hers, wanted to immerse himself deep
inside her, to assure himself she was safe.

Bryn's hands were frantic on him, tugging at his
wet clothes until they had him out of them, his body as
naked as hers. 'Are you cold?' She was managing a one-
sided, breathless conversation between kisses. 'Come
to bed, I can warm you better there.'

Kitt bore her backwards to the blankets. 'I thought
you'd never ask.' He followed her down with a laugh,
feeling alive, feeling the fear that had gripped him the
last hours effectively banished. Her legs were open to
him, welcoming him into their cradle. His erection, already full, surged pikestaff-hard at first contact with
her soft flesh. This would not take long. Three thrusts,
maybe four and he'd be spent. There was no finesse as
he entered her hard and fast, primal thrust after primal
thrust as he buried himself inside her.

He found her ready for it. Her legs wrapped about his hips, taking him deep, her core wet and slick, ready to accommodate his rough entry, even revel in it. Beneath him, her body arched, bucking in the hasty pleasure of their coupling, her climax as feverish, as intense as his when it came. This was not about first times or last times, lucky guesses or second chances, this was about drinking the ambrosia of life.

· He lay embedded inside her long afterwards, reluctant to leave the shelter of her feminine harbour. They were entwined completely, intimately. When at last he moved, it was to roll on his side and take her against him, her buttocks curled against the curve of his groin. Consummation and comfort; he craved them both. He'd had his consummation, wild and ferocious, but he still sought the comfort of holding her close, the assurance that she was there, whole and safe. 'Bryn, I nearly lost you today. I'm so sorry.' It was easier to talk without seeing her face. She was warm against him. It felt good, it felt right. *Moments of happiness are not sustainable*, he reminded himself.

'Nothing happened. I'm perfectly fine, not a scratch to show.'

But the distance between 'not a scratch to show' and being blown to smithereens, or having her throat slit, was a matter of mere inches, the matter of luck changing in a heartbeat. If he'd tackled her a second later, if the Jamaican captain had singled her out instead of Passemore, if the captain had not turned his back, if a hundred other variables had gone awry, the day could have ended very differently. Only a fool would pretend otherwise.

He said as much out loud, but Bryn merely turned in his arms, to see him face-to-face, her body pressed to his. 'I'm no fool, Kitt. I know just how close it was today.'

The quiet intensity of her voice was nearly his undoing. He enfolded her in his arms. What had he been thinking to let her come? He should have sailed straight back to Bridgetown the moment she'd tumbled out of his wardrobe. But he knew what he'd been thinking. He'd wanted her too much and he'd known he could have her, at least for a little while. He'd been selfish and in his selfishness he'd risked her.

He should tell her, say the words, but he found the only words that would come was a litany of 'I'm sorrys'. He was sorry for things he couldn't begin to tell her. He was sorry for exposing her to danger, for exposing her to his life, sorry that he couldn't change it. Most of all he was sorry that the world of Kitt Sherard had no place in it for a woman like Bryn Rutherford, a decision that was made long before he met her.

Bryn pushed back a bit to take his face between her hands. 'You saved us all today. There's nothing to be sorry for.' Then she slipped beneath the warm cocoon of their blankets and burrowed to the bottom, her hands announcing their presence on his calves. Her lips followed them up, past his knees, to his thighs, until there was only one place left for them to go. Kitt's breath caught in anticipation of what she meant to do.

Her hand came first, running the length of him, preparing him, until he felt himself come exquisitely to life beneath her fingers. Then came her mouth, her sweet delectable mouth. Her tongue stroked his tender head with quick, teasing flicks across his slit. Kitt could feel himself bead for her. He closed his eyes, letting the pleasure sweep him away, letting it drown out the im-

possible wanting, the guilt of his selfishness. He could
have this moment, this gift. She ran her tongue the
length of his under-ridge and he moaned; she mouthed
him, sucking hard until he sobbed with the ecstasy of
it, rocked with the ecstasy of it until the blankets had
fallen away, revealing Bryn in all her beauty between
his legs, each stroke sending him closer to the edge of
his release.

Kitt arched, barely able to articulate a strangled caution to Bryn, but she was ready. She caught him in
her hand, holding him as he spent, his phallus pulsing,
throbbing with its climax. The moment was as intimate
as they came. He'd never been held through it, never
seen a woman watch him come with awe riveting her
face. He wanted to remember her this way for all time.
How had she known this was exactly what he needed?
She'd given him acceptance to simply be himself.

She would try and change him. Bryn wondered—
would he understand that's why she'd done it? Beside
her, Kitt's breathing was slow and even. 'Happy?' She
ventured the brave word in the dark. She snuggled
against him, her head finding his chest as surely as his
arm wrapped about her, drawing her close.

'Content.' Kitt sighed as if to emphasise his point.

'I'm…content, too,' Bryn echoed. She would rather
be happy, but content was a more realistic word. Content
implied she was satisfied with what she had, while understanding it was all she *could* have even if she wanted
more. Kitt pressed a kiss in her hair. It made her bold or
perhaps the tender gesture made her desperate. 'What
happens when we get back to Bridgetown?'

Difficult words, but they had to be spoken. They'd
pretended they both knew what would happen, they'd

even pretended they were satisfied with that. Well, at least she had and she suspected he'd pretended to be satisfied, too. The man who'd made love to her tonight would never truly be satisfied with such an understanding any more than she. How much longer would they go on denying the truth? If they didn't address it now, it would be too late.

'You know what happens, Bryn. This is over. It has to be.'

'Is that what you want?' Bryn asked softly, trying to ignore the slow pain growing in her heart.

'It's what has to be. Today should have shown you how impossible it is for it to be otherwise. We were lucky. We won't always be lucky. And, yes, these sorts of situations will happen again and again just like the day I met you.'

'The assassins chasing you into the garden?' She forced a laugh, trying to find a way to argue against his decision. Surely he wasn't climbing balconies *every* day.

'Even before that.' Kitt sighed in the darkness. 'That day, we had a rum drop-off to complete. It was supposed to be simple, but it was a trap designed to ambush us. The man who warned me about the assassins died in my arms. Now it seems we have another layer. The captain in my hold was kind enough to inform me that Hugh Devore is the mastermind behind the Sunwood swindle. Apparently, while he's not out ambushing my rum sales, he's coaxing wealthy gentlemen into investing in a plantation that doesn't exist.'

An ambush over a typical trade, a dead man's warning, being chased by assassins and climbing a stranger's balcony. All in a day's work, quite possibly all in *every* day's work. She would never know what he would be facing when he went out. What was worse? Knowing or guessing? Today's reality had been fairly frightening. 'You're trying to scare me off,' Bryn said quietly.

'Is it working?'

'It's not that I don't understand, Kitt, it's that I want to try anyway.' She was out on the very furthest limb of her tree of confidence now. It was a thin one, it might snap at any time and send her plummeting. *Don't betray me, Kitt. It took everything to say those words.* She was not a weak woman, but she felt vulnerable just now.

'You do me a great honour, Bryn.' His answer was neither refusal nor acceptance, but something in between and it would have to be good enough.

The rain had stopped in the night, leaving behind a brisk breeze that blew them steadily and quickly towards Bridgetown. At the rail, her hat once more firmly on her head, Bryn watched the port loom ever closer in the afternoon sun with growing trepidation. Had anyone missed her? She'd told the servants she was going to stay with a new friend. It hadn't been a lie, only she'd been gone longer than she'd planned. The servants would know she'd packed to be gone a day or two. Instead, she'd been gone five, nearly six. Was that all? It felt as if a lifetime had passed. Still, all should be fine. Her father was not scheduled to be back until tomorrow.

'We'll drop anchor here.' Kitt materialised at her elbow, breaking into her thoughts. 'I'll row you in, unless you'd prefer Passemore or O'Reilly?' He was letting her decide where it ended. They'd not talked of 'it' since the prior night. She'd spent her bravery the night before. If he was going to leave it up to her, she'd hang on to him as long as she could.

'I'd prefer you if you have the time.'

'Are you nervous?' Kitt leaned beside her on the rail, his blue eyes on hers, the gesture feeling personal and sincere. How many times had they met on this spot on the rail since leaving port? She would miss this. He'd become friend and lover combined into one. It would be difficult to go back to being less.

'I'm thinking how disappointed my father will be to hear about the island.' He would be disappointed. It was a severe blow, but it was also a lie. She hadn't solely been thinking of her father's reaction although she probably should be. Back to Bridgetown meant back to business, back to being the banker's daughter. Her father needed her.

Kitt did more than row her in. He carried her valise and he walked her the distance from the docks to the house at the end of Bay Street. But he said nothing, their walk accomplished in abject silence. Bryn reasoned it was better for him to be silent than to say things he didn't mean or make half-promises he had no intention of keeping. It would hurt more if he lied to her. In truth, it was hard to imagine it hurting more than it did. She was hurting pretty badly right now, as if something was being ripped from her.

She'd thought she'd be safe this time. Kitt wouldn't betray her and he hadn't. He hadn't used her, hadn't seen her as a means for personal gain, he hadn't needed anything from her. He'd given her gifts beyond compare, experiences that exceeded her dreams. Because of all that, it wasn't supposed to hurt, there wasn't a reason for it to. *Since when did love need a reason? Admit it, you fell for him. All the promises you made yourself about adventure and happy ever afters being momentary could not protect you.*

They reached the gate separating the house grounds from the street. He swung it open for her and handed her the valise. 'I'll call on your father in a couple of days when he returns and talk with him about the island. I'll see what we can salvage. But then I'll go back out again. It's important we find Devore.'

Devore—oh, yes, the grand villain in all this. Bryn dragged her mind back to practical matters. For a moment she'd forgotten about that island, the missing one, the one they'd set out to find. Instead, her heart had leaped, thinking it saw a flicker of hope. She'd been thinking about a different island, about salvaging something else, an entirely different reason to talk to her father.

Kitt began to speak, but the front door suddenly opened with some force. Bryn froze, her mind going blank except for one thought: her father was home, James Selby with him. She'd known there was going to be hell to pay, but she'd hoped for a little time, a reprieve in which to marshal her resources, to think through her explanations. Apparently the devil was keen to collect his due.

Chapter Twenty-One

'Thank goodness you're all right!' Her father hugged her tight. His warm welcome was more than she deserved. 'When you didn't come home as expected, Sneed sent for me. We had no idea where you'd gone.'

'I'm fine.' Bryn pasted on a smile, guilt surging at the worry she'd caused. He'd cut short his business trip because of her. He had every justification to be furious. He could have shouted at her, could have berated her, could do far worse than that and yet he'd hugged her, his concern for her safety overriding all the other implications of her absence.

Her father's grip on her loosened and she could feel his attention shifting over her shoulder to Kitt. 'Thank you for seeing her home, for watching over her. Please, come join us on the veranda for a glass of falernum.'

It was masterfully done. Her father had set in motion the script by which he wanted her homecoming recorded for the public, for the servants, for James Selby. He was saving face for her, standing between her and disaster. He was saving face for Kitt, too, treating him as a trusted business acquaintance for all to see.

Beside her father, Bryn could see Selby visibly stiffen,

his eyes narrowing as they fixed on Kitt. Selby didn't believe the fiction, but he'd go along with it to curry favour with her father. There was nothing he could take issue with at the moment. 'Bryn darling, why don't you rest, have a bath brought up if you'd like.' Her father attempted to gently dismiss her. After all he'd done, she didn't want to defy his authority, but she would not leave the aftermath of this homecoming to a protective father, a jealous suitor, and a man who'd faced down pirates in a storm, not when that aftermath was about her.

She looped an arm through her father's. 'I will last a little longer.' She shot a look at Kitt. 'We have news that you both need to hear and I'd like to be there for it.'

Selby bristled and she realised too late the connotation he'd put on her words. Bryn rushed on hastily. 'It's about the Sunwood investment.' She wasn't about to blurt out the island didn't exist on the front lawn.

Hearing it over falernum wasn't much better, but at least it was private and it certainly served to distract everyone from the unanswered question of what she'd been doing with Kitt for five unchaperoned days. Of course, she'd rather have had a more pleasant distraction for them. Selby turned a startling shade of white and her father went very still as Kitt laid out the findings.

'I sailed out to the co-ordinates Selby gave Bryn.' Kitt gave Selby a sharp look. If Selby had lied, now would be the time to come clean. For her father's sake, Bryn almost hoped that would be the case, although it would certainly damage Selby's reputation. But Selby said nothing. 'I even thought I may have written them down in reverse,' Kitt added charitably, more face saving, this time for Selby. It was generous of him given that he owed Selby nothing and Selby was looking daggers at him.

'I sailed out to the other set of co-ordinates as well although they seemed too far out to be believable. But I wasn't ready to give up. The map did show a set of islands in that direction and there were islands there, just not developed islands.' Kitt paused and looked directly at her father. 'I thought you'd want to know right away.' He would not apologise for being the bearer of bad news. 'I am sure you understand this could mean trouble for the bank if it got out you and Selby had been taken advantage of.'

Her father nodded slowly, his shoulders, which had borne so much, starting to slump. Bryn's heart broke for him. They'd been so close to the fresh start he'd coveted, the bank nearly operational, the charter fulfilled, only to have it all poised on the brink of ruin.

'No one has to know,' Selby said quickly. 'We'll simply stop investing and that will be the end of it.' That was how Selby's rather facile mind worked. Everything was black and white, but Bryn saw the grey space. They couldn't simply walk away from this.

'We know who is behind this. I have the name,' Kitt said tersely, trying to avoid direct disagreement with Selby. 'We have to go after him. We are ethically obliged.'

Selby glared. 'You dare much to speak of ethical obligations after spending five days alone with a woman of good reputation.'

Bryn winced and took a hasty sip of falernum. Her father shot her a look. 'Were you with him? Is that where you went?'

'Yes.' She would not lie. She fixed Selby with a hard

stare, daring him to defy her. 'You do yourself little credit by painting with a sordid brush.' That was the difference between them. Selby was interested in self-protection, but she was interested in protecting others. She would not make Kitt pay for her bold plan.

She turned back to her father. 'Captain Sherard did not invite me. When I learned he was going out to see the island, I hid aboard the ship. I did not make my presence known until he was at sea and could not turn back.' The explanation seemed to placate him, but her father was an astute man. There would be more questions in private.

'I was glad I risked it,' Bryn continued staunchly, avoiding Kitt's eyes. 'Now you have two witnesses to the fact that the island doesn't exist, just in case there is any challenge to Captain Sherard's word.'

'I would not expose your presence needlessly,' Selby put in hastily. 'Sherard's word is enough for me.' He was quick to grovel after his misstep.

'As it should be,' her father spoke sharply. 'As the primary investors for the bank, we all rise and fall together. Dissension in our ranks cannot be tolerated. Anyone who cannot accept that is welcome to leave our association.'

'I couldn't agree more,' Selby affirmed. Bryn saw the faintest signs of a smile twitch on Kitt's lips. This was the victory she'd angled for with the announcement she'd share with all and sundry she'd been aboard the ship. She'd forced Selby to have to publicly acknowledge Kitt's word and accept his verdict. It was a secondary triumph to have removed herself from needing to make that testimony.

'So do we go after the villains?' Kitt circled the conversation back around to the point at which Selby had derailed it. 'I can have my ship ready and at your disposal the day after tomorrow.' He could have an official mandate for this next voyage.

'I think we must. I will assemble the board of directors tomorrow and explain the situation to them.' Her father blew out a breath, a man dreading but prepared to take responsibility for his errors. Her father had never shied away from his duty. He would not shirk it now.

Kitt leaned forward and spoke in earnest. 'Definitely assemble them, but do not play the martyr. Tell them you and Selby had made the investment as a trial in the hopes that if it was successful the bank could choose to be involved later. Tell them we've since learned it's a land swindle and we are setting out to bring the criminals to justice.'

Her father's face began to brighten. 'Yes, that could do the trick. There are no lies there. Your own involvement proves that. James and I truly *had* hoped to bring Sunwood to the investors' attention. We will look proactive in our response and in the immediacy of it. Thanks to you, Captain, we learned of the fraud right away before more than initial money was sunk into it.'

Bryn felt some of the knots in her stomach loosen. Kitt had managed the situation in a way that would not only save face for her father, but for the bank. Her father would look like a hero. The venture would be saved. She wanted to throw her arms about Kitt, wanted to thank him, but there was no chance. The men stood up and shook hands. Kitt barely looked at her, giving her the briefest, remotest of polite farewells. He might as well have been taking his leave of any hostess.

Selby gave every impression, however, of wanting to linger. Her father diplomatically disabused him of the notion with a firm hand on his shoulder. 'James, I am counting on you to call the meeting. Invite everyone for eleven o'clock tomorrow.' It was his *congé*. James smiled politely, his shoulders squaring with the importance of the task.

Her father had one last parting thought for him. 'James, a man is defined by the choices he makes in his hour of crisis.' In other words, James's future on the board would be contingent on his ability to embrace the phrase 'discretion is the better part of valour'. Nothing that occurred in this house was to be bandied about with anyone, not his magpie of a mother, nor with the other investors.

Her father's brave façade faded the second James Selby passed through the gate. He turned to her with worried eyes, looking every day of his fifty-five years and then some. She could do without reminders of his mortality. 'Why did you do it?' he asked quietly, sinking down into a chair in the little-used front parlour.

'Captain Sherard had indicated after the toast at dinner he was concerned about the nature of the investment. That made me worry, too, and I couldn't just sit back and wait.' But it had been more than that. The words tumbled out. 'You were leaving, going off with your new friends and partners on a trip you hadn't told me about, you were investing in plantations without a word of it to me.'

She twisted her hands in her skirts. 'You didn't need me any more and here was an opportunity to show you I was still useful.' She didn't feel twenty-three at the moment. She felt about eight, very small, very vulnerable. She'd felt vulnerable with Kitt, too, that last night. She didn't particularly like it. Exposing one's feelings was nasty, uncomfortable, risky work. No wonder Kitt was so reluctant to do it.

Her father's features softened, his eyes misty. 'You don't need to be useful to me, Bryn. You're my daughter, you're my whole world.' He waved a hand to indicate the house about them. 'We're here for you as much for me, after all.'

Complete acceptance of who she was flaws and all, the kind of acceptance she'd offered Kitt. The similarities struck her hard. Had it been as difficult for Kitt to accept as this was? Her father put a hand on each of his knees and straightened. 'This would be easier if your mother were here. She would know what to do, what to say. I'm afraid these sorts of delicate conversations elude me, they always have.' She sensed he was gathering himself. 'Do I need to bring Sherard up to scratch?'

'No, we had an agreement,' Bryn answered evenly.

Her father raised his eyebrows. 'Might I enquire as to the nature of the agreement? I may be old, Bryn, but I know what happens between men and women in close quarters. Captain Sherard has a certain reputation and you are a beautiful woman, so full of life like your mother. Do not play me for a fool.'

'Sherard is not the marrying type. I will not have him forced into anything he does not want,' Bryn said with finality. She wanted Kitt, but not like that—not bought and paid for with her father's money and influence. There were a hundred men she could have had in London under those terms. Such an arrangement would trap them both. Neither of them were looking for that sort of marriage.

Her father tapped a finger on his leg in thought. 'Sherard might not be the marrying sort, but James Selby is and he's made no secret of his esteem for you.' She started to protest. They'd had this discussion before. Her answer hadn't changed. Her father held up a hand to stall the interruption. 'Selby is a good man, a steady man, Bryn. With my guidance, he will become more astute. He is young yet, unpolished. He is bound to make mistakes like the Sunwood project in his eagerness to prove himself. But I will make him my protégé. He can be taught. If you need a husband, he would do admirably.'

What he meant was if she was pregnant, if there were consequences for her five days with Kitt. She looked down at her hands, her face colouring. Her father was offering to buy her a husband, to set that man up for life with the Rutherford connections and the banking charter all to make her and her child respectable. It was a generous offer, a loving offer that spoke again of being completely accepted flaws and all. 'Selby wouldn't be so bad,' her father argued with soft persuasion. 'Sometimes the quiet ones are just what wild souls need. They can have a calming, balancing effect.'

'Like you and Mother.' She looked up and shook her head. 'But that was true love.'

Her father looked uncomfortable for a moment, a look that was gone as soon as it came. She might have imagined it. 'Perhaps it's time for a confession. It was always love for me, but I think true love came later for her.'

Bryn wanted to argue—she had cut her teeth on stories of her parents' fairytale romance—but something in her father's gaze stopped her.

'I had no chance. I was a younger son, I was retiring.

I liked my numbers, I liked calculating odds. I had little use of society in practice. She was such a bright flame, always the centre of everyone's attention. My cousin the marquis was much the same, handsome, wild. Everything came easy for him, even Esme. When things come easy, it is hard to appreciate them. He did not appreciate Esme as a gentleman should appreciate a lady.

'There was a compromising incident, there was scandal, my cousin blamed Esme and would not do the right thing. Scandal is always more bearable for a man, especially when he has a title. Not so for a beautiful untitled woman with little claim to society beyond her looks. The Rutherfords understood my cousin's hesitation to marry so far beneath himself, but my brother was earl by then and he was eager to see the family redeemed. Suddenly, as the only unwed male close at hand, my odds started to improve. I couldn't believe my luck. Then you were born and I knew I was the luckiest man alive.'

Bryn knew she'd been born early in their marriage. A new suspicion took her as she let the story settle. 'Am I yours?'

He grinned. 'Most definitely. You were born twelve months almost exactly after the wedding.'

'And the scandal? Was there any truth to it?'

He nodded. 'Yes. She had been…well, indiscreet with my cousin, but that's not the point. Everyone makes mistakes. We don't love them the less for it.'

'You never held the past against Mother,' she said, implying that Selby would. He was all that her father said, but he was also petulant. His remark this afternoon indicated as much. He would hold Kitt Sherard over her head whenever he needed leverage for the rest of their lives. No amount of money or prestige her father threw Selby's way would change that.

Her father rose, perhaps sensing they'd reached another impasse on the subject of James Selby. 'Think on it, just in case. I'll have Cook make your favourite for dinner tonight.'

Bryn didn't want to think on it, but it was inescapable. No matter how far down in the bubbles of her bath she slid, she could not escape her thoughts. The story her father had told her threw her world off balance. It forced her to call into questions assumptions she'd taken for certain truth, assumptions about love, about marriage.

Whenever the villagers had recounted her parents' courtship, they'd conveniently left off the events leading up to it, the cousin mentioned only as a secondary character in the tale who had surfaced as competition for the charming Esme's hand, but who had been out-wooed by the quiet hero. There'd been no mention of Esme's desperate circumstances, or of the callous marquis's rejection, only of her father sweeping Esme off her feet in a whirlwind courtship.

She saw also how much her own situation paralleled her mother's. She, too, was wild. Her mother had feared her daughter would follow in her footsteps, throwing herself away on the squire's son who might also be too wild to care about the consequences. No wonder her mother had wanted her with someone stable, someone well situated like her father.

Bryn ran a cloth over her arms, washing them free of bubbles. It was no wonder her father favoured Selby. He saw himself in Selby. Perhaps she should, too. Her father was far wiser and far worldlier than she'd given him credit for. And, apparently, she was far less. True love didn't exist. Practicalities did. Perhaps the James Selbys of the world were the best a girl could hope for. Even her parents' marriage hadn't embodied the ideal, no matter what the local legend purported.

Perfection didn't exist because it *couldn't*. It wasn't a happy prospect. It was, however, a sobering one that required more answers than she had and those were answers that included the past, whether Kitt was willing to dredge it up or not.

This wasn't only about romance and love. In a larger sense it was about truth, something Kitt had been skating around. She had, too. She'd convinced herself it didn't matter in her new paradigm of living for the present, of living for herself. But it did.

If she was to go forward with Kitt, if she was to force him to admit he cared about her, that he didn't want this to end, there had to be truth. There had to be explanations about his past, which did exist whether he wanted it to or not. Everyone had one, even the man from nowhere. That his past involved an encounter of some sort with a land swindle seemed to make it even more pertinent considering their circumstances. These were answers she had to have no matter how painful they might be. Nothing more could happen without them.

Chapter Twenty-Two

'*I have a warrant for the arrest of Chase Melford on grounds of fraud.*' Kitt was dreaming of the past, of promises. They were all gathered in his father's office: himself, his mother, his father, his brother, older by two minutes and the heir. '*He is named as an active collaborator in the Forsythe scandal.*' His brother's face, Chase's face, was ashen as he listened. His brother probably was guilty and probably had been oblivious to what he had done. Finances weren't his brother's strong suit. He had other talents. Chase wasn't reckless, but he didn't often think about the long-term implications of his actions. He was heir to an earldom, he didn't have to.

Then had come the charges. If found guilty, he would face imprisonment. A title, his father's connections, wouldn't protect him now. Too many of the nobility had fallen in this scandal. In their desire for vengeance they would not protect one of their own if that one was guilty or if that one would provide a convenient scapegoat. It was said the Earl of Audley's heir had suffered a nervous breakdown over his investment in the non-existent island somewhere out in the Caribbean. Kitt had been friends with Audley's other son, Ashe Bedevere.

Kitt had thought his brother would faint at the mention of imprisonment. His brother would not survive this. The family would not survive this. But he would. He could save them and he could save himself, give himself the freedom he'd been craving. This was his chance, *their* chance.

Kitt crossed his legs and drawled indolently, 'You've got the wrong man. It's not him. It's me. He's entirely unaware. One might say I wooed in his name, to quote a little Shakespeare.'

His mother moved to protest, but a sharp look from his father silenced her. 'We are identical twins.' He explained the obvious to the inspector. 'It was no hard thing. I'm the one who convinced our friends to invest.' He quelled Chase's argument with a look only a twin would understand, a silent message: *let me save you. I love you. The family needs you to survive this intact.* Chase's eyes had met his: *Are you sure? I will trust you. I love you, too.*

The inspector had been hampered then by legalities. The warrant had the wrong name on it and could not be enforced. He'd left with a threat to return. 'I'll be back.'

I'll be gone, Kitt thought with a quiet calm—the magnitude of what he'd done hadn't fully settled, but the need for action had. His mind was already working. How much time did he have before the inspector was back? An hour?

The moment the door shut behind the man, Kitt was up the stairs, calling for a valise and all the money he could find in the house. He fired off instructions. Trunks could be sent to Ren later and Ren would get them to him. Chase was beside him, arguing all the way between orders. But not his practical father, who remained below, staring up at him from the bottom of the staircase with admiration and sadness before he moved to comfort his wife. His father understood it was the only way to save the family.

The transformation in his status amazed even him and he'd been the one to put it in motion. Only the night before, he'd been the darling of the ballroom, charming maids and matrons, his biggest concern in life being how to avoid his mother's matrimonial shenanigans. Less than twenty-four hours later, he'd become *persona non grata*, running for his life. 'My son, you can never come back—do you know what you've done?' his father had said, embracing him one last time.

He knew precisely what he'd done and he knew why he'd done it: to take all the stain upon himself, to save the family. Within an hour, he'd left it all behind, even his own name. Michael Melford could be traced. Kitt Sherard—a man from nowhere—couldn't be. So he'd become Kitt Sherard—Christopher from one of his middle names and the patron saint of travellers, Sherard for his mother's maiden name. He was a man with nothing but what he made for himself.

There was more to dream about, but the sun wouldn't let him. He had to wake and deal with what the day brought, starting with a meeting with the board of directors to sort this whole mess out. That wasn't the only sorting to be done. There was sorting to do with Bryn as well. Had things gone well for her after he'd left? Did she understand he'd meant it when he'd said 'no expectations'?

Kitt splashed water on his face and reached for a clean shirt. He'd not played fair there. He knew what she thought—that he wouldn't marry her because he refused to abide by society's dictates in that regard. The reality was quite different. He couldn't marry her because of the risk to her and to his family.

How could he tell her what he'd done? What if she knew the nightmares he dreamed? If he told her the truth, she might understand. But one more person knowing Kitt Sherard was nothing but a mask for another man put them all at risk. If England ever discovered him, he was dead. He could offer Bryn very little. They could never return to London. This was a secret that had to be kept for ever.

Kitt finished dressing and broke his fast downstairs with the other boarders. He spoke little, his mind on the upcoming interviews, on other fantasies. Would Bryn be surprised to know he would have her if he could? The realisation had stunned him the first time he'd thought it. But the more he took it out and examined it, the less shocking it became. He took it out now as he walked to the meeting.

He had fabricated domestic fantasies aplenty of a future with Bryn lending her touch to his home; Bryn wading in the surf, her skirts held above the waves, her hair flying loose about her shoulders as she laughed with him; Bryn in his bed, the big mahogany one at the villa with the down bedding. Bryn with his son, *their son*, on her hip. Ah, that was the most dangerous image of all. A child. One more person to protect. It was the most potent, too, the one with the power to lure him away from the lonely discipline he'd worked so hard to acquire.

* * *

He was not the first to arrive at Rutherford's. Harrison and Crenshaw were already there, and Selby. He shook hands and greeted everyone, his eyes distracted already as they searched the room for Bryn. He wondered if she would sit in. She had valuable information to contribute, to be an alibi for his story if nothing else. But perhaps it was best she didn't. There was no need to bring their association to anyone's attention, especially if Selby's reaction yesterday was anything to go on. Selby had immediately jumped to sordid conclusions.

Unfortunately, those conclusions were accurate, but irrelevant to the situation. They only served to muddy the waters. The first priority was to get permission to go after Devore. Technically, he didn't need permission. He'd go after Devore regardless. Permission would simply determine on what grounds. Did he have permission to make the land swindle part of his vendetta or would this remain a private affair between the two men?

The rest arrived and took their seats around Rutherford's long dining-room table. Bryn was not coming, but Rutherford left the doors open ostensibly to catch the breeze. Kitt hid a smile. Bryn was in the house and he'd wager his fortune she was listening somewhere.

Rutherford made an initial statement about the situation and turned to Kitt. 'Mr Sherard undertook a short voyage to the supposed destinations. I'll ask him to share what he found.'

Kitt nodded and began to speak. 'The Sunwood Plantation does not exist at these co-ordinates…' He unrolled a map and pinned it down with candlesticks. He pointed to different places, tracing his voyage. It seemed like he talked for ages. He shared what he had found, how he had found it and gone on to a second set of co-ordinates to be sure. There was outrage and questions. He fielded the questions patiently, explaining how the scheme was set up, how this was not the first time. It was easy enough to do out here in the uncharted ocean with thousands of islands.

When he finished, silence descended on the table. Selby had been uncharacteristically quiet, as well he might, since it was his rashness that had brought this upon them. Now, Selby leaned forward, locking eyes with him. 'How is it that you know so much about land swindles? You seem highly informed for a man of your background.'

Kitt braced himself on his arms and leaned across the table. 'What are you saying, James? Is there an accusation you wanted to make?'

'I don't know—should I be concerned about one? You have to admit your recommendations are not the best.'

Kitt raised an eyebrow at this. Those were fighting words. There was much he would tolerate for himself, but he would not hear a word against Ren. They had been friends since their school days, not that he could call on that allegiance now without giving too much away. To do so would indicate he had noble connections in England as opposed to the fiction he and Ren fabricated here—they were business partners. How else would the lofty Earl of Dartmoor know a rum runner? 'Careful, James. You question Dartmoor's reputation.'

Crenshaw broke in. 'Gentleman, an internal squabble is hardly beneficial to us at this point. We have more important concerns. Selby, I think there is no purpose in doubting Sherard's information in this instance.'

Kitt gave Crenshaw a curt nod of thanks and backed away from the table. 'You all have much to discuss and you know my opinion. Rutherford, I'll avail myself of the hospitality of your garden while you talk amongst yourselves.' He shot James a look. 'I don't want to unduly influence your decisions.'

Rutherford began to protest that he was on the board of directors, too. Kitt raised a hand to stall any further comment. 'I am and I have offered my opinion. My boat and my services are at your disposal. Perhaps you would discuss things more freely in my absence.' He wanted to go in search of Bryn and there was truly nothing more he could say. He would go after Devore no matter what their decision.

In the garden, the air was cooler, the heat of the afternoon had not yet settled. The smell of sweet hibiscus was on the breeze and it soothed his temper. He drew a deep breath, letting some of the tension go from his body. Selby deserved a thrashing for his comment. He stilled. Someone was in the garden with him, behind him. He could feel them.

'I want to know the answer to Selby's question.' Bryn's voice was quiet.

'You were eavesdropping. I thought you might be.' He could not look at her. If he did, he'd be lost. He held himself rigid, willing her not to move into his line of sight.

'Don't make this about me, Kitt. You told me you were involved in a land swindle. I did not press you then for an answer, but I am asking for one now.'

'Why should I tell you? If you're asking, you've already assumed the worst. Obviously you have doubt.'

'I have what you've allowed me to have.' There was

some steel, some heat in her voice. 'I think you want me to believe the worst. When I first met you, you led me to believe you were nothing more than a house-breaker, only for me to discover you a few hours later in the company of gentlemen.'

Kitt snorted. 'Your logic is ludicrous. Why would I want that?' But she was far too close to the truth.

'It's how you keep people at a distance, how you en-sure you're alone.' Bryn didn't hesitate with her answer. She'd thought this out and that frightened him. What else had she thought out? What else had she realised despite his attempts to obfuscate it?

'I'm not in the habit of keeping beautiful women at a distance.'

'Only the ones that upset you. I disturb the balance of your universe,' Bryn argued.

'I suppose you upset a great many men then.' They were moving ever so slowly away from the intent of her conversation. Kitt was beginning to feel a little relief. Maybe he could distract her after all.

Then she ruined it. She pulled on his arm, forcing him to face her. 'Dammit, Kitt, tell me—did you swin-dle men out of their money or was it you who was swin-dled?'

She was furious. Her face was flushed, her eyes al-most feverish in their intensity. He'd pushed her further than he'd realised. 'Tell me. Everything depends on it.'

Everything did. The board's belief in his informa-tion, his credibility, more than that, his future depended on it. If he told her, he could win her, he could outbid Selby. But she'd never be able to tell another. Could he trust her with that? Why did everything that happened between them in this garden come down to trust?

'I can't tell you because my life depends on it, Bryn,' he said simply. He felt tired, defeated, as if he'd fought this battle for too long.

Bryn sat down on the bench and motioned for him to sit beside her. He didn't. He didn't want to be that close to her. 'It's hard, isn't it? To trust another. You wanted me to trust you. It didn't seem so difficult when you were asking it because you knew I could trust you. But I didn't know. Now, the shoe is on the other foot. I know you can trust me, but you don't know, not for sure.' She reached for his hand, not willing to accept his resistance. 'I trusted you with my body and with my reputation. That is a woman's life. You can trust me with yours, Kitt.'

But he wasn't going to. Bryn felt defeat lurking. She was going to lose, not just this argument, but *him*. He wasn't going to tell her and she simply couldn't tolerate that. He knew it, too—this was a decision not only about sharing his secret, but a decision about them. It was his last defence in pushing her away. Then suddenly, he sat and he began to talk.

'My name hasn't always been Kitt. My brother was involved in the Forsythe scandal in England in thirty-one. Do you remember it? It was over a Caribbean island that was supposed to be colonised. Unwittingly, my brother invested and convinced several families to invest heavily as well. As a consequence, a lot of people lost a lot of money. Some lost their lives. Some had invested so deeply they committed suicide. One young man had a nervous breakdown. He never recovered. He's in an asylum today.'

She watched Kitt's profile, the firm line of his jaw working as he spoke. It took all her discipline not to prompt him. He would share in his own time. 'I could save my brother, but I couldn't save them. My brother and I are identical twins born two minutes apart. I took the blame and I fled. He and my family would be exonerated by my departure and by my assumption of the guilt. People will pity them, but people will hate me. I can never go back to England. Some of those people may even hate me enough to hunt me. I may not have to go back to England to seek death. It may find me. Do you understand? People believe I cost them their loved ones, their livelihoods.'

Bryn nodded. She understood other things, too—the depth of commitment to family it took for him to make that sacrifice. The hidden depths of nobility, real nobility, that had nothing to do with rank. His sacrifice made hers look minute in comparison. He was a bold man, a brave man, who had doomed himself to exile for the sake of his family. She was not foolish enough to argue platitudes with him, that perhaps there was another way or that maybe in time things would be different.

'Maybe I could have saved more of them if I had stayed.' Kitt's gaze was faraway. 'Perhaps I could have helped some of the families, maybe I could have done more if I'd stayed, but I couldn't bear to see my brother suffer, couldn't bear to see my family become outcasts. No matter how many people I helped, I wouldn't be able to save my family. In the end, I chose my family over others—the few instead of the many. And maybe I chose my own freedom over all of it without fully understanding the price.'

He turned to look at her. 'Now you know why I know so much about land swindles.' She knew a lot more than that.

Chapter Twenty-Five

He looked glorious! For however long she lived, the image of Kitt would be burned on her mind. He was Poseidon rising from the sea, or Apollo come to earth. His skin gleamed in the sun, sleek and greased from liberal quantities of oil, his bare chest crossed by a bandolier of pistols, a long knife sheathed at his waist. But it wasn't the weapons that made him formidable. It was the set of his jaw and the hardness of his eyes. This was no Poseidon or Apollo. This was Ares, god of war, come to do battle. Hope surged. Poisoned knife blades diminished in the face of this avenging warrior.

'Let her go, Devore!' Kitt's voice rang out with authority across the beach. His men faced Devore's in a menacing line, each of them bristling with weapons. Kitt's message was clearly communicated: this could be a blood bath. His men were prepared to fight for her. 'It's me you want.' Kitt held his arms wide in a pointless gesture of peace. He was armed to the teeth. It didn't matter there wasn't a weapon in his hand at present. He could have one there in seconds.

When Devore said nothing, Kitt called out his offer

'Thank you. Your secret is safe with me, always.' She squeezed his hand. He had told her much, but not everything. He was protecting her still. It had not escaped her attention that he'd omitted names, his real name particularly. But it was enough. He would tell her more when he was ready.

Kitt rose. 'I should go. I'll be leaving to go after Devore in a day or two no matter what they decide in there. Until then, it would be best if we kept our distance from one another, I think.'

If he came back. She heard the underlying message. Going after Devore was dangerous. She'd seen that danger first-hand. 'Do you have to go?' It was a stupid question, but it made Kitt smile.

'If Ren or Emma, or you, want to be safe, I have to go. Devore is a menace to us alive. He's a menace to your father and the bank as well.' He bent forward and placed a kiss on her cheek. 'I will see you again and we will talk when it is settled.' He swept the back of his hand along the line of her cheek. 'Don't look so glum, Bryn. You have victories enough to celebrate today.'

It was a significant victory to know he was not guilty. At the end of the day, he was a good man who cared for others no matter how he tried to muddy the waters to the contrary. Her conscience was free to love him and she would. For now, that would be her secret. She reached up for his hand where it lay against her cheek. 'Be safe.' She would tell him the rest *when* he came back.

Chapter Twenty-Three

It was safe to assume Sherard knew the island didn't exist and by now he must surely know they were behind the plantation swindle. Hugh Devore paced the floor of what passed as his office, nothing near as elegant as the one he'd had on Barbados. That was one more sin to lay at Kitt Sherard's feet: the lack of any luxury, any comfort. It had taken months to get this far. Just when they were making progress, Sherard had to interfere again.

It proved he was right. They should not have waited to go after Sherard. But Blakely had made a strong case of operating from a position of strength and Devore had agreed. At the time, it seemed sound. Now, Hugh Devore wondered otherwise. A position of strength also meant there was more to lose. They had the business to protect from exposure. The scales had tipped. No longer were they hunting Sherard, he was also hunting them. Their offence had been minimised.

'We have to act now and we have to act fast.' Devore spun on his heel to face Blakely and the first mate. Damn, but his forces were reduced. He had to act fast for other reasons, too. He'd lose the first mate once the

man's brother was free. He had no illusions the pair
would stay around after this last run in with Sherard.
He'd temporary lose his ability to chase Sherard on
water until he could find another captain.

'Beyond revenge, killing Sherard won't stop the swindle from leaking out,' Elias Blakely put in weakly. He
was getting nervous and Devore worried about losing
him, too. Blakely had no ethical qualms about swindling
people on paper when it was just numbers in a ledger,
but when lives were on the line, the man became positively squeamish.

Devore whirled on him with a hard stare, enjoying
how it made the man squirm. 'Is revenge not enough?
Have you forgotten what Sherard has done to us? Have
you forgotten what you had? The luxury in which you
used to live? Sherard took that from us, dropped us off
on an island with only what we could carry. He made
us no better than worms.'

'He let us live,' Blakely answered. 'We escaped a
trial.'

'At a price!' Devore roared. 'It is no small thing.' This
was not the time for Blakely to have cold feet. But he
was right about one aspect: there were more people involved. Silencing Sherard would not prevent others from
knowing. By now Sherard would have told Rutherford
and Rutherford would have told Selby.

If he was lucky, it would stop there, the two investors being too embarrassed to confess it publicly to the
bank board. If he was unlucky, the bank board would
know, too. Devore felt a moment of stinging regret. If
not for Sherard, if not for the failed sugar cartel and the
debacle at Sugarland, he too might have been asked to
sit on the board as one of Barbados's leading financiers.

Heaven knew he'd had the money to do so at one time. Sherard could pay for that, too.

Blakely piped up one more time, a sure sign of how nervous he truly was—nervous enough to stand up to him rather than face Sherard. 'We should take what we have and go. Barbados is dead to us, we can never go back there. In fact, the whole Caribbean is dead to us. Sherard will not rest until he finds us. We should go up to Florida or to New Orleans and start again.'

It wasn't a bad idea, but being chased off left a sour taste in Devore's mouth. He nodded, a plan starting to form. Blakely was right. Now that things had come to a head, there wouldn't be anything left here for them even if they did have their revenge. 'All right, two days, Blakely. You have two days to organise our departure.'

Blakely gave a tremulous smile, hardly daring to believe he'd won an argument. 'What will you be doing?'

Devore fingered the sharp blade of his letter opener. 'I will be picking up a passenger, a little insurance to make sure Sherard keeps his distance.' He motioned to the first mate. 'You're with me. You and I have a trip to make to the mainland. I've decided a new start requires a new bride.'

The start of 'life without Kitt' hadn't gone well. Bryn had lasted in the house all of a half-hour after yet another bankers' meeting began before she'd grabbed her market basket and stormed out to shop. Not that it counted as truly storming out. There'd been no one to see. The men had all been gathered around the big table in the dining room, deep in conversation. No one had paid her any attention or known she was gone, or for that matter even known she was in a temper. Not even Kitt, who had greeted her with stiff politeness when he'd arrived in the company of Mr Harrison and Mr Crenshaw as if they'd not shared an incredible conversation the day before, in some regards a life-changing conversation. Apparently, 'life without Bryn' was going better for him than 'life without Kitt' was going for her.

She'd not thought it would be like this. She'd imagined something more tragically romantic when she'd pictured them meeting in the interim—eyes full of soulful, secret looks of longing, of regret that there couldn't be more all in hopes that some day it might be possible. Good lord, she'd never thought of herself as the swoony type. She was supposed to be more practical than this, more like Kitt. It would get better. In a week or two this would all be over. She and Kitt could move on to exploring other possibilities.

Bryn selected some fruits from a stall and put them in her basket, realising too late one of them was rotten. She had to pay attention! She couldn't wander around absentmindedly thinking about Kitt. She'd get herself run over by a cart or...

'Miss? Could you come with me?' a big beefy man said at her elbow. Where he'd come from was anyone's guess. She'd not been aware of him when she'd started shopping, then again, she'd not been aware of much. His tone was polite, but he was not familiar to her. 'I have a message I need you to relay.'

Bryn studied his features, trying to recall if she'd seen him before, someone perhaps from the gala dinner. No, she did not know him. 'I'm not expecting any messages. Forgive me, but we have not been introduced. Perhaps you should arrange a meeting with my father directly.' It was a bit haughty of her and she smiled to soften the politely delivered blow, but her instincts cried out that such a tactic was necessary. Something about him made her uncomfortable. Perhaps it was simply that he stood too close to her, crowding her. 'If you'll excuse me? I'm meeting some friends.'

He didn't budge. His eyes narrowed, sending a chill through her in spite of the warm sun. 'Liar. You left the house alone and you're meeting no one.'

Cold fear came to her. She'd been followed and she hadn't even known. This was her fault. This was what she got for letting her thoughts daydream over Kitt. She needed to get away. She had no weapon to hand, no real weapon at least. Her hand closed over the rotten piece of fruit in her basket. It would do.

Bryn took a step back and threw the slimy missile, hitting him squarely in the face. He yowled in disgusted surprise, his hands clawing at his face to wipe away the oozing fruit, his attentions distracted momentarily. Bryn dropped the basket and ran…straight into a solid wall of unfriendly muscle who wasted no time wrestling her into a quiet alley away from the eyes of the market. There was no time to scream, barely even time to fight before she was shoved rather roughly into a dark interior, the door of the old storehouse clanging shut behind her taking the light with it. She could see nothing, but her captor was still with her. She could hear him breathing in the dark.

'What is the meaning of this?' she railed, trying to get her bearings, her mind reeling. She was certain now that this was an abduction attempt. Had anyone noticed? Was someone from the market even now on their way to her father?

'You will see, the boss has plans for you,' came the reply, thick with an island accent.

'Who is the boss?' she tried, desperate for information. Anything she could learn would help her escape and, if not escape, then help her negotiate. What did they want?

Light flooded the little chamber for a moment before it was cut off by a bulky form. 'I am the boss.' The man from the market. She recognised the voice and the shape.

He approached, walking with a pronounced limp. That limp should mean something to her. Her mind raced, trying to recall the memory. He was close, crowding her again in the dim room as he had in the market. She stood her ground, refusing to back up. In the small space there was nowhere to move, no way to evade him that wouldn't make her look foolish. To back away would appear cowardly and give proof to her fear. Better, she reasoned, to meet him with her chin up.

He chuckled at her show of defiance. 'Sherard has himself a spitfire this time.' He put his hand beneath her chin, turning her face this way and that in the dimness. 'A pretty one, too.'

Devore. The name came to her. Kitt had told her once that Devore limped as a result of a bullet he'd put in the man's knee. She understood much of this now. Thwarted at sea in an attempt to keep Kitt from reaching land, knowing Kitt would expose the swindle, Devore had decided to take her hostage. Perhaps he thought to use her as leverage for Kitt's silence. Perhaps he thought to blackmail Kitt into abdicating his claim of fraud. Perhaps she was to be the lure to draw Kitt out into the open. Perhaps he simply wanted to strike back and take something of value. He might have misjudged her worth if that was what he hoped.

'You assume too much if you think Kitt will come for me,' she said with a nonchalance she didn't feel.

He started to move about her in a predatory circle, his eyes crawling over her form with undisguised lascivious intent. 'I don't assume too much at all. I saw him on deck with you that first night out, before you knew we were there.'

Her cheeks burned, but Devore wasn't done. 'Now that I know what you like, I'll be sure to provide you with the same service.' Bryn cringed inwardly at the thought. Outwardly, she remained stoic, her eyes forward, focused on the wall. Even with a theoretical understanding of her role in Devore's private battle with Kitt, his next words were chilling.

'I've decided…' Devore came to stand in front of her. She looked past him to the space over his shoulder '…that we shall be married. That will put you beyond Sherard's reach as long as I live.'

'He will kill you!' Bryn spat, her words hastily and poorly chosen in the wake of Devore's shocking revelation. The proposition invoked no small amount of fear.

'Ha! So he does care? I thought so.' He smiled evilly, grabbing her wrists and dropping a loop of rope over them. He tugged and she felt the rope bite into skin as he jerked her forward. 'Philippe, the blindfold please, we're ready to go.'

Brave or not, Bryn did struggle then, putting up a fight as the other man bound a cloth over her eyes. She wanted to know where they were going, wanted to seize any opportunity to get away. But she was no match for his muscled brawn any more than she had been in the marketplace. But it was Devore who ended it with a stiff slap across her face that left her stunned by the show of brutality.

'There will be no resistance, my dear. If you try my patience, you will learn there are worse things than a slap in the face.' His calm tones belied the violence he'd just meted out. 'Philippe, I think a gag is in order, too. I'll wager this one's a screamer.'

The gag smelled and she involuntarily turned her face away in an attempt to avoid it. But Devore pressed it to her mouth and nose, forcing her to breathe deeply of the foul rag. Her head began to swim, her mind registering too late this was no mean gesture designed to be a show of power. She felt consciousness slipping away, the one thing she was desperate to hang on to, the only thing she had left that gave her any control. A small, panicked moan escaped her. 'No...' But that was all.

Kitt was desperate to hang on to his sanity. The bankers' meeting had gone on for what seemed an interminable amount of time. How much more was there to say? Devore was guilty of fraud, he needed to be brought in. Yet these men were determined to turn the decision into a two-hour discussion. Didn't they see they were losing valuable time? Even now, Devore might be sailing away with his profits. If he escaped them, the bank's reputation would be ruined before it even started.

But the bank's reputation wasn't Kitt's only concern. He was losing time, too—he wanted this settled so he could focus on Bryn. What could he risk offering her? It had been torture to see her that morning, to be in her house, to know she was near and not be able to reach out to her. He wanted this latest adventure to be over. He wanted to know she was safe.

He'd barely slept the previous night. His thoughts had been haunted with 'what ifs'—what if he gave up his business? He didn't *need* to run cargo. He was wealthy enough to live off investments and live more tamely. But that wasn't him. It would be like giving up his soul. And yet Bryn moved him, touched him at his core with her love for adventure, with her loyalty. To turn his back on what she offered him was no small thing. He'd felt the absence of her in his bed quite acutely for reasons that went beyond sex. By the time the sun had risen he was no closer to an answer.

Sneed entered the dining room, quietly passing an envelope to Rutherford. Kitt followed the interaction with his eyes, his mind desirous of any distraction. The conversation had long since bored him. Rutherford looked perplexed, turning the note over in his hand.

'I believe this is for you, Sherard.' Rutherford looked down the table at him as Sneed brought the unopened envelope. Kitt took it, apprehension running through him. This was no ordinary note. Passemore brought the mail to the boat or to the house. How would any note know to find him here? Or why?

Kitt slit the envelope and read. It was a wedding invitation done up on formal, heavy cream paper. His gaze stalled on the first line at the sight of Hugh Devore's name. His heart began to pound. The next line confirmed his fears. The bastard had taken Bryn. Devore had her even now and had done who knew what to her while they'd sat discussing their options. And it was his fault. He'd exposed her to Devore. Devore somehow knew Bryn mattered to him, although he'd certainly given Devore plenty of chances to learn of it. He'd been careless. This was a direct blow, not so much about the swindle, but about personal revenge. Devore blamed him for his wife's desertion. Now he sought to take a woman in place of the one Kitt had taken from him.

Stay calm. Show these gentlemen nothing, he counselled. Panic would do no one any good, certainly not Bryn. He looked up at Rutherford and the others, eyeing them in turn. 'While we have been discussing our situation *ad nauseam*, Devore has taken action.' After hours of noise and babble, silence fell on the table, awkward and heavy. Kitt tossed the invitation into the centre. 'He's taken Rutherford's daughter.'

Chapter Twenty-Four

Rutherford paled. 'We must go after him.' He'd already half-risen in his seat, prepared to rush to Bryn's aid, all foolish, noble loyalty. It twisted the knife of guilt a little more in Kitt's gut. He'd jeopardised Bryn.

'It's what he wants.' Selby spoke coolly from his place at the table, his voice drawing everyone's attention.

'Of course it's what he wants,' Rutherford said impatiently. 'He means to ransom Bryn for our silence on the matter of the island.'

'No, it's what *he* wants.' Selby jabbed a finger in Kitt's direction. Kitt bristled. What fresh conspiracy did Selby seek to convict him of now? 'Sherard would like nothing better than to marshal your legitimate resources to fight his less-than-legitimate-war with Devore. Why risk himself when he could have the bank intervene instead?'

Kitt watched Harrison's eyes narrow. 'What is this about, Sherard? Is there any truth to it? There had better not be a secret agenda.'

'Do you expect him to answer that truthfully?' Selby cut in before Kitt could respond. 'Devore wants revenge for Sherard and Dryden exiling him and the Gridley gang last summer.'

Kitt shifted uncomfortably in his seat. Selby had said too much. Couldn't the man see he'd nearly betrayed Bryn? A smart man at the table would see the missing link of logic. Crenshaw decided to be that man. 'I thought this was about the land swindle. What does abducting a banker's daughter have to do with Sherard's little vendetta? I thought Rutherford had the right of it: Devore wants to trade the daughter for our silence.'

Selby paled, recognising his mistake too late. To explain further meant publicly pairing Kitt with Bryn. Kitt tensed, waiting for Selby to back down. 'Well, Sherard was the one that discovered the island was a hoax,' he said weakly.

Kitt decided to enter the fray. These men would talk themselves to death, meanwhile Bryn was in some very real peril. 'We have to go after her. We can sort out the particulars of my motives later.'

'We don't know where he's at,' Selby said sulkily.

'Yes, we do. It's on the invitation.' Kitt pushed the card towards Selby. Tortoise Island, six o'clock. It was just past three now. Barely enough time to get his ship under way and go, but perhaps Devore was counting on that; there wouldn't be enough time to ride for Ren and rally the plantation workers. There would only be enough time to assemble Kitt's crew and whichever investors might choose to come.

Selby picked up the invitation and tossed it back down again. 'If it's so obvious where to find her, it must be a trap.'

'Of course it's a trap,' Kitt said through gritted teeth. He was going to strangle Selby in a minute. 'That doesn't mean we don't go.' That sounded very similar to something Bryn had said to him not so long ago. Then, he'd been the Selby in the room.

Kitt pushed back from the table. 'The *Queen* sails at four. If anyone feels inclined to come, be on board. The tide won't wait. If we mean to make Tortoise Island by six, we need to catch it.' They needed the wind to hold as well. He didn't want to alarm Rutherford, but it would take all the speed the *Queen* could muster to make that deadline. He was starting to suspect that had been Devore's plan all along—to have them arrive too late.

Not that the marriage would be binding. Devore would be a bigamist if he claimed marriage to Bryn. It wasn't the theoretical that worried Kitt, it was the practical. Devore wouldn't hesitate to consummate the marriage such as it was and Bryn wouldn't hesitate to fight it even though she'd be no match for Devore's brute strength.

Kitt strode down the front steps of Rutherford's town house at a near run, stuck on the image of Bryn resisting. A litany took up residence in his mind: *Don't fight, don't fight.* But he knew she would. She wouldn't give in even at risk to her personal safety. Bryn was stubborn and tenacious. Heaven help him, it was what he loved about her.

Something pulled on his arm and he turned to see Selby beside him, jogging to keep up. 'Sherard, stop and face me like a man!' Selby nearly shouted. That did it. Kitt had all he was going to take from the likes of James Selby, who had arguably brought all of this to a head with his foolish investment.

Kitt seized him by the front of his jacket and hauled

him up against a fence post, roaring his displeasure. 'Take your hands off me or I will squash you like an ant!'

Selby was not daunted. 'Are you happy now? You have everyone running to do your bidding, to rescue Miss Rutherford for you, to finish your vendetta for you. Do you care for her at all or is she just a means to more of your sordid ends?'

Ah, Kitt understood the man's rage. He should have known. Perhaps he *had* known and had conveniently chosen to ignore the facts. Selby was in love with her. Of course he was. What man wouldn't worship Bryn Rutherford from afar? Or up close if he could? Like he had. A man like Selby wouldn't dare the latter. Still, Kitt was in no mood to tolerate Selby's assumptions.

'I should call you out for that!' Kitt snarled, his face close to Selby's. Let the man see his anger. It would make his forgiveness seem all the more generous. 'Your feelings for her do you credit, but your emotions do not.' He shook Selby once and stepped back. 'Curb your temper before it makes you foolish.' He could spare no more time for Selby. He had a boat to make ready and a woman to redeem.

Beyond that, he didn't dare to think of what came after. Bryn would be despising him by now. No matter how moving their last conversation had been, no matter how many subtle promises had been made, no professions of love would override the fact that the danger he put her in was very real. It was no longer hypothetical as it had been on the ship. She was experiencing it first-hand and she would not thank him for it. She could not ignore that part of his life. If she was smart, she would understand why she couldn't be part of it. If *he* was smart, he'd give up his fantasies. He couldn't have her. He couldn't let her live this way for him.

He was regretting having been so cool towards her that morning. She might even be wondering if he would come for her. He hated that the most, that Bryn would doubt him, but he'd given her no reason to believe otherwise. How many times had he warned her he would not play the gentleman? But surely she knew someone would come? Maybe that didn't inspire much confidence if she thought those someones would be her father and Selby, hardly two knights in shining armour when it came to overcoming the likes of Devore. *I am coming, Bryn.* He cast his gaze to the sky as he hurried towards the harbour. The winds would hold. They had to. He would reach her in time. He had to. Nothing else mattered.

Kitt would reach her in time. He would come, if not out of his own volition, out of her father's. Bryn stretched and twisted on the cot, trying to find relief for her sore arms without upsetting her stomach with any sudden movements. Whatever had been on the rag had made her nauseous. When she'd come to the journey had been over. The blindfold and gag had been removed, a sure sign they were no longer necessary. But she was just as helpless. She was stuck on the cot, her hands still tied and the rope connected to a ring fixed in the side of the hut.

Were they still on Barbados? Had they sailed somewhere else? If she managed to get free, where would she go? At the moment, such considerations seemed moot.

The hut opened, admitting the hulking form of Devore. He was carrying a box. 'You're awake, just in

time. Do you know what is in here?' He lifted the lid
and set the box down across her lap. He parted the tis-
sue and pulled out a gown. 'Your wedding dress, isn't it
lovely? I got it in a trade a while back with a merchant
ship.' He shook out the expensive confection. 'It should
be close enough to your size.'

'The same way you were trading for Kitt's rum? By
ambush?' Bryn managed to get out past her dry lips.
'I'd rather go naked.'

'That can be arranged, my little virago.' He set the
box down and walked to the crude little table and the
pitcher that sat on it. 'Thirsty?' He poured a cup of water
and Bryn tried to appear uninterested while he drank
it front of her, giving a wet, satisfied smack of his lips
when he finished. 'It's cold. It's very good water actually.
Would you like some? Perhaps we could reach an agreement? You put on the dress, and I'll give you a drink.'

Bryn was far more interested in what the deal implied. Her hands would be free! Free hands created possibilities. Her mind was whirring. Free hands could
smash the water jug, free hands could pick up a pot-
tery shard from the broken jug and wait for a moment
to swipe the jagged edge across Devore's leering face.
She would take the deal, but she didn't dare appear too
excited by it or Devore would suspect something. With
great reluctance she eyed the water jug, her posture
feigning defeat as she managed one hoarse word. 'Yes.'

Devore bent over her, slicing a thin, wicked blade
through the ropes, the big paunch of his stomach in her
face as he cut. He laughed at her discomfort, but he held
out the cup of water and watched as she drank it. The
water was good. She let it slide down her throat, but her
enjoyment was short lived. He yanked the empty cup

away. 'You've had your drink. Now, put on the dress.' His eyes gestured to the box on the cot and he settled into the hut's one chair.

Dread settled over her. He didn't mean to leave. He laughed again, this time at her hesitation. 'Don't give me this maidenly modesty act, Miss Rutherford. You have no modesty. I saw you with Sherard, with him buried between your legs.' He played with his knife, drawing her eyes to the long blade. 'Get on with it before I decide to not be nice, although I should warn you, I like it when you fight.'

Bryn slid down the short puffed sleeves of her gown, her fingers slowly working the laces at her back. For now, what choice did she have? To undress herself was better than having someone else do it for her, a scene she rather thought Devore would enjoy a little too much. The man was repulsive. When the time came, she would have no trouble slicing, gutting, cutting, whatever it took. She had no empathy for this cretin who took so much pleasure in degrading others. That time would come. There was a rescue party on its way to her. Devore had arranged it, a final showdown between him and Kitt. The only question was how would Kitt compete against Devore's men. She was merely the bait to draw Kitt out.

'Now the chemise,' Devore growled, a hand riding his crotch. 'No sense wearing anything beneath that wedding dress when I'll be taking it off you soon enough.'

Bryn closed her eyes. *Just get it over with. Watching can't hurt you.* It was with some relief that she slipped into the dress, her skin covered once more. There was a rap on the door of the hut and she clutched the loose dress to her. One of Devore's henchmen entered.

'Best get on with it, Boss. We've got Sherard's ship in our sights, just rounded the headland.'

'The headland!' Devore roared. 'How did he get so close? We were supposed to have seen him long before this.'

The man shrugged, backing away from Devore's wrath. 'You can go see for yourself, Boss.'

Devore lurched to his feet, grabbing her by the wrist in a vicious grip. He dragged her towards the door. 'It looks like we'll have to speed things up a bit.'

'You're in an awfully big hurry to die,' Bryn snapped, tripping behind him, her feet tangling in the skirts. 'You can't possibly think you're his equal in combat. He's faster, stronger, younger, he'll wear you down.' Perhaps she could sow some doubt that would turn Devore from this course.

She shouldn't have provoked him. Devore hauled her to him, drawing his knife, the blade the only thing between them. 'This is the great equaliser. I don't need to be stronger or faster. I only need to prick him with the smallest of cuts and the poison will do the rest, a nice trick I picked up from the natives.'

'Killing Kitt won't stop people from knowing about the swindle. You can't kill all of us.' It was all bravado at this point. The knife was a frightening weapon indeed. The relief she'd felt in hearing Kitt had arrived was replaced by a paralysing fear. Kitt could die without even knowing what had wounded him, without knowing that she loved him.

'I'm not interested in stopping the news,' Devore sneered. 'I'm interested in revenge. When I've had it, I will sail away with my new bride.' He brandished the knife dangerously near her face. 'And when I've tired of her or she has displeased me one too many times, I will discard her, too. How long do you think you'll last, my dear? A few days, a week? Years?'

Bryn wanted to make a grand gesture as she stumbled ignobly behind Devore out into the sun. Perhaps a braver soul would opt to prick herself on the deadly blade right now and end it by taking away Devore's leverage, or say something grand like 'I'd rather die than contemplate years with you', but it wasn't true. She wanted to live so very much. She wanted to swim with dolphins, shower beneath waterfalls, and make love on white sandy beaches with Kitt. All of it with Kitt. If that made her a coward, then so be it. She would find a way to warn him.

Devore brought her up short at the treeline where the jungle gave way to beach. 'Don't think about warning him. I have a blade for you, too.' He motioned to a big, swarthy man with scars on his chest. 'If you cry one word of warning to him, Baden here has orders to give you a nice scratch. I wouldn't risk it, my dear. Can you imagine the guilt Sherard would carry with him knowing you died for him? That alone would kill a man. It's not a pretty death either. I've seen men afflicted by the poison. It isn't pretty nor is it fast enough. It grabs hold of your bones and it won't let go until you scream, your body contorting, twisting this way and that looking for relief. Surely marriage to me would be a far better alternative than that.' He yanked her chin up, forcing her to meet his gaze. 'You never know, you might just find you have a taste for a man like me.'

Bryn spat in his face, allowing herself one small piece of defiance. 'Never.'

He laughed. 'Well, that's for you to decide. I'm off

to greet our guests. Baden, you might want to tie this one up in case she gets any ideas about running. I want her to have a front-row seat to Kitt Sherard's demise. His luck has just about run out. He's only got this far because I allowed it.'

Bryn's eyes darted past Devore's bulk, trying to catch a glimpse of Kitt, of what Devore had planned. Devore turned, following her gaze, the tension in his form belying his confidence. For the first time, Bryn realised he was afraid. If she'd been able to look past her own concerns, she might have seen it earlier: the brutality, the bullying, the poisoned knife, the tactics of a coward. That didn't mean he wasn't dangerous. The knife especially posed a very real threat, coward or not.

She caught sight of Kitt, a band of men fanned out behind him as he gained the beach. Her breath hitched. Devore had every right to be afraid.

one more time. 'Me for her!' He slipped the bandolier from his shoulders and let it fall to the ground. Bryn's throat tightened. This was a trade Kitt had made before, for his brother. She knew in a horrifying moment of truth that Kitt loved her. He had sacrificed himself once for his brother out of love and now he intended to do the same for her. No, that wasn't what she wanted. She didn't want him to simply turn himself over, to submit to Devore. She wanted him to fight, to make Devore pay.

Apparently it wasn't what Devore wanted either. 'I don't want a trade, Sherard. I want you to suffer,' Devore called out. 'Submission is too easy. There's no pain in it. I want you to suffer as I've suffered. I lost everything that had worth to me, thanks to you, and just when I'm getting back on my feet, you come along again to kick me back down. Well, no more.'

Devore stepped back to her side, his knife flashing in his hand, the tip hovering beneath her chin. Bryn drew back, trying to make herself as small as possible, but Devore held her fast. This was not the plan! 'This blade is poisoned, Sherard. One prick and she dies. I am taking her with me aboard my ship as I sail into a new life. If you follow us, she dies. If you attempt to do me any harm, she dies. Do you understand?'

He understood Devore's repetitive litany too well. Any misstep from him and Bryn died. Kitt's hand flexed around the handle of his own knife, a throwing blade, specially balanced for accuracy and speed. He just needed an opportunity. Bryn lived as long as he let Devore go. But that required leaving Bryn in Devore's hands and that was intolerable. Bryn would not suffer for him, because of him.

It was clear Devore wasn't bluffing. Bryn's pale face was proof enough Devore's threat was real. Kitt assessed the options with lightning speed. Devore would kill her right there in front of him or kill her later, perhaps, with the slightest provocation. Letting Devore go now didn't buy Bryn more time, only more danger. He needed a clean throw, he needed Devore to step away from Bryn so there was no risk of him accidentally pricking her. And yet, if he could somehow put Bryn in charge of Devore's blade, it would give her power, a tool to defend herself with. Would she understand his message?

'You are more of a coward than I thought, Devore.' Kitt began to pace, hoping to distract Devore with his ceaseless movements. 'Taking a helpless woman, using her to blackmail me into compliance and resorting to poison, all speak of cowardice. I would have expected better from you. Perhaps you've lost your courage without Gridley around to call the shots. Perhaps he truly was the brains of the operation. Are you afraid to face me man to man? What will your men think of their boss if you refuse?'

Kitt drew a circle in the sand and stepped inside. 'I dare you to join me. Man to man, knife to knife.' He couldn't afford to look at Bryn's face. He would lose his focus, his detachment. He'd felt it slip the moment he'd seen Devore's knife slide beneath her chin. He didn't need her panic to know the risks. He was the more agile of the two, but Devore had a poisoned tip—it more than made up for the bulk and limp of him. Devore didn't need to be fast, Devore only needed him to be careless. Kitt knew he had no margin for error.

There was a rustle in the ranks of Devore's men. 'C'mon, Boss, give the bastard what he deserves,' someone called out. The sentiment was taken up with cheers along the line. Kitt grinned. Devore would not be able to back down now. Devore stepped into the circle. Despite the danger to himself, Kitt let relief ease his thoughts and focus his body. Bryn was safe for now. As long as he kept Devore in the circle, Bryn was safe.

Kitt feinted, testing Devore's tactics. Devore growled and threw a handful of sand. Kitt was ready for it and darted backwards. His men roared their disapproval of the underhanded ploy. He heard Passemore call out something derogatory. The proverbial sabres were starting to rattle. His men would fight. Passemore had instructions to launch a full attack if he fell, to get to Bryn at all costs.

Kitt and Devore circled. He watched the man's bad leg, he watched the sweat bead on the heavier man's forehead. Devore would want to have this over quickly. Devore lunged, lowering his head like a bull, his head aimed for Kitt's midsection, his free hand attempting to grab Kitt's wrist. Kitt dug his feet into the sand and took the blow, grabbing the man's shirt and wrapping his fist in the fabric to throw him. Devore tried to grab hold of Kitt, but couldn't. There was no shirt, only slippery skin that offered no traction. Devore lost his footing, momentum overbalancing him. He went down, Kitt's blade slicing into him as he fell.

It was chaos on the beach then. Devore's men rushed the circle, only to meet Kitt's crew, weapons drawn. Kitt pulled his knife free, his one thought on getting to Bryn.

All sorts of accidents happened in mêlées like this one and the fighting was far too close to her.

Kitt punched and stabbed, cutting a path towards her, his thoughts immediate: get Bryn, get to the boats, get to the ship. There were no thoughts beyond that. One brute remained between him and Bryn. Kitt drove his knife deep into the man's belly without hesitation. His next cut was through Bryn's bonds. They were free, the boats fifty yards ahead of them.

They ran, his hand tight over her wrist as he dragged her towards safety. He didn't care, he just wanted off the beach, just wanted Bryn safe. He shouted to Passemore to cover their retreat and swept Bryn into his arms, carrying her through the surf to the row boat. Others joined him to get the oars under way. Minutes later, Passemore had the rest on board and they were away, leaving the bloody beach behind them.

He had her. Bryn was safe! She was in his arms, because he wouldn't let her leave them. But victory had struck him dumb. All of his thoughts had run out. He'd not thought beyond the beach, hadn't allowed himself to think of them both leaving the beach alive. What next? He didn't know. That wasn't quite true. He *did* know what was next, the one thing he'd promised himself he'd do if he got her off the beach. He'd see her on a boat to England, back to where she belonged. After today, her father would certainly support such a decision. As long as she was here, there would be those who would try to get to him through her. He couldn't expose her to that. They'd barely lived through it once. He couldn't imagine living through it again. He loved her too much. He was going to do the only thing he could. He was going to give her up. But first, he had to walk away and that was proving hard to do. His mind was made up, but his body was not.

'Thank you,' Bryn said quietly into the silence that had grown up between them. They were at the rail of the ship, the rest of the crew had gone about their jobs, their busyness giving the two of them privacy without leaving the deck. 'You were brilliant today, so fearless, so brave.'

'I was scared,' Kitt said more sharply than he intended. He would not be made into a hero over this. It was his fault this had happened in the first place, that she'd been in danger at all.

Bryn's hand was light on his arm. 'Of course you were. I think that is what real courage is about; going forward even though you're frightened, even though the outcome is uncertain.' She paused and bit her lip. Kitt waited for her to continue. 'Which is why I want to try and be courageous now. I promised myself I would do something if I saw you again. It was all I could think of to keep myself from going crazy with fear when I was with Devore. I don't pretend it's something you want to hear, but it's something I need to say.'

Bryn turned to face him, forcing him to look at her. His stomach rolled into a tight ball. This was where she told him how much she despised the man he was, how much she regretted what had passed between them. Kitt steeled himself. He'd known from the start it would come to this. A woman like Bryn Rutherford was far too good for a man like him. Today, she'd seen him kill without hesitation. When all of this had started, it hadn't mattered. But in this awful moment, he'd never wished so much to be a different man, to have a different life.

'When Devore was making his threats, I kept thinking of all the things I wanted to do and all the things I had done. The best things were the things I'd done with you. And everything I had yet to do, I wanted to do with you. I didn't look for this to happen. I thought I'd be safe with you, but I'm not. I fell anyway, Kitt. I love you.'

I thought I'd be safe with you, but I'm not... He understood that part. He'd expected that much. It was the part after that caught him by surprise. *I fell anyway... I love you.* It took a moment for him to realise she'd not meant it literally. She meant the safety of her feelings, of her heart. She didn't despise him. Quite the opposite. She loved him. It was a stunning gift, one he couldn't accept.

'I cannot offer you anything decent, Bryn.' His resolve was wavering. He'd never get her on a ship to England at this rate. 'I can't keep you safe. There will always be the potential of another Devore. Even if I gave it all up, I can't erase my past and whatever may lurk there.' *Maybe he could, maybe there wouldn't be any more enemies, maybe no one would look for him. Maybe his identity was safe. Maybe...* The possible began to chase the impossible around his mind in a dizzying circle of reason. 'I just don't know what I'm capable of. If I did, it would be different.' Kitt fumbled with his thoughts, overwhelmed. When things seemed too good to be true, they probably were.

Bryn's grey eyes lit up. She meant to do battle. For him, Kitt realised. 'I don't want it to be different or you to be different. I don't want "decent". I've had my share of what passes for decent gentlemen. You are far more than decent with your love of family, with your loyalty.' She fixed him with a hard stare. 'I want you,

Kitt Sherard, rough edges and all. The question is do you want me?'

'Rough edges and all?' Kitt gave a faint smile, but it was no laughing matter. His insides were still roiling, but for a different reason. Did he dare take the leap? He wanted to. If he leapt or not, Bryn had his heart. Nothing would change that, not England, not a thousand miles of sea.

Suddenly, it was all too much. He needed her desperately, needed to feel her around him, needed to be inside her, to know she was his beyond words. 'Come with me.' Kitt's voice was gruff, filling with emotion. His hand closed about hers, leading her to his cabin, the door barely shut behind them before he claimed her with his mouth, her back against the wall.

'Kitt.' She moaned his name into his mouth, her hands cradling his face, her body pressing against his, wanting this as much as he did, needing it perhaps more.

'Are you sure, Bryn?' He drew a ragged breath. 'Devore, he didn't…?'

'No, he did nothing that could truly hurt me,' she murmured, Devore and his filth couldn't touch them, couldn't haunt them any more. Her hand slipped to his trousers, cupping him, stroking him. 'There are some rough edges of yours I like more than others,' she whispered at his ear, her teeth catching the tender part of his lobe. 'Undress me, Kitt. I want to be naked with you.'

He slid the gown from her. He'd burn it the first chance he had, but for now he wanted to worship with his hands, with his lips, his tongue, wanted to erase every trace of Devore's touch from her skin. She was his, and only his. Primal fire consumed him as he took her down on the bed. He'd nearly lost her today. One slip of the knife and she would have been gone, beyond any skill he had to bring her back. There are some things a man couldn't fight with pistols and blades. Those were the things that scared him the most.

He came down between her legs, revelling in how she opened for him, how her legs went about him to draw him close. *This* was one of those things. He had no illusions now that being with Bryn would grow less intense with familiarity or time. That scared him, to lose himself so completely in another. It also ignited him, fired him deep at the core of his soul. This was living at its most frightening, but loving at its finest.

Kitt thrust deeply with all the surety of a man who knew he was home. He let his body say what his words could not. She arched against him and he came hard, wringing a satisfied cry from her as she clung to him, their bodies overcome with pleasure, overcome with life. It had been a near-run thing today. He vowed silently it would never be so near again. He rolled to his side and pulled her to him as his heartbeat slowed, the enormity of what he'd committed to coming to him in post-climax clarity.

'It will be hard, Bryn. Life with me won't be easy.'

Bryn smiled up at him. 'I know. I like it hard.'

Kitt laughed. 'You're a naughty wench when it comes right down to it.' He sighed and blew out a breath. 'It's been quite a day: rescuing damsels, a fight to the death…falling in love.'

Bryn traced a circle around his nipple. 'All in a day's work for the notorious Captain Sherard from what I hear.' She paused and levered up on one arm to look at him. It was one of his favourite poses, her hair hanging over one shoulder, her eyes fixed on him. 'You haven't answered my question and Carlisle Bay looms. I want you, Kitt. Do you want me?'

'Do you doubt it?' He'd worshipped her with his body. What more was there to prove? Meaningful words were not his strong suit. He could banter all day, flirt all night with empty words. But meaningful words? He'd denied himself those for so long.

'I do not doubt it. I don't want *you* to doubt it or yourself. Say the words,' Bryn coaxed.

Kitt met her gaze solemnly, his voice quiet, intuitively understanding this would be the most reverent moment of his life. 'Yes, Bryn Rutherford. I want you, for ever, for always.'

There would be vows and public declarations later to satisfy the law and the church, but these words satisfied their hearts and meant so much more. Somewhere in the back of his mind, a little voice whispered, *it's a trap.* Yes, indeed. Love was a trap. A glorious, well-sprung trap in which he was utterly caught.

Epilogue

No one ever said loving Kitt Sherard would be easy, but it was an amazing journey as he revealed little pieces of himself to her. Bryn understood she would not get it all at once, but she had a lifetime to learn him, a lifetime to love him whoever he was—notorious Kitt Sherard or Michael Melford. She loved both the rogue and the gentleman, but most of all, she loved the man they'd combined to make. That man waited by the warm surf of the beach to claim her as his bride.

Beside her, her father gave a misty smile as he walked her down the runner of red carpet covering the sand. 'Your mother would be proud of you. You have followed your heart and that's all she would have wanted.'

Bryn smiled, too moved for words. Kitt was her heart, her future. Her father placed her hand in Kitt's and stepped back. He joined the guests gathered on the sand—all three of them and one of them asleep: Ren Dryden and his wife, Emma, who held a baby in her arms.

Kitt squeezed her hand, smiling down at her as the vicar began the ceremony. 'Dearly beloved, we are gathered here today…' Dearly beloved, yes, indeed, Bryn thought. They could have had a grand wedding at St Michael's in Bridgetown, filled with citizens wanting her father's favour, wanting to bask in Kitt's success in bringing the land swindle to justice. But Bryn had wanted something more meaningful, a private celebration of their love with people who mattered.

She hardly heard the ceremony. She was too caught up in Kitt's gaze. It held hers with a look that communicated his pledge to her better than any words. If her voice shook as she said her vows, it was to be expected. It wasn't every day a woman was loved so thoroughly or so well. It was an overwhelming prospect to know she'd wake up to this man, to this love, for the rest of her life.

Waves rolled lightly over their bare feet as the vicar pronounced them husband and wife. This was the life and it was hers to claim, hers and Kitt's. Kitt tipped her chin upwards and covered her mouth with his, sealing their vows with a kiss, sealing them together, for ever.

* * * * *

REQUEST YOUR FREE BOOKS!

 HARLEQUIN® HISTORICAL:
Where love is timeless

2 FREE NOVELS PLUS 2 FREE GIFTS!

YES! Please send me 2 FREE Harlequin® Historical novels and my 2 FREE gifts (gifts are worth about $10). After receiving them, if I don't wish to receive any more books, I can return the shipping statement marked "cancel." If I don't cancel, I will receive 6 brand-new novels every month and be billed just $5.44 per book in the U.S. or $5.74 per book in Canada. That's a savings of at least 16% off the cover price! It's quite a bargain! Shipping and handling is just 50¢ per book in the U.S. and 75¢ per book in Canada.* I understand that accepting the 2 free books and gifts places me under no obligation to buy anything. I can always return a shipment and cancel at any time. Even if I never buy another book, the two free books and gifts are mine to keep forever.

246/349 HDN F4ZY

Name	(PLEASE PRINT)	
Address		Apt. #
City	State/Prov.	Zip/Postal Code

Signature (if under 18, a parent or guardian must sign)

Mail to the **Harlequin® Reader Service**:
IN U.S.A.: P.O. Box 1867, Buffalo, NY 14240-1867
IN CANADA: P.O. Box 609, Fort Erie, Ontario L2A 5X3

Want to try two free books from another line?
Call 1-800-873-8635 or visit www.ReaderService.com.

* Terms and prices subject to change without notice. Prices do not include applicable taxes. Sales tax applicable in N.Y. Canadian residents will be charged applicable taxes. Offer not valid in Quebec. This offer is limited to one order per household. Not valid for current subscribers to Harlequin Historical books. All orders subject to credit approval. Credit or debit balances in a customer's account(s) may be offset by any other outstanding balance owed by or to the customer. Please allow 4 to 6 weeks for delivery. Offer available while quantities last.

Your Privacy—The Harlequin® Reader Service is committed to protecting your privacy. Our Privacy Policy is available online at www.ReaderService.com or upon request from the Harlequin Reader Service.

We make a portion of our mailing list available to reputable third parties that offer products we believe may interest you. If you prefer that we not exchange your name with third parties, or if you wish to clarify or modify your communication preferences, please visit us at www.ReaderService.com/consumerschoice or write to us at Harlequin Reader Service Preference Service, P.O. Box 9062, Buffalo, NY 14269. Include your complete name and address.

HH13R

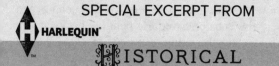
"Yet you insist you were watching me purely with the eye of an artist?"

His thumb was stroking her wrist, so lightly she wondered if he was even aware he was doing it. The tension between them became palpable. Beguiled, as much by her own newfound desire as by Jack's proximity, Celeste could think of nothing to say but the truth. "I watched you because I could not take my eyes off you. I was fascinated."

His eyes darkened. His hands slid up to her shoulders. She leaned into him as he pulled her toward him. It started so gently. Soft. Delicate. Celeste leaned closer. The kiss deepened. She could feel the dampness of his shirt and the heat of his skin beneath it. A drop of perspiration trickled down between her breasts, and she felt a sharp twist of pure desire.

She curled her fingers into his hair. Their tongues touched. Jack moaned, a guttural sound that precisely echoed how she felt, filled with longing, and aching, and heat. Their kiss became fierce. He bent her backward on the bench, his body hovering over hers, blocking out the sunlight. He smelled of soap and sweet summer sweat. His legs were tangled in her skirts. Only his arms, planted either side of her, prevented her from falling.

She was also in danger of falling, metaphorically speaking, from a far greater height if she was not extremely careful. Celeste snapped to her senses. Jerking herself free, she sat up. Jack's cheeks were flushed. His hair was in wild disarray. His shirt was falling open at the neck to reveal his tanned throat. The soft linen clung to his frame, revealing tantalizing glimpses of the hard body underneath. She wanted more. It was good that she wanted more, but with this man? No, she must be out of her mind.

She edged a little way along the bench, shaking out her skirts. "I hope you are not expecting me to faint?" she asked, more sharply than she intended.

"Despite our extremely brief acquaintance you do not strike me as someone much given to histrionics."

"You are perfectly correct, I am not. Even when kissing complete strangers."

"Not quite complete strangers, mademoiselle. We have at least been formally introduced." Jack shook his head, as if trying to clear the dazed look from his eyes.

Find out what happens next in
THE SOLDIER'S DARK SECRET,
available March 2015 wherever
Harlequin® Historical books and ebooks are sold.

www.Harlequin.com

HARLEQUIN®

A *Romance* FOR EVERY MOOD™

JUST CAN'T GET ENOUGH?

Join our social communities
and talk to us online.

You will have access to the latest
news on upcoming titles and special
promotions, but most importantly,
you can talk to other fans about your
favorite Harlequin reads.

Harlequin.com/Community

 Facebook.com/HarlequinBooks

 Twitter.com/HarlequinBooks

Pinterest.com/HarlequinBooks

HSOCIAL